ANALYST SESSION

Terence Gallagher

Introduction

This novel is set in England in the 1980s. While the characters and events portrayed are fictional, the political and social environments in which the story plays out are real. Margaret Thatcher came to power in 1979. By the time of her resignation in 1990, she had utterly transformed the UK. Martin Housegood, the fictional embattled Prime Minister of this tale, is a dyed-in-the-wool Thatcherite. The Iron Lady believed in deregulation, privatisation of key national industries, and free markets. When she took office, the gas, electricity, and coal industries were entirely state-owned. When she left, all of the energy industries except coal had been privatised.

Thatcher's social policy was driven by her conviction that public expenditure needed to be reined in. A change to how old-age pensions were indexed in 1980 saw a steady reduction in purchasing power for pensioners as the decade wore on.

Margaret Thatcher embraced monetarist policies to curb Britain's high inflation rate, which was running at 10 percent when she took office. She raised interest rates to 17 percent. The pound sterling appreciated in value, making British exports like automobiles and consumer electronics more expensive vis-à-vis their foreign counterparts. UK manufacturing in particular experienced a major contraction. In 1984, Bruce Springsteen recorded "My Hometown," which lamented the loss of manufacturing jobs in his native New Jersey. It could as easily have been a lament for the job losses experienced in the UK's industrial heartland in the 1980s.

Smartphone today is a thousand times faster than, and can store a hundred times the data of, a typical mainframe of that period. Today the ability to process data is cheap and ubiquitous. In the 1980s it was scarce and expensive. What has not changed in the past forty years is the capacity of large information technology projects to fail and, in some cases, fail spectacularly. Roughly one in two IT projects are deemed a failure either because they finish over budget, are significantly late, or do not meet their business objectives. The sorry tale of the benighted project recounted in these pages is, regrettably, an all-too-common occurrence.

Terence Gallagher
Dublin, July 2020

Chapter One

This morning, as he had pretty much every morning for the last fifteen years, he got up about seven o clock and left his wife Deirdre asleep in bed. He made himself a cup of coffee, listened to the news on the radio, and departed to catch the bus down to the tube station. There, at a working men's café, he had tea and two sticky buns, surrounded by truckers and other blue-collar workers, being slightly out of place in his suit and tie.

He joined the other commuters crowding to get on the downward escalator, which led to the trains. He heard the sound of compressed air as the tubes came and went in the station, and resisted the impulse to hurry because he knew that it was tough to tell whether the train was going in the right direction to Leicester Square or going in the other direction to Cockfosters. He remembered how, when he had first come to London, he had always succumbed to the irrational impulse to somehow rush to the platform, impelled as it were by the noise of the arriving or departing train, just in case he might miss the opportunity to catch one just about to leave. Now he took his time, standing on the right, rather than walking, on the moving stairway. The rush-hour tube was as crowded as ever, and as usual, he didn't manage to get a seat largely because he lagged behind the people jostling to get into the train. He resigned himself to hang onto one of the straps at the centre of the coach and knew that because of the delay, there would be a kind of stop-start progress on the line down to Embankment. He made the necessary change at Leicester Square and caught the Bakerloo line, coming out of the tube station at ten to nine. The daylight was just beginning to break in the early December morning.

Andrew Sweeney caught sight of himself in a shop window as he walked towards the offices of the Metropolitan Electricity Board. What did he see? A nondescript figure dressed in a grey raincoat with a scarf pulled around his neck against the December cold. Thinning hair going a little grey at the temples, stooped somewhat for his five foot eleven inches. Not a very good physique, not fat really but indeed not the figure or shape of a man who keeps himself in very good condition. Glasses, horn-rimmed, clean-shaven. The kind of person you pass by on the street and pay no attention to.

The offices of the Metropolitan Electricity Board, a twenty-story building, glass, with a modern box-like architecture, stood pretty well on its own in a deserted area which had been levelled in the Second World War. Only sporadic attempts had been made since to rebuild. He walked past the security guard, who glanced up briefly from the Sports section of his newspaper, where he was trying to work out the best tips, and best bets for the Haydock race meet and caught an elevator to the fourth floor of the building where he worked.

The office layout was a semi-open plan, analysts, and programmers in their own cubes in the open area. The more senior men got cubicles by the window. Offices for managers were along the back wall. They were kind of horseboxes with glass above waist level, so there was no privacy. But then that's what open plan was all about.

'Hi Andrew, how was your weekend?'

'Not bad, Phil, and yours?'

Phillip Evans was an analyst in his fifties and had been there longer than himself. Of all of the people that he worked with; Phillip was one of the few for whom he felt any affinity.

'Went to go see the Arsenal match on Saturday. Great game! What did you do?'

'I took Michael to the Imperial War Museum. He's into soldiers and guns and that kind of thing. I suppose it's his age'.

Phillip looked at him a bit surprised.

'I thought a pacifist type like you wouldn't have much interest in exposing your son to war memorabilia, Andrew?'

He smiled and replied ''Well, I am hoping it's just a passing phase, not being one of these enlightened parents, I try not to project my values too heavily on to my son'.

'Well, we have the project status meeting in a half hour'. Phillip grimaced. 'What say a pub lunch at noon?'

'Not the best start to a Monday but then given that it's the project status meeting. I guess I'm going to need a drink 'Andrew answered.

Andrew Sweeney walked to his cubicle, took off his raincoat and scarf, hung the neatly on a hanger and placed them on the coat hook provided. He started the log-on process to his terminal. Today it only took two minutes, which was pretty good. Other days the wait could be as long as ten. They were expecting more processing power to be delivered but the shipment was two months late already. He checked his electronic mail. Only a few administrative memoranda had come in overnight. Nothing urgent or requiring his immediate attention. He knew he would be questioned about the testing he was doing of the billing cycles for the new system at the status meeting. He decided to spend half an hour before the meeting reviewing this.

The results of the new test run were back. He had submitted the test on Friday night just before he left. The test results were clean. This meant they could move on to the next cycle – Retroactive Billings.

He walked over to Peter Spencer's cubicle. Peter Spencer was his irreverent assistant, twenty-six, from Birmingham and a keen rugby player at the club level.

'Hi Peter, how did your match go Saturday?'

Peter looked up at him, a broken nose and two front teeth missing gave him a slightly sinister and lopsided smile.

'Kicked hell out of the bastards, my opposite was carried off on a stretcher. That's the sort of rugby match I like'.

'I just checked our results' Andrew replied. 'The test has run clean so we can move to Retroactive Billing'.

Peter was enthusiastic.

'Great! Get Mavis and Gladys right on to it!'

Andrew looked at him.

'I wish you would stop calling them that Peter. We're bound to get into some sort of trouble with discrimination in the workplace or the like.

Mavis and Gladys were, in fact Martin and Gwynn. They were two computer science students from the London Polytechnic who worked part-time for the Board to get job experience. Currently, they were assigned to the test team and entered test condition data for the various cycles. Since the work was clerical data entry the nicknames had come up. They took this in good part but it was quite incongruous. Martin and Gwynn were on the rowing team of the Polytechnic, and like all rowers had a lanky, muscular build.

'The most complicated part of the cycle is going to be Retroactive Billings over a rate change 'Andrew indicated.

'You'll need to explain that to Martin and Gwynn, Peter, so they have some idea of what exactly it is we are attempting to accomplish. They're here to advance their computer science education. I wouldn't like to think of them being treated as just mindless data entry clerks.

Peter answered, 'I'll try but for as many times you go over it with me I still find the algorithm to be the product of a demented mind'.

Andrew sighed.

'The easiest way to remember it is to understand the business rationale that underpins it. What we're trying to do is balance and predict the load on the national grid. Commercial customers contract that each month they will not exceed a specific utilisation of megawatts and based on that they get a certain rate. If they should exceed their usage in a given month, then their annualised rate goes up to a new band and their previous months bills have to be recalculated and the differential billed to them. The situation becomes compounded if we have had a rate increase in any of the preceding periods because now we have to bill retroactively but also take into account the rate change. We should plan to go over some examples of this this afternoon so you, Martin and Gwynn are straight on what we are trying to do'.

Peter tugged at his forelock and said 'Yes Sir, Mr Squires, Sir'.

Andrew registered the literary allusion. Peter although he affected a north country rustic manner, was in fact, very well read.

Joe Fortisque walked by. 'Time for the status meeting Andrew'.

'Be there is two minutes Joe'. Andrew gathered up his papers.

The conference room was at the far corner of the floor. It had glass on all four sides, two sides giving a view of the immediate surrounding area which was a wasteland. You could choose either to look at the motorway flyovers on one side or razed building lots on the other.

Joe Fortisque, in his fifties, was the director of the Commercial Division of the DP department – there being two divisions, the other, the Engineering Division, had to do with scientific and engineering applications.

The status meeting scheduled for nine thirty finally got going at nine forty-five, the ten participants drifting in at staggered intervals.

Joe began 'It's now the third of December and we plan to convert the system for start of business the second of January. So, we are getting down to the wire here boys. Let's see where we are. Conversion team, what's the status?'

Dave Sugden, head of the conversion team was in deep conversation with his lieutenant and didn't hear the questions. Joe became irritated.

'Dave, for God's sake, could you just listen up? I asked you a question.'

Dave looked up startled. 'Oh, sorry Joe I was just trying to get a last-minute update'.

'Status, Dave'.

'Well as you know, we are converting the database in sections based upon the leading digit of the customer number. Essentially, we've segmented the database into ten segments. We successfully converted one over the weekend and everything appears to have gone smoothly. We got the data over.'

'How long did it take? 'Joe asked.

'Sixty hours 'Dave answered.

Joe looked at him. 'You can't be serious. We have a window of exactly seventy-two hours to convert the entire database. And you're telling me that one tenth of it took sixty?'

'I told you it was going to be a tight squeeze, Joe'.

'Dave, a tight squeeze is one thing but what you've just told me is that three weeks from conversion date the conversion run is going to be off by an order of magnitude in terms of elapsed time'

Dave snapped back. 'We're off by an order of magnitude , Joe , because the bigger machine that was supposed to have been delivered four weeks ago still isn't installed yet'.

Joe looked defensive.

'Okay, okay. I talked to the manufacturer and they are going to deliver this weekend, hopefully, we'll be configured a week from today'.

Andrew interjected mildly. 'The conversion process is input/output bound. A faster processor isn't going to make that much of an impact. The new disk drives will.'

Joe looked at Andrew appreciatively.

'Thanks for making that point Andrew. I will call the manufacturer and make sure that he understands the importance of delivering the disk drives. While you're about it, where are we with systems testing?'

'Well, we have a fair way to go. A lot of work to be done but we are moving now to commercial billing. We've regression tested all of the previous cycles over the weekend and they have run clean. That means eighty percent of the systems test is running error free, with twenty percent to go and a month before we convert'.

Joe looked and said, 'So, you think we will get there then?'

Andrew replied, 'It'll be a close call but what with seven days a week and putting in the overtime, I think we should make it ok.'

Joe smiled. 'Well, that's one piece of good news anyway. But where are we on user training?'

Bob Masters looked at him 'A bit of a hiccup, Joe I'm afraid. We discovered that the training development teams hadn't been updating the screens for changes that have been made to the system. So, we've been training the users on an outdated version of the software'.

Joe went pale. 'What are you trying to tell me Bob?'

'What I am saying Joe, is that we didn't update the training materials to stay in sync with changes that have been made to the software as a result of the testing. As you know, the testing has produced some significant changes and these have not been reflected'.

Joe looked at him. 'That's not what I asked you Bob. In simple terms are the users ready for the new system or aren't they?'

Bob looked at him and said slowly,' The other side of it is that the union is pretty upset about the fact that members have been wasting their time training on the wrong stuff. They're already pretty unhappy about the workforce reductions that the new system is going to bring in. This is just the last straw as far as they are concerned.'

'Maybe we should look for a postponement of the conversion date Joe', Bob said.

Joe, who had been pale now proceeded to go bright red.

'Bob, that's horse shit. We've already slipped the date six months. The fifteenth of May I had to go to Brett Johnson and explain to him how his system that we had said would covert on June the first was not now going to convert until January the first. And, moreover, the workday estimate we gave him of a 20,000-day system had mushroomed into a 30,000-day system. I'm not going in there and tell him that we have fucked up again. I want to keep my job. I assume you would like to keep yours. I don't really care what we have to do in the next month to get ready for this conversion, but we are going to convert January second.'

Andrew noticed that Dave had been doodling while this spirited exchange was going on. He had drawn Brett Johnson complete with Swastika, Nazi salute and a ten-gallon hat. Andrew thought the caricature somewhat unfair. Brett Johnson hailed from Philadelphia and besides, he was really only following direction for Chaddick Spencer III. Chaddick Spencer III was Managing Director of the Metropolitan Electricity Board. He had held several senior management positions in utility companies in the United States before being appointed Managing Director of the newly deregulated Metropolitan Electricity Board. This was part of the privatisation agenda of the Tory government.

The status meeting went on for another half hour. The remaining teams reported average progress.

Joe, however, seemed abstracted with trying to take in the full implications of what Dave and Bob had previously told him. Joe terminated the meeting at 11:00. 'From now on we are going to have daily status meetings until this system coverts' he announced.

'The floggings will continue until morale improves 'Dave muttered under his breath.

'Dave, Bob, this time tomorrow I want an action plan from both of you describing how you're going to deal with the situation in your areas and how you propose to bring these into line in time to convert on the first of January'.

Dave began to splutter 'Joe, that's not a lot of time'.

Joe shot back 'I'm not asking you this, Dave. I'm telling you. That will be all.'

Andrew gathered up his papers and walked slowly back to his desk. On his way he passed Jimmy Prescott, surreptitiously fiddling with half a loaf of bread in his desk drawer to make breadcrumbs for the pigeons he fed at lunch time.

'How's the Delinquent Accounts Receivable Report coming along Jimmy? 'Andrew asked mischievously.

Jimmy shut the drawer of his desk suddenly, catching his fingers as he did so. 'Shit 'he muttered under his breath.

'Not bad Andrew. A couple more weeks and I should have some pretty decent analysis'.

Jimmy had been working on a report which was intended to illustrate how the new integrated customer database would allow much more efficient algorithms to be developed for the collection for delinquent accounts. He had originally been given two months for the assignment and had so far spent six months at it with nothing to show. With less than a year to retirement age obviously the pigeons had captured more of his attention that the delinquent consumers of the Metropolitan Electricity Board.

Andrew chuckled. 'Sounds great Jimmy 'and walked on.

He reserved a conference room for the afternoon and spent the next half hour preparing examples of retroactive billing for Peter and the two university students.

Phillip stopped by his desk at twelve and mimed lowering a drink.

'Ready for a spot of lunch?'

They walked companionably out of the building.

'Where to today, Phillip? 'Andrew asked. 'The usual?'

The usual was the Swallows Inn. 'No 'Phillip answered, 'Let's try the new place, the Priory, that's just opened. I hear they do a good pint of Guinness Andrew'.

Andrew grunted skeptically.

'Guinness doesn't travel very well out of Ireland, Phillip. There are only a couple of places that I know of in London that serve a good pint of Guinness. One is up in Finsbury Park; the other used to be in Piccadilly Circus and it closed down about a year ago. Curious place though; it was all underground. When you went to the Gents, you could see through the skylight up to the kebab shop where they sold kebabs to the tourists. You could see the lamb roasting on the spit'.

Phillip choked, 'Bloody hell, what about the hygiene?'

'Nobody seemed to care particularly much 'Andrew answered. 'If the stuff is spiced, who knows what you are eating?'

The Priory turned out to be pretty up market. It came complete with antique looking brasses, dark paneled wood, booths of upholstered leather and deep pile carpet. It also had a much more exotic range of lunchtime dishes. The Swallows Inn ran to a Ploughman's lunch or a toasted ham and cheese sandwich. The Priory did soup, cheeses, quiche, vegetarian salads, buffet, the whole works. It did, however, have the ubiquitous fruit machine. Andrew pumped three pounds of coins into the machine for little or no return.

Lunch time conversation focused first on the league standings from the previous weekend's soccer matches. It then drifted inevitably to the status meeting they had just had.

Phillips assessment was uncompromising 'The whole project has been a cock up from the start to finish. It was a political decision to bring in the Americans and the project schedule was politically driven from start to finish. Nobody bothered to do a bottom up analysis on what it was really going to take to convert to the new system. Chaddick Spencer figured out what he would need to do to get the bonus attached to his contract and announced that we are going to have the system converted and generating the cost savings in two years. And our guys, spineless bastards, kept saying it was possible'.

'Well Phillip, it's going to be a tough couple of months trying to get the system converted on this schedule. I will grant you that, ', Andrew concurred.

'Funny how these big projects seem inevitably to turn themselves into death marches 'Phillip muttered.

'Fancy another pint Andrew?'

Andrew shook his head. 'Ah no Phillip, I would be worthless for the afternoon if I did. Age is catching up with me I suppose. When I first started here I would knock back three pints of real ale no problem. The work I did in the afternoons, after a session like that, wasn't worth a tinker's curse. At least I didn't nod off though which is what I'd do now'.

'You're right there 'Phillip said. 'Work is the curse of the drinking classes, as dear old Oscar Wilde said; I suppose we should finish up then so we can start heading back'.

They got back to the office about one thirty. Andrew spent the rest of the afternoon drilling Peter and the students on the billing algorithm that they would be testing. Even though the department was supposed to be in crunch mode as they readied themselves for the new system, one could hardly have said that there was an air of frantic activity. Perhaps less newspapers were lying open on people's desks, no one was working as if their lives depended on it.

The tea trolley came around at three o clock as it did three times a day. Once for breakfast, then at ten in the morning, then three in the afternoon. It served a wide variety of snacks, sandwiches, scotch eggs, rich fruit cake and of course, tea and a brown substance described as coffee. Andrew remembered a couple of years back, one of the attendants being very enterprising, started selling bingo cards from the tea trolley but this caused a distraction as people scratched and matched to see if they had won anything. The management, when they got to hear of it, felt it came uncomfortably close to gambling on company time, so a stop was put to it.

Chapter Two

Andrew finished work about seven and walked slowly back to the tube station. There was a florist on the way and even though they were out of season, and therefore very expensive, he bought a dozen long stem roses for his wife Deirdre. The look of pleasure on her face when she received them, he felt, would more than compensate for the expense.

The tube journey, as always, was conducted in silence, most of his effort was spent trying to prevent the roses from being crushed. After fifteen years in London, he had gotten used to the fact that the English did not converse on public transportation. Mostly they immersed themselves in their newspapers and studiously avoided eye contact. This was a marked contrast in behaviour to the Dubliners with whom he had grown up. There was generally a lively hum of conversation on Dublin buses. It was an aspect of Irish life he had missed when he had come to London, but over the years he had grown accustomed to it. Rather than missing the companionship of conversation, he now became agitated when someone tried to talk to him on the tube.

It was a grey driving rain when he arrived at Palmers Green Station. He huddled with the others at the bus stop, regretting that he had not brought his umbrella. The tissue paper with which the roses were wrapped began to disintegrate. Traffic moved slowly. London, it seemed to him, got more congested every year and the rain only made things worse. The bus, when it did come, took him along the high street then past the rows of pre-war, terraced houses until he came to Fulton Avenue which was where his apartment was.

He owned the first floor of a rather large semi-detached house on a quiet street.

'Hi Deirdre, I'm home'. She came into the living room bare foot, wearing a silk dressing gown and drying her long black hair which still had no trace of grey even though she would be thirty-seven the following month.

A more critical observer might have said that the long hair no longer suited her features which had grown sharper as she had grown older. The soft fresh-faced look of youth had faded with the passing years. For him though, it simply didn't matter.

'Flowers, Andrew, Roses! Oh, you shouldn't have! Leave them on the table and I'll just go and get a vase and place them in water'.

'Oh, by the way I had trouble cashing a cheque this morning at the bank. It was very inconvenient really. I was to have lunch with Peggy Middleton and in the end we had to split the bill across our credit cards. You know how the waiters don't like that'.

'There was over a thousand pounds in the current last week Deirdre' Andrew observed mildly.

She pouted; her shoulders sagged 'Oh, I don't know Andrew. You know I had to pay for Michael's riding lessons and then there's the ballet class. Oh, and I bought a Waterford Crystal lamp for the living room. All I spent on myself was a few pounds for a silk scarf'.

Andrew sighed. Why did his son need riding lessons he wondered? Michael had never exhibited the slightest interest in horses or any other animal for that matter.

'It's alright Deirdre', he said, 'I'll transfer some money into the current account to cover us until the end of the month'. He quickly suppressed the familiar feelings of anxiety and guilt. Her cherished smile returned.

'Thank you Andrew, I will be careful. For the next week I will live like a mouse and so will you, beans and toast for tea every day'.

The phone rang and Deirdre answered it. 'Oh, hello Alice, how are things? One moment, I'll just take the call in the bedroom. Andrew, its Alice Winthrop, the drama soc you know. I'll only be about ten minutes. Be a dear will you and read Michael his bedtime story. He already had his bath'.

He waited for Deirdre to pick up the extension in their bedroom and then placed the phone on the received in the hall. He went into Michaels room; the boy was quietly waiting in bed, his story book for the night already picked out.

He was a thin child, tall for his age with pale blue eyes and light brown hair. Andrew never failed to be struck by the marked contrast between the quiet boy in front of him and the troubled and disturbed infant Michael had been. A long traumatic labour, over twenty hours, culminated in a caesarean delivery. He and Deirdre had gone to Lamaze classes together but it was no adequate preparation for the actual experience.

Michael had colic as an infant and then as a child was prone to violent tantrums. His sleeping patterns were extremely disturbed; it took hours to coax him to go to sleep. Michael would wake up at five o clock every morning screaming. Andrew would spend two hours before he went to work trying to keep him amused. When he came home late at the end of the day he would face an exhausted and extremely distressed Deirdre, worn out from having to deal with the child. Hyper Attention deficit, the doctors called it. Blue-eyed, fair-haired children were prone to it and there was a strong correlation between its incidence and a traumatic labour. It was comforting to at least be able to put a name to what they had been experiencing. Michael could not be left with a baby-sitter or placed in day-care. He became heartrendingly upset and they just couldn't do that to the child.

His mother had offered. 'Well it's the will of God. If you lived in Dublin of course, I could help out, but as it is, I'll pray for you'.

Somehow, Deirdre and he had got through the experience and little by little Michael had begun to settle down, to gain more control over his emotions. He became able to react in a more measured way to the surroundings and the environment in which he found himself. He still had his moments but then what eight-year-old did not. Deirdre and he determined not to have any more children and Andrew had undergone a vasectomy.

'They had a prize giving today Daddy 'Michael was not given to small talk.

'Yes Michael? Andrew answered.

'Why do people bang their bones together when they are happy?'

'Bang their bones together? 'Andrew answered slowly.

'Yes, like this 'and Michael clapped his hands. 'Oh, you mean clap Michael 'Andrew answered. Why did people clap? Make noise to indicate happiness or satisfaction or congratulations. It was just like Michael to see an everyday event and consider it from an entirely original perspective. Andrew was at a loss to give him an answer.

'I don't know Michael, it's just something that people do to show that they are happy or pleased'.

The storybook was about a race of creatures that went around polluting planets and the impact that they had on a group of peaceful herbivores whose world they had thoroughly destroyed. It had a strong environmental and conservation message. Michael followed along quite well; he read a number of the sentences completely. When they had finished Andrew made to leave the room.

'We forgot to say our prayers Daddy!, Michael reminded him.

His mother's voice echoed in Andrews head. 'What kind of father are you? Bringing the child up without any kind of religion at all I suppose'. He ignored the inner voice. Sometimes when he was very tired he found himself, involuntarily answering back as if his mother were in the room.

He had bought a book a few years back on transactional analysis. 'I'm ok-you're ok'. The thesis of the author was that the scripts of a childhood are played back constantly in our adult lives. It was a point of view with which he found himself in complete agreement.

They said their prayers and Michael settled down to sleep. When he got back to the living room, Dierdre was still on the phone. The roses lay unattended on the table. Sadly, he put them in water. He could hear her peals of laughter coming from their bedroom. He sighed and went to the kitchen to see what was in the refrigerator. He made a meal of leftover lasagne and coleslaw. After he cleared away he brought out two Waterford glass goblets and a chilled bottle of white wine, reasonable vintage, from their holiday in France the previous Summer. He put on a tape of Rubenstein playing Beethoven's Fourth Piano Concerto. The haunting sounds in a minor key reminded him of the first time he had heard the piece. He was fifteen years old and painting the ceiling of the spare room of his childhood home in Dublin. His mother was getting ready to take in a lodger. 'We need the money 'she had said. He had turned on BBC Radio Four and was introduced for the first time to the work.

He dozed fitfully in the chair; after about two hours on the telephone Deirdre came back animated and buoyant from her conversation.

'Sorry dear, I was just catching up on the gossip. Cynthia Frobeshire is getting a divorce'.

'Cynthia who? 'Andrew asked.

'You know, Cynthia Frobeshire. The one that hangs around horses a lot'.

Andrew registered the name. 'Oh, that Frobeshire. Her family have spent so much time with horses they've begin to look equine themselves. She has a wonderful set of teeth in her head'.

'You bet 'Deirdre responded. You'd take more than your life in your hands if she decided to give you a blowjob, Andrew'.

He smiled. It was one of the things that had attracted him to Deirdre in the first place. Her capacity to say the outrageous.

'I got out a bottle of wine for us, I thought we might split it before we went to bed'.

'What a wonderful idea Andrew 'Deirdre responded enthusiastically.

She curled herself up in the chair next to him. 'Pour me out a glass. I've got such a lot to tell you'.

It was what he lived for. These occasional interludes when Deirdre relaxed and happy would confide in him about her social activities in the wide circle of acquaintances she had garnered. She was a witty, vivacious raconteur and still stunningly beautiful. Even after thirteen years, he still didn't quite know what she saw in him. She was an outrageous flirt, sometimes he wondered if she had ever had an affair. In his blackest moments he wondered if Michael were even his son. But at this moment, basking in her contentment and happiness, all of that was forgotten.

Andrew first met Deirdre at a debate at Trinity College where they were both students. The motion was something like 'This house supports legalised abortion in Ireland'. Andrew spoke against the motion. He had diligently researched the moral and legal issues surrounding legalised abortion in Ireland. He had marshalled the arguments related to the rights of the unborn child, the right to life, respect for the individual and so forth. His contribution was moderately well received by the house and he sat down quite pleased with himself. Then Deirdre came to the ballot box.

The first impression she made was a visual one. She wore a long black dress, with only a silver amulet around her neck by way of ornament. The effect on her mostly male student audience was electrifying. Men were standing on their chairs in the back of the room to get a better view of her. Whereas his speech had been dry and forensic, hers was packed with emotion. She detailed the pitiful plight of young girls in rural Ireland condemned to take the boat to England to obtain an abortion in the event that they had fallen pregnant through ignorance of contraceptive techniques, or more likely, their sheer unavailability. She castigated the double standard in Irish life which was big on Christianity and yet treated these unfortunate girls by ostracising and humiliating them. She talked about a woman's right to determine what to do with her own body. She then proceeded to demolish his argument by launching a personal attack on him.

'The previous speaker has presented arguments against this motion which would do the Catholic hierarchy proud. But let's put forward a hypothetical case. Let us say that he managed to get a girl pregnant. This of course is only for the purpose of the debate. Just looking at him I wonder whether he has the testosterone levels or indeed the sexual proclivities to accomplish it.

It was grossly unfair but the audience loved it. 'If it happened out of wedlock, shock, horror! What would he do? The honourable thing? Would he marry the girl? Or would he be just as well pleased if she took herself off to England and got rid of the embarrassment? Let us say they were married and let us say that after a difficult pregnancy it became an even more difficult delivery and the choice came down to the life of the Mother or the life of the child. What would he do then? The logic of his position, ladies, and gentlemen, is that he would sacrifice his own wife in favour of the unborn child. Women have a right to decide what happens to their bodies. The moral prohibitions against abortion are a reflection of a male dominated society. Men are quite happy to get women into trouble. They're just as happy today to have rules about what women should and should not do with their bodies. I put it to you Ladies and gentlemen, that the legal and moral prohibition of abortion in Ireland is just an extreme example of male chauvinism'.

The audience was mostly male and notionally Catholic, so in the end the motion was defeated. At the wine reception in the committee room afterwards Deirdre came up to him smiled and said 'Great speech, I congratulate you'. Not a word of apology about her attack on him. He experienced simultaneously an array of emotions, which ranged from lust, to infatuation, to resentment. They developed a 'hi, how are you 'kind of relationship after that when they bumped into each other in college. The next major encounter of significance was when they were on a Trinity team for an inter-collegiate debate. Deirdre regaled him with amusing stories of her professors and who was sleeping with whom in her class. Most of the people were just names to him. He never encountered them in his own social sphere. The debate was being reported by a number of national newspapers, so there were some journalists and photographers present. It wore on interminably. Deirdre had gone on talking. Then she startled him by saying 'Jesus, this is boring. You know what I could so with now, Andrew. A good fuck. What do you think my chances are with that photographer over there? Great thighs got a wedding ring on his finger but I don't think that matters'.

He was speechless and shocked. Was its moral outrage or wounded vanity that she obviously did not regard him in any sexual way. After that, the tenor of their relationship became that she would treat him as a confidant almost like one of her girlfriends. Telling him the ins and outs of her various romances; explaining to him how the boyfriends made out in bed, how they measured up or not as was more often the case. He listened to it all noncommittally. It was not the relationship he wanted with her but, he reflected, it was much better than no relationship at all. Then came Trinity term of their final year and he worked up enough courage to ask her to the Trinity Ball. Much to his amazement, she agreed. He took her for an expensive dinner at the Shelbourne Hotel and then they went on to the gala event. He was not much of a dancer, but he did his best. Deirdre had many admirers and was happy to dance with several of them. Towards the end of the evening she became particularly attached to the captain of the rowing team. One moment she was on the dance floor, next she was gone. He looked all over the campus for her but couldn't find her. Bitterly he walked home alone. About a week later the unrepentant Deirdre showed up. She had, it appeared, gone to the yachting captain's rooms that night and then taken off with him for the Henley Regatta in England the next day. He tried not to show how hurt he really was.

Towards the end of college year, he interviewed for a number of positions in Ireland and also in the UK. He got a place in the Irish Civil Service to his own surprise. He survived an interview panel of grey-haired men sporting pins which proclaimed them to be either fluent Gaelic speakers or total abstainers from alcohol for twenty-five years or, more chillingly, both. It was a tough job market; the offer he got from the UK was from the Metropolitan Electricity Board. To get away from his mother's oppressive influence, he chose the job in England. It was, he told himself at the time, just a temporary job to get his feet wet, to get some job experience and then move on to something more lucrative.

He asked her to marry him before he left for England. She was incredulous. She never thought of him in a romantic way she said. He wasn't her type; besides, she had no interest in marriage. For the first couple of years he returned to Ireland two or three times a year. Deirdre graduated from college with a degree in General Studies. She decided to try for a career in the theatre. She went to drama school in Dublin and supported herself by waiting tables. She had a succession of short-lived romances with a variety of men. She became increasingly dissatisfied and depressed with the lack of progress in gaining an entrée to Dublin's small theatrical community. He asked her to marry him a couple more times. Two years after they graduated she surprised him by saying yes. He never really understood her motivation. He suspected that he was offering her an opportunity to get out from Dublin and try her luck in London. He wasn't really sure how much she really cared for him but it didn't matter.

Deirdre, it turned out, was extravagant and his salary modest. In their first year there were constant arguments about the finances. He tried interviewing for positions with merchant banks in the City, where the pay and benefits were much better. Somehow he never seemed to get the jobs. He guessed it was because he just didn't interview well. Also, if the truth be told, the English gave him an inferiority complex. He was very conscious that he was an immigrant in their country. Deirdre chaffed at the constraints on their lifestyle. A couple of times their account had been seriously overdrawn and he had been summoned to a very unpleasant interview with the assistant manager of the National West Minister Bank where they had their account. More than anything else, he worried that she would grow tired and walk out on him. Then one day he developed the idea. They were re-doing the billing system at the Metropolitan Electricity Board and he was the programmer analyst in charge of the billing program. A few of his mates down at the pub had been joking that the controls of the company were so lax that probably anyone could fiddle with them. It was deceptively simple; the billing program was specified so that if a customer's bill ended up after multiplying out the units by the rate with a fraction of a penny, the total was rounded down to the nearest penny if the fraction was less than a half, rounded up if the fraction was more than a half.

He programmed the algorithm so that the bill was always rounded up and the fractional difference he sent to another account. The Metropolitan Electricity Board had an electronic funds transfer with its bank. He programmed the financial reporting system to show that everything balanced out. The company had ten million consumers billed quarterly; into his own numbered account went on average fifty thousand pounds a quarter; two hundred thousand pounds a year. It had been going on for ten years.

Prior to committing to the act, Andrew had never done anything illegal. He understood how to divert the funds, but not how to do so in such a way as to make it difficult to trace them back to him if anything ever came to light. For a week he spent every night in the public library devouring whatever he could get his hands on about money laundering or financial fraud. He considered and discarded schemes for establishing dummy corporations in the Bahamas or the like. Quite simply he did not have the contacts or expertise to pull something like that off. The best bet seemed to be to convert the proceeds to some sort of highly negotiable asset which could then be disposed of without too many questions being asked. His research also impressed on him how important anonymity was. Transactions, where possible, should be conducted by telephone, through third parties or in writing. The fewer people who could identify him later the better off he was.

Electronic funds transfer saw to it that the fifty thousand a quarter that he had embezzled for himself went to an account at the Chase Manhattan Bank in London. The account was in a fictitious name. He took a lease on a one-bedroom apartment in Potters Bar, furnishing it cheaply. Then he advertised through a real estate agent for a tenant, an older woman living alone. The rent he asked was very low. It gave him the post restante address he needed. Using the little personal savings, he had, he passed himself off as a buyer of precious gems. He bought £3000 worth of diamonds, small, low carat, unremarkable for 'industrial use'. He used the initial cash transaction to establish himself with Montague and Sons of London, dealers in precious stones. He indicated a desire to purchase 'modest' consignments on a regular basis. The Chase Manhattan Account would be used to provide settlement funds. The consignments were to be delivered by messenger to his apartment in Potters Bar. His tenant was authorised to sign for them as he was out of the country a lot. Part of the conditions of the lease were that the tenant forward all mail and packages to a PO box in a Post Office close to Heathrow airport. As he explained over the phone to the retired schoolteacher who originally answered the advertisement 'I travel internationally a great deal. I want someone responsible to take care of my apartment. Also having my mail forwarded someplace near Heathrow means I can get it when connecting through the airport. That's why I am keeping the rent low'. His tenant, unable to believe her luck at getting a furnished apartment at a third of the going market rate did not enquire too much about the details.

He waited for the first billing run to deposit the diverted funds to the Chase Manhattan Bank. About a week later, he called in sick to work. He told Deirdre he would be away overnight at a computer conference. That morning he went to the PO box near Heathrow and retrieved the mail from Potters Bar, including a box containing £50,000 of industrial quality diamonds. Later that morning he flew to Geneva and opened a numbered account in the Bank of Geneva. Then he flew to Amsterdam. He sold off the gems to dealers there in four lots. In each case, he gave the account in Geneva as being his settlement account for the transactions. Once a year after that he went abroad to Amsterdam, sometimes by ferry, sometimes by air. Planning everything out had seemed like an esoteric chess game. Actually, executing it had been gut wrenching. Every step of the way he had wanted to back out. Only his certainty that Deirdre would tire of their modest lifestyle and leave him propelled him forward.

From time to time he had sent written instructions to Switzerland to have funds forwarded to a Building Society in Ireland. He explained the extra income to Deirdre by saying that a sister of his father's who had died had left him the bulk of her estate. Bridget Reilly had never married and he was her only nephew. He was careful not to do anything too extravagant or obvious with the extra money, but over the years it had allowed him to gradually build and sustain a lifestyle he could not possibly have supported on his salary alone. The guilt was always with him like a dull ache that flared up every time he would put more money into their account. He stopped going to Confession and Communion because of it. What was the point? He couldn't get absolution unless he committed to make restitution and if he made restitution they would be plunged back to the subsistence level that had made he and Deirdre so unhappy at the start of their marriage. Tomorrow he would see to it that the additional finds were transferred from the Building Society in Ireland to his National West Minister account.

    Deirdre chatted happily on. They finished one bottle of wine and opened another. They went to bed about one o clock after having checked on Michael. That night they slept in each other's arms, something they didn't do very often.

Chapter Three

Brett Johnson and Chaddick Spencer walked up to the fourteenth tee. The older man was of medium height and going bald. He had a powerful physique though running to fat around the midriff. The younger, tall, over six foot, was thin, and not very muscular.

It was Saturday; they had started the round at nine o clock, one of the first on the course since in the dead of Winter daylight only broke around eight thirty. The golf course was about four miles outside of Guildford where Brett Johnson lived. His boss Chaddick Spencer and his wife had come down for the weekend.

'Need to move along these last few holes, Brett 'Spencer said. 'Otherwise we will be late for this pub lunch with our wives. You and Patricia have a pretty nice set up down here. Wish my wife liked the country. She would never go for it though. We have to live in the city she says. Take advantage of all the culture and that shit.'

Spencer teed off first and drove the shot down the fairway but over to the left. Johnson had not the same power in his shots but was more accurate and so the pair were pretty evenly matched. His shot went straight down the middle of the fairway but ended a couple of hundred yards further away from the green than Spencer's.

'How are we doing with the new system Brett? 'Spencer asked.

'Well I got a status from Joe yesterday.' Johnson responded. 'He says we should be ok if we get the new computer in on time. He asked me to approve a bunch more overtime though'.

Spencer shrugged. 'I don't give a shit about the overtime. We just need those systems in. The whole business plan depends on it! These guys have been working in regulated industries so long they don't know which side is up. For years they have never had to focus on anything much beyond drawing their paycheck. That's why you and I are here, fella. The guys in power over here, the Conservatives, seem to have gotten the message that this country has to get more competitive in a global market or its on its way to becoming a banana republic. So, they privatise a bunch of things including the utilities industry. The only problem, cleaning up the town is going to need a ramrod. And that ramrod is going to have the unacceptable face of capitalism. So, what do they do? They hire a bunch of mercenaries to do the dirty job for them and that's where the likes of us come in. The Metropolitan Electricity Board is an inefficient operation. We could get their job done with a third less of the labour force. That says you could give the shareholders a decent return without raising the price of power to the consumer, maybe even cut it some'.

'But what about the displaced workers?' Johnson asked.

'Son, I have got news for you. Those jobs are going away anyhow. If not those jobs, then somebody else's jobs in this country. Electric power is a cost of production. The way things are in the world today, there's plenty of people to compete for almost anything you might care to produce. And if you don't keep your costs of production under control, you wake up one morning and discover that your next door neighbour, the French or some country over in Asia or even the good ole US of A is making your product for a lower cost and selling it to your customers. Now the Conservatives appear to have figured this out. The only problem is that in the short term there's going to be some blood on the carpet in these regulated industries. So, they hire themselves a hatchet man like me and when the dirty work is done, they give me the shove and put in some establishment Brit. That way they can blame a lot of the unpleasantness on the insensitive American asshole, who doesn't appreciate the finer points about the fabric of British Society'.

'I think that's being too cynical 'said Johnson, 'I think they hired you because you're one of the best in the business'.

The older man looked at him. 'That's what I like about you Brett. You got a good heart and you keep it that way. But I am telling you son, I figure I got about three years in this contract and after that I am history'.

He gave a wolfish grin. 'Not that it matters, the golden parachute in my contract is going to give them indigestion , big time'.

They continued with their game. At the eighteenth tee, a fine drizzle began to fall. It ended with Spencer winning the round by two holes. As they walked back to the club house the older man asked 'So, what are you doing for Christmas, Brett, you are going back home?'

'No, with the new system converting over New Years, I didn't feel that I could take the time. Patricia's parents are coming over to spend Christmas with us'.

'I guess Deborah and I are staying here too. Of course, she has me on the Jenny Craig diet so I don't know what I am going to get for Christmas dinner.' Spencer patted his paunch. 'I guess it will be some kind of bean sprouts.

The older man paused. 'You know you are a lucky guy Brett, to have your wife and kids around. This time of year, particularly, I miss my kids. Jeez, I miss being n New York. I miss going to the ice hockey games with the kids, going to the Garden, seeing the Rangers kick the shit out of some other team.

I miss the smell of pretzels and roasting chestnuts on my way to Grand Central Station. Deborah is a trophy wife; I was thinking with my dick. Madge put up with a lot of nonsense from me over the years but she turned a blind eye to a lot of things. She certainly wasn't going to stand still for Deborah. Oh, Deborah is top drawer right enough. Her father is an investment banker. She went to all the right schools, to Vassar and to Brown and she's fifteen years younger than I am. She was pretty insistent that we get away from the States. She doesn't have too much time for my kids. I'll get them next Summer; they're coming over for a couple of weeks, but it's tough being over here. Ah, fuck it. I'm getting sentimental and maudlin in my old age. Let's get going to this pub lunch'.

Johnson really didn't know how to respond. His boss had never really spoken about his personal life before. He asked what he hoped was a neutral question.

'If you're from Texas, what made you so fond of New York?'

His boss looked at him. 'That's right, a farm about fifty miles outside of Austin, Texas. I didn't travel around much when I was a kid. Austin, which we got to every couple of months, was the big city for me. Then coming out of high school I applied for the Point, had the local congressman recommend me and there I was. First time I saw New York was a weekend pass me and a bunch of other cadets got. We came down on a Greyhound bus. Coming, out of the Port Authority onto Eighth Avenue, just blew me away. I fell in love with the place, the excitement, the energy, all those people. All my time at the Point I went down to New York every chance I got. And when I was in Nam I promised myself if I ever got out of the place alive, New York was where I was going to live.

'Well, I can relate somewhat to that ' Johnson responded. 'When you phoned me up about this job, Pat and I thought about it and figured it would be a great experience both for us and the kids. Neither of us have ever been out of the States. We did our homework, of course, and we read books on London, but nothing prepares you for the actual experience of it. How are your kids, anyway?'

'The boys, oh, they're doing fine I guess. I talked to them last weekend. I don't get to see as much of them as I would like. I would really like to but Deborah isn't too wild about my spending time with them. She says we are going to start a family of our own one of these days. She'd want to get on with it, I'm no spring chicken.'

Johnson at that point felt sorry for his boss. 'Why don't you tell her you are going to see them and that's all there is to it?'

He said it impulsively without thinking about it. Then he reflected. 'My God, I have just given him a piece of advice. He doesn't take advice'. Johnson waited for the explosion. Surprisingly, it didn't come.

'I've thought about it a lot lately, must be the time of year. I thought about telling Deborah that we are going back to the States for Christmas, for instance. I've thought about asking for a divorce. The only problem is that she has this prenuptial agreement that I was fool enough to sign. The way it's set up, if I pull the plug she walks away with pretty much everything. Ironic, isn't it, graduate of West Point, survived two tours of Nam, Chief Executive of a major UK company and this east coast Wasp has me trussed up tight as a turkey at Thanksgiving.'

They entered the clubhouse as the chimes of the clock from the nearby village church struck twelve.

The December days dragged on with the seemingly incessant grey driving rain. A few days before Christmas it began to snow. At the Metropolitan Electricity Board, the department worked itself into a frenzy of activity getting ready for the year end conversion to the new system. There was, however, a certain schizophrenia about it. People worked very long hours but then took off to one of the many parties that were being held for the holiday season and in some cases would arrive looking rather sick the next morning. One programmer with a particularly crucial piece of the software to test came in with the flu, a temperature over a hundred and slept on a trestle bed in order to get in as much testing as possible. His supervisor asked constantly how many errors were left in the program and occasionally about his temperature.

The daily status meetings became catalogues of disasters averted and endless overlooked details. The arrival of additional computing capacity plus the reorganisation of the customer database had got the conversion processing time to a reasonable window. It had been anticipated, however, that on a customer base of ten million there would be twenty to thirty thousand records with errors that couldn't be converted over until some correction could be made to the file to clean it up. The first mock run of the file produced not twenty thousand, but two hundred thousand such records. Clearly, the data entry effort to clean all this up in advance of the conversion date was beyond the capacity of the department. At the status meeting they decided to simply plug something into the new database and flag the error records as needing correction later. Yet another problem arose. When it became apparent that the customer service representatives out in the district office would now have to spend many more hours of their day in front of a visual display unit, their union threatened to strike since they said this represented a health and safety issue. Frantic negotiations took place between management and the union which resulted in a compromise, job rotation. The impact for management, however, was that the intended savings out in the district offices in terms of personnel needed to perform the workload were not going to be so dramatic.

Someone printed up the wrong version of forms related to a version of the software that essentially had been obsoleted four months previously. User training was going abysmally. Mock business days which attempted to simulate in a training environment what it would be like to process business against the new system, demonstrated that transactions which the users were expected to complete in four to five minutes with the aid of the system were actually taking them ten to fifteen minutes. The workforce implications were horrendous. More training courses were hastily scheduled and the more complex screens had to be reprogrammed.

For Andrew, the period was spent in an agony of indecision. He had the opportunity to reprogram the billing algorithms to eliminate the computer fraud. What he could not count on, however, was whether in running comparisons between results of the old system and the new someone might not inadvertently discover a discrepancy. The old system had been so much smaller. He had control over all aspects of it. Security over the software libraries was much more lax. Now whereas he had made sure that he still controlled the programming of the critical billing algorithms there were other aspects of the system, particularly in the areas of financial reporting, which he did not control. He decided with much trepidation to leave well enough alone.

He repressed his guilt and anxieties as best as he could. Christmas fell on a Monday that year; the previous Friday there was a Christmas lunch in the staff canteen. Normally, the department adjourned to one of the local pubs after Christmas lunch, but this year because of the system conversion most of the people went grumbling back to work. Retroactive Billing was in reasonably good shape so he, Peter and the two interns quit about five o clock and went down to the Swallows Inn.

The pub was festooned with holly and fairy lights. There was a busy hum, even louder than usual, it being the Christmas season. Martin and Gwynn, as they had a charity row on Christmas day confined themselves to two glasses of lager a piece. Peter and Andrew matched them with pints of bitter. The interns called it quits at eight o clock. But Andrew was anxious and worried about the impending system conversion and whether the financial reporting would bring any irregularities to light. He found himself ordering more drinks compulsively. Peter, if he noted the unusual behaviour, chose to say nothing, and seemed happy to accompany Andrew in his binge.

Their conversation wandered over a variety of topics. Peter was going on to a Christmas party after the pub closed. The party was being hosted by an acquaintance of a girl that he had bumped into after one of his rugby matches. Peter over the five years he had been in London had, as far as Andrew could see, entertained a succession of girlfriends, none of the relationships lasting very long. In a couple of instances, he had moved in with a girl. Peter's relationships with the opposite sex seemed, from his accounts, to be generally fiery. A lot of crockery got thrown around. One particularly feisty girl had broken a picture over his head in a domestic argument. When Peter described the women he went out with he talked exclusively about their physical attributes. He favoured big bosomy women and had a complete library of Madonna videos and CDs.

Peter started out the conversation with his usual rhapsody about how well stacked his latest acquaintance was and mused about what his chances were later on that night.

'Well, this thing is going to go on into all hours of the morning and there will probably be dead bodies all over the floor. I don't know with all that going on whether I'm going to get my leg over or even get a chance at it'.

Andrew rolled his eyes towards the ceiling, tipsy. Peter continued 'Particularly this time of year I think, jeez wouldn't it be great to have a steady girlfriend? These one-night stands are all very well but they are not too good for your health this day and age. You pretty well have to wear a condom if you don't know the girl and then if you had a few before you get down to business, if you know what I mean – put it this way, condoms and alcohol don't mix'.

Andrew looked at him. 'Peter have you ever thought about talking to the girl before taking her to bed?'

'You mean chatting her up? Sure, I got some great lines.'

'No Peter, I mean talking to her. Trying to figure out what interests her, whether you have any common interests.

Peter looked dumbfounded. 'Most girls aren't interested in the kinds of things I am interested in. They couldn't give a toss about how rugby is played. They don't know the soccer results.

Andrew tried again 'Peter in any long-term relationship you are going to spend a lot more time out of the bed than in it. If you tried to find a girl that had some common ground with you and thought of you first as a companion rather than as a sexual partner you might find that the relationship would last longer'.

Peter was not to be persuaded. 'If I wanted a companion, I would buy a dog'.

'My shout now Andrew, what are you going to have?'

'Make it a whiskey this time Peter. If I keep drinking beer, I will float out of here before the night is out'.

While Peter went to get the drinks, Andrew went to the Gents.

'So, are you going back to the Emerald Isle at all over the vacation? 'Peter asked when they sat back down.

'I'd be trapped in the same house as my mother 'Andrew answered. 'Not on your life. Besides, we have too much to do over here'.

It was the booze talking. Normally Andrew was very circumspect about his domestic situation. Peter didn't pick up on it. 'Yeah, I understand, families can be a pain. Is there anything you miss about Christmas in Ireland?' he asked.

Andrew reflected 'I suppose I miss meeting up with my cousins, getting all caught up with the family gossip. You know the usual. Who is splitting up, who is sleeping with whom? I miss my friends from college. But then we've all moved on, have families and so forth so I don't really see much of them even when I do go back. One thing I don't miss is going to the graveyards on Christmas morning.'

'Come again? 'Peter looked befuddled.

'Oh yes, you have traffic jams outside Glasnevin Cemetery on Christmas Day with all the people trying to get in. Just so as you are aware Peter, the cult of the dead didn't pass away with the Egyptians. It's alive and well and living in Ireland.'

Peter chuckled 'I always knew you Irish were a rum bunch, I will go up north on Sunday afternoon, spend Christmas and Boxing day with the parents. Where we come from you spend Christmas morning down at the Working Man's Club getting shit faced, then go home, have a big feed, sit back and watch the Queen's speech on the box'.

'Well, the Irish don't stint on the alcohol either, Peter. Generally, what happens is that you go to the graveyard, come back depressed then knock back a few hot whiskeys to cope with the cold and the depression'.

'Time now, ladies and gentlemen please, time now'. The bartender rattled his glasses and yelled at the top of his lungs in the hopes of dispersing the raucous crowd. It was already twenty past eleven, twenty minutes past closing.

'I'd best drink up 'Andrew said, 'or I will miss the last tube home'.

He joined the stream of people leaving the pub on their way to pick up cars or like him, heading for the tube station. Elephant and Castle was not too crowded but Piccadilly Circus, where he had to make the change, was a mess thronged with Christmas travellers. He kept well back from the front of the crowd, even though it meant he would probably stand all the way out to Turnham Green. There had been too many stories about people being pushed onto the tube line by the relentless crush of the crowd coming down the access tunnels.

Toward Finsbury Park the tube had emptied out sufficiently so that he could get a seat. He wondered blearily though the haze of alcohol what the conversion to the new system would bring. He went through it in his mind, the options, and alternatives if anything should come to light. He dozed off.

He woke to the sound of the driver calling out 'Cockfosters, end of the line, everybody out please, everybody out'.

He had slept past his station. This had not happened to him in ten years. The lavatory was closed so he had to relieve himself in the bushes outside. Then came the hunt for a telephone booth that was working and which accepted coins as he had no telephone card. He eventually found one which even had telephone directories. He contacted a mini cab company. There was going to be an hour wait because it was the weekend before Christmas but he really didn't have too much choice so he agreed. In the end, he didn't get home until two thirty and Deirdre was fast asleep.

The next morning, he felt wretched. He was supposed to take Michael to see Santa Claus. They didn't get going until after one o clock in the afternoon so he had to settle for Santa Claus at one of the less upmarket stores. The lines, at places like Harrods, would be far too long.

Andrew drank copious quantities of water and took aspirin every two to three hours in an effort to cope with the hangover. He rather suspected Michael knew about Santa Claus but they both maintained the fiction as it was a good excuse for them to go out together.

On Christmas morning, they all went to Mass; something Andrew did with Michael every Sunday. Deirdre occasionally went, generally for the big feasts, Easter, and Christmas. When they got back she began organising the dinner. Michael was in his bedroom happily playing with the construction kit his parents had bought him. Andrew brought Deirdre a glass of wine.

'Well, I suppose I better get it over with'.

'Get what over with 'Deirdre asked as she chopped carrots.

'Phoning my mother'.

'You make it sound like you are going to the dentist Andrew'.

'I know. I don't know what it is about having a conversation with her, but it always ends up with me going on a huge guilt trip'.

'Mothers always know what buttons to push Andrew. Yours is just a more extreme example of the breed'.

Andrew sighed and went to the telephone. The phone was answered on the first ring. She must have been waiting beside it.

'Merry Christmas Mother'.

'Oh. I just got in from visiting the graveyards. My parent's graves are a disgrace; I don't know what we are paying Perpetual Care for. I spent a half hour on my knees cleaning the headstone. It's taken me all morning; you know what the bus service is like in Dublin on a Christmas Day. I had to wait forty-five minutes for a bus home'.

'Could Uncle Joe not have taken you to the graveyard Mother?'

'He's coming to collect me for Christmas dinner. Isn't that enough? I don't care to impose on people to that extent Andrew'.

'Mother 'Andrew said with a hint of exasperation, 'he's your brother'.

'Makes no difference, I would like to have some independence'.

'Could you not have taken a taxi then?'

'You have no sense of money Andrew, but then you never had. I'm a widow with one child in Canada and another in England. I can't afford to be running around in taxis.

'How are you feeling? 'Andrew tried to change the subject.

'My arthritis is bothering me but I get by. Have you been to mass yet? 'his mother asked.

'Yes, we have. We just got back'.

'Did Deirdre go too?'

'Yes mother, Deirdre went too.'

'Well, that's something at any rate.'

'Michael liked the sweater you sent him very much.'

'I'm glad. It took me a while to knit it with my hands and all. It wasn't too big for him?'

'No, just the right size'.

'Well, I had best not be running up your phone bill 'his mother said, 'Your Uncle Joe will be by shortly and I still have his presents to wrap.'

Andrew thought he should prolong the conversation. He took the cowards way out. 'I will phone you for New Year's Eve then mother. My best to Uncle Joe and Auntie Martha'.

'Another year older and deeper in debt 'his mother responded gloomily. 'There's the doorbell, that will be him. Goodbye Andrew'. She put down the phone. The thin querulous voice echoed in his head all the rest of the day.

Chapter Four

The system converted the day after New Year's. At first everything appeared to go reasonably well; there were not many customers in the branch offices and so the clerical staff were able to keep up with the demand. As the week wore on, however, backlogs began to mount up and the lines for customer services grew longer and longer. Remittance processing, where customers paid their bills by cheque, began to experience problems. The process had been completely revamped utilising the very latest in optical scanning technology, but the new machines seemed very temperamental. They had performed well enough in the acceptance testing but continued operation over several days had caused then to start breaking down with distressing regularity. The cash flow of the enterprise in the first week, instead of getting better, proceeded to get worse.

The project teams were holding daily status meetings. As the first week progressed the atmosphere at the meetings went from mild euphoria to concern and now towards the end of the first week's operation, a feeling of barely concealed panic was pervasive, coupled with a sense that the situation was slipping out of control. For Andrew, the week though nerve wracking, had gone quite well. Customer billing cycles which had been run twice so far, had proceeded without event and the bills had been cut.

On the eighth of January, Joe Fortisque pushed up the status meeting scheduled for one pm to eleven am and announced that they would work through lunch. It was a subdued group that had gathered in the conference room; there was little of the kibitzing that normally went on and everyone took their seat quietly. Fred opened the meeting without preamble.

'We had a major incident over on Finchley Road on Saturday. One of our customer services people was assaulted by a customer. It would appear that the bloke had to queue for three and a half hours last Monday to pay a reconnection fee and was assured that we would have his electricity back in forty-eight hours. His wife is pregnant. Well, by last Thursday he still wasn't reconnected and was getting no satisfaction over the phone. So, the following morning he went down, queued again for three hours to be told by our clerk that we have no record of his previous transaction. Our employee was hauled across the counter and the fellow proceeded to punch him out and had to be physically restrained. We prevailed on the clerk not to press charges. Matters are going from bad to worse and it's only a matter of time before this kind of thing gets into the newspapers. 'The attendees around the table looked stunned.

'Ok people let's get down to it. Dave, you were to report back to us with the cause or causes of the backlogs of our district offices. What did you find out?'

'Well Joe, there are a few things. First, the training that the service representatives received covered cases that were too simplistic. The mix of transactions that we get over the counter in real life covers a greater range of situations. The service reps are unfamiliar with all of the features of the new system and it takes them a while to complete the transactions. To illustrate, we estimated that measuring the time it takes for the customer to come to the counter to the time that he leaves with his transaction completed, five minutes would have elapsed. In fact, it's taking more like eight to nine. In a couple of districts, communication controllers weren't working correctly and this was causing the poor response time at the terminals which of course, contributed to the delays. That particular problem has been corrected. The last major cause of the delays is the number of validation errors we are getting when keying in the transactions. We were anticipating a one to two percent error rate. What we are getting is more like four or five percent.'

'Why is that? 'Joe asked wearily.

'Well there are a couple of reasons and I can't quantify how much each one is contributing. Some of it is just errors in the validation routines so we are getting false rejections. The second problem is more intransigent; it has to do with the state of the converted database.'

No one liked the sound of this. Dave took a deep breath.

'Well the validation routines were specified on the assumption that we had a clean customer database. You remember about a month ago we were having difficulty getting the conversion to run in the available window. A lot of that had to do with the errors we were getting as we tried to convert because the old database was corrupt for quite a number of customers. We decided to strip out the validations and just convert those customers as is so we could hit the window. Well now every time we tried to process a transaction against one of those corrupted records, of course it bounces'.

'God in heaven 'Joe was now at the white board and was jotting down the laundry list of problems as they were being recited.

'Dave, why are we not able to post cash to customer accounts?'

'Very simple, customer duplicates'

'Say what? 'Joe looked astounded. 'How can there be duplicate customers?'

'Well, in the old system the key was type of service in customer number, so if you had a domestic meter that was different from a commercial meter and then you put the customer number on that and you got a unique key. We decided to go to a customer view of the database so that now we have customer and it doesn't really matter how many types of service we provide it's just that one customer. The problem is that in the old system we set up a lot of customer numbers that were the same. It didn't matter then because we still had the service type identifier which provided the unique key now, of course, that isn't the case'.

'How could we have possibly converted over duplicate customer records?' Joe exploded.

'Well 'Dave responded reasonably, 'We had put in the validations in the conversion routines to catch that but then as you recollect we took those out for performance reasons'.

Joe collapsed in his chair. 'This is a total balls up. And I have to go in and give status in an hours 'time 'Joe sighed. 'Can we roll it back?'

Everyone looked up startled. 'What do you mean roll it back Joe?'

'I mean revert back to the old system and process all the transactions that we have done this week?'

'It would be a monumental effort to reprocess all of these transactions Joe 'Dave murmured.

'it will be a big effort whichever way we go 'Joe responded. 'And at least if we go back to the old system we can have a comfort level that it will work'.

Arthur Forehand who was in charge of operations, raised his hand sheepishly. 'I was hoping not to have to tell you this Joe but I am afraid that we can't go back'.

Joe looked at him aghast.

'You see we were strapped for disk space and one of the guys inadvertently deleted the production load modules for the old system'

In God's name Arthur, that's insane. What possessed him?'

'Well it was a new fellow and it was over the holiday period. There was an awful lot going on Joe, trying to get ready for the conversion. I'm not condoning it. It just happened'. 'We take back up surely?' Joe had by now gnawed away half of his pencil in agitation.

Arthur sighed. 'Well about six months ago we put in a new automated archival system which basically schedules backups of the datasets in an automated fashion. Before we had to initiate the backup process manually. Only problem is you have to identify the datasets to the archival system that you want backed up and as luck would have it a couple of datasets where we had some of the production system didn't get named so we were only backing up partially. There are some key modules that we don't have any copy of.'

Joe was a broken man. No one spoke for over two minutes. The silence yawned like a chasm. Joe Fortisque seemed to Andrew to have aged ten years. He seemed physically shrunken. Finally, Fortisque roused himself 'It looks like we have no choice but to go on, so we are going to have to take each of these problems one by one and decide what we can do to address them'.

Coffee and sandwiches were ordered in and everybody settled down for what was obviously going to be a long and painful meeting. The inescapable conclusion was that more resources were going to have to be applied to the system, systems resources to reprogram a number of the processes to take account of what they now knew , user resources in terms of extended overtime for the customer representatives and the clerical staff dealing with the remittance processing . The new system, far from allowing them to reduce their personnel costs , would inflate them significantly for the foreseeable future. The meeting broke up with everyone clearly understanding that what lay before them was a future of unrelieved long hours and unremitting frustration. Joe tottered off like a man condemned to brief his boss. Andrew wandered back to his desk. Peter stopped by soon after he sat down.

'Well Andrew , what news from the status meeting ? 'Andrew smiled wryly at him. 'I think we can safely conclude that the wonders of modern technology are not all that there cracked up to be Peter.'

Peter chuckled, 'you don't say. Well at least in our little part of the world things appear to be going okay. The customer billing cycle ran clean last night. Had a few problems printing the new style bills but we got that sorted out. '

'We kept a copy of the print file I suppose ? 'Andrew asked.

'Oh sure 'Peter responded.

'Okay have them run me some sample bills from a section of the file so I can do a manual check. It doesn't do to be complacent Peter. '

'A worrywart like you , no one is ever going to suggest that of you Andrew. I'll have them do it right away. '

Joe Fortisque met Brett Johnson in his corner office which had a view of the Thames. The lanky American was surrounded by basketball memorabilia.

'Well Joe what have you got for me ?'

'Well Brett, as I'm sure you're aware , we've been having some teething troubles bedding down the new system. Nothing we can't put right of course. But sometimes it's easy to lose perspective about the fact that this is a major overhaul, the first we've done of its kind in twenty five years and also a major organisational change.'

'Why is this not giving me a warm feeling Joe , I'm a big boy , I know it's bad news. You don't need to sugar-coat the pill. What exactly is going on?'

'There's two big pieces to it. In order to convert on time, we made the decision to defer cleaning up some of the shit in the old customer databases until after we went live. The new system was programmed on the assumption that there was clean data in the customer databases. What's happening is that we are getting an awful lot of errors because of that and slowing down the processing and the backlogs are building. The second big piece of the problem is that the training we gave our people was too simplistic for the real-life situations and so we are not getting the productivity levels that we anticipated. '

'So, what are you going to do about it Joe?'

'A couple of things. We are going to reprogram part of the system to make it more tolerant of data problems that might be encountered on the customer database and we're simultaneously going to put in a big effort to clean up the database. I'm recommending that you authorise extended overtime to do this. For the training problem, we're going to put together some additional training courses and materials which we will give to the people after hours and on Saturdays. '

'This is going to send the budget overrun, through the roof Joe.'
'I know that but at this point we don't have any other alternatives. '

'And when are we going to get back to steady state ?'

Joe looked at him. 'Well obviously I'm going to have to run some numbers and we need to get a better handle on just how much work is out there. But I couldn't promise you that we could be back to normal much before six months. '

'I'll go and brief the Man Joe but you know that there's going to be a post-mortem on this and it just isn't going to be pleasant. '

Joe sighed.

Johnson went to brief his boss who was practicing his putting when he arrived at the office.

'Damn, that was a close one. '

'Chaddick, we have got problems. '

Chaddick Spencer chuckled. 'I'm not paying you a six-figure salary to tell me that. What kind of problems?'

Johnson recited the litany of woe

'So, what are you going to do about it ?' Spencer was no longer smiling. Johnson rehashed what Fortisque had told him.

'How much more is this going to cost ?'

'We're building up the numbers in detail of course , but ballpark, another five million pounds. '

His boss stopped putting. 'This is horseshit. I have a board meeting one week from today. Two years ago, I went to these guys and told them that in order to position the Electricity Board as a commercial for-profit enterprise they needed new systems. This was going to cost ten million pounds and take eighteen months but the new system would pay for itself in direct savings in one year and indirectly it would position the enterprise to go into new lines of business not to mention dramatically improving customer service. '

'Six months ago, I had to go and tell them that the system is going to be six months late and guess what it's going to cost twenty million but not to worry it will pay for itself in two years. Now I have to go in front of these guys and tell them it's going to cost them twenty five million and we're not going to see any hard savings for another six months and it's going to take two and a half years to pay for itself. In their oh so polite British way those guys are going to hand me my head and I don't blame them. '

'This is what you're going to do Brett. First of all, you're going to fire Fred Flintstone's AKA Joe Fortisque's ass and you are personally responsible for this project from today forward. Then we're going to focus on the receivables. We currently have aged receivables fifty percent of them sixty days past due and mostly from the big commercial accounts. This is what you're going to do from now on. Any account that is more than 30 days past due is disconnected. The only exceptions are hospitals and defence installations. I'll tell the board that we're going to take an aggressive posture on the receivable side. The additional cash flow we generate is going to offset the new overrun and basically the cost benefit projection would not have altered since last June. '

Brett was grey. 'I understand how you feel about Joe , boss, And I guess after this last experience I have to agree with you that he has got to go. But this thirty day and disconnect thing.'

His boss exploded. 'I don't give a rats ass what do you think Brett. I warned you about these guys six months ago when we had the first fuck up. I told you to stay on top of them and you didn't. Now I'll run cover for you at the board level but let me make this perfectly clear. I've known you a long time Brett but one more screw up and it's your ass.'

He was rummaging in his drawer 'Jesus where did I put my antacid?'

Chapter Five

Robert Petrie pulled wearily into the driveway of his semi-detached house in Putney at half past eleven. Age thirty-two he was the Conservative MP for the district, having won the seat in a by election from the labour party which had held it uninterrupted for thirty years. The constituency was largely working class. The truth be told, it wasn't that Robert had so much won the seat as that the Labour candidate had lost it. Reg Phillips was a well-known figure on the London City Council and well respected in the constituency. Unfortunately for him, one week before polling day he had become embroiled in a highly visible and widely publicised financial scandal. It came as a welcome surprise to the conservative party head office, not to mention his own constituency association, when Robert actually won the seat.

His wife Marjorie was in the kitchen drinking cocoa and reading the days newspapers.

'Sorry I'm so late Marge. After the division at ten o clock I needed to spend some time with Phil Andrews, working out our pairing for next week.'

Phillip Andrews was the Labour MP with whom Robert usually 'paired'. Pairing was an arrangement whereby two members of the opposing parties would agree to be absent from the house on a prearranged schedule. This meant that the overall voting balance in a vote of the house would not be affected by their absence.

Robert and Marjorie wanted to take a long weekend the next week and go up to Scotland for the skiing.

'What are you voting on?' Marjorie asked.

'Oh. The third reading of the environment bill. It passed handily enough; we had a majority of fifteen.'

'Was the PM there?'

'Oh yes. Large as life and looking very pleased with himself. The legislative agenda is running like clockwork this year. Even if we do only have a majority of four.'

The conservative party currently had a majority of four over all of the other parties combined in the house. This meant that most votes were closely contested and so the MPs needed to be on call each evening at ten o clock when the divisions were taken.

'Any chance for a spot of cocoa?'

'Of course, I made a pot of it 'Marjorie answered, 'help yourself.'

'I wish to God they would get around to looking at Commons reform ' Robert sighed.

From time to time there were discussions between the major parties about reforming House of Commons procedures. The custom of always voting at ten o clock at night was very wearing on the members of Parliament. Robert, being a London MP, was at least able to go home. The MPs for the rest of the country were obliged to spend several nights a week in the Capitol. This put a strain on a lot of marriages. Marjorie was not impressed with the complaint.

'Well, you knew what you were letting yourself in for Robert when you gave up your nice job in the City and decided to run for Parliament'.

'You're right Marge but I must say you're being very good about it.'

Marjorie smiled. 'Oh, I'm a political hack just like you Robert but both of us can't go into politics. With what they are paying you one of us has to see to the household finances.'

Robert's salary as a backbench MP came to thirty thousand pounds. This was a third of what he had been earning as an investment broker in the City. Marjorie was communications director of a large retailing firm. He and Marjorie had both been politically active and this is how they had met in Oxford at the young conservative club. The decision that he go into politics had been a joint one. Marjorie had read history. Robert economics. Both had been serious students and their relationship had been born out of commonly held beliefs and time spent working together on political activities. Fundamentally both believed what was good for British business was good for the country in general. They saw a restricted role for government.

'Coming to bed?' Robert asked.

'Yes, I guess so. Let me just wash up the cups. Marjorie did not like leaving things in the dishwasher overnight.

'How did your committee meeting go today?'

Robert was on the labour and industry committee for the house. He was currently working on a bill which would align UK law governing worker compensation with EC regulations. 'It's pretty heavy sledding. Of course, there isn't any unanimity about what exactly the protocols from Brussels mean. I'd say it will probably be another month or so of work before we are able to send the bill back to the House. How was your day Marjorie?'

'Well, we announced the quarterly results today and they were pretty mediocre. The Chairman gave one of his 'Times are Hard 'speeches. You know the sort of thing. Increased competition, problems with the Exchange rates, weak demand. No suggestion of course that the management might just be a bit inept.'

Robert grinned at her. 'Marjorie, bite your tongue.'

'Oh, put a sock in it Robert. What I do is less communications than propaganda.'

'One mustn't complain. It pays the rent.'

'What are you doing tomorrow?' She asked him.

'Well, there's a charity bazaar at the local church. They want me to open it so I'll do that. Then there's a clinic being held at Waverly Flats. I'll be home by six.'

Marjorie was elated. 'Good you get to cook dinner then. I fancy some goulash and see if you can't bring home a decent bottle of wine.'

They both undressed as they carried on this conversation. They kissed each other goodnight and fell asleep in their large double bed, but first evicted the cat. Her peculiar pleasure on these cold winter nights was burying herself under the bed clothes.

At the Metropolitan Electricity Board, the struggle to keep the new system up and running continued through the month of January. Brett Johnson replaced Joe Fortisque at the daily status meetings. Joe's sudden dismissal had cast a pall of gloom and unease over the project team. Brett was clearly unfamiliar with the detailed workings of the various parts of the data processing organisation. Much of the status meeting was taken up explaining the roles and functions of various people within the department. The edict of cutting off delinquent accounts thirty days past due date was implemented but not without fierce controversy. Many in the department felt it was a knee jerk reaction.

Chapter Six

The vicar of St James was a stooped prematurely balding man who wore glasses and a permanently worried expression. He greeted Robert Petrie profusely at the church hall where various ladies of the parish were busily setting out their wares on tables arranged around the room.

'Very good of you to come, Mr Petrie. I'm sure the bazaar organisers appreciate it and I certainly do. We are hoping for a good turn out today and of course lots of people will drop by after service tomorrow. The church heating system is over thirty years old and on its last legs so these kind of fund-raising events are very important to us.'

Petrie made a mental note that he would now have to buy something and hoped he could find an item somewhere in the stalls that was not too hideous.

'Very pleased to have been involved vicar. I think it's very important to support these community activities.'

A small round woman of middle years appeared at his elbow. That was Mrs Rutledge, the constituency association treasurer.

'Ah Mr Petrie, you have arrived. There's just fifteen minutes before the opening. I'll quickly introduce you to a couple of ladies.'

Petrie was steered purposefully away.

'The vicar is an awfully good sort, but he does monopolise one so', Mrs Rutledge confided.

Petrie felt like pointing out that he had hardly had the opportunity to speak five words to the vicar but he restrained himself. It doesn't do to fall out with the treasurer of your constituency association, he reminded himself mentally.

'We just need to open the bazaar and spend about an hour circulating ' Mrs Rutledge said . 'I know you must be a busy man but of course it is important to spend time at the grass roots level.'

Petrie agreed. 'Yes, and after this I am going over to Waverly Flats to meet with some people.'

Mrs Rutledge looked a little startled. 'Waverly Flats? I wouldn't have thought that there would be many conservative votes there but still, I suppose, it doesn't hurt.'

'Well, it's a marginal constituency 'Petrie temporised.

Mrs Rutledge thought a moment and then brightened up. 'You're right of course Mr Petrie. You must go out to the highways and byways and gather up all the sheep sort of thing. Yes, very wise, very wise, marginal constituency. Now this is Mrs Blenkinsop, together with a very nice collection of brasses.'

Mrs Blenkinsop was certainly well into her seventies and peered at Petrie with rheumy short-sighted eyes.

'Hilda dear, this is Mr Petrie. He's our local Member of Parliament. You remember I told you that he is going to open the bazaar?'

'What party is he? 'Mrs Blenkinsop asked.

'Oh Tory of course, Hilda. You know that.'

'Voted Tory for forty years and never missed an election.'

Petrie murmured something conventional about it being a wise choice and hoping she would vote for him at the next opportunity.

When the time came to open the bazaar there were about a hundred people in the hall ranging from the vaguely curious to the totally disinterested, to the people with nowhere else to go and nothing else to do on a Sunday morning. Petrie made some vague generalized comments about the social significance of community and how encouraging it was to see support for this effort to preserve the national heritage, which was very important. He reflected after he said it that perhaps repairing the central heating system for the church was stretching it a bit in terms of preserving the national heritage but no one seemed to be paying particular attention to what he was saying. The vicar was smiling beatifically so he felt that what he had said probably covered the situation. After the opening ceremony, he took tea with a number of ladies of the parish and then wandered around the various stalls trying to find something that he could buy. He settled on a delph figurine of a milkmaid milking what he thought was a particularly well endowed cow. He made some further small talk with the vicar and then left gratefully for his next appointment at the Flats.

The Flats were only a half a mile away from the church but it was as if he had entered another world. In place of the stone church and the neat terraced houses which surrounded it, the Flats stood on a bombed-out site. At the side of them was a dis-used railway track, the line long since closed down. Most of the windows had wire grating over them and a number had been completely boarded up. It seemed to Robert Petrie that the smell of stale urine pervaded the place.

Petrie was conscientious about visiting his constituents and in the two years he had been in Parliament had traversed the length and breadth of his constituency. Occasionally with these things people showed up to argue about his politics but more often than not it had to do with welfare benefits or immigration policy. Fundamentally, he was dealing with people caught up in the workings of government bureaucracy. He spent a lot of his time explaining basic benefits to people, and providing them with information as to where to get assistance. In cases where he thought the constituent had a legitimate grievance he carefully noted down the salient points and afterwards wrote a letter on Commons stationery to the appropriate department, seeking information. Anything he found out he communicated to the constituent.

When he had first started these rounds, he had been genuinely shocked at some of the conditions people were living in. A number of the stories, particularly those where young families were separated because of immigration restrictions, were heart breaking . Little by little he had become accustomed to it, growing as it were a shell or veneer to make him insensitive to the pain underlying some of these people's lives.

There were about forty people waiting for him when he got to the Flats. The meeting was being held in the community room. Tea and biscuits were laid on. He introduced himself and assured everyone that he would stay until he had talked to them all. He looked at his watch and it was past two. He had promised Marjorie to be home by six and wondered if he would make it.

It was the usual crop of concerns and complaints, unemployment benefits, child benefits. Some people were truculent, some tearful, a number of them thanked him for taking the time and assured him that they would vote for him at the next election. Around five thirty when he was thinking of finishing up and going home an old woman shuffled up to him supported on the arm of a younger, though still middle-aged, friend. Petrie sighed inwardly but managed to say, for what seemed the umpteenth time 'Hi, my name is Robert Petrie. I'm your Member of Parliament. What can I do for you?'

'Nice to meet you young man. Dora Heard's my name. I'm sorry to be troubling you but it's that I'm having difficulty getting qualified for disability benefits.'

'What can I do for you? 'Petrie asked with a practiced smile.

'Well, these last few years I have been diabetic and there's been problems with the circulation to my feet. I had a fruit and vegetable stall for forty years at Fenchurch Street but I guess the standing around got too much for me and I got a problem. When I went to the Doctor he said that I had a touch of gangrene so they cut off a couple of my toes. I get around sort of, but I can't walk any distance.'

'What is the problem precisely? 'Petrie asked.

'Well I filled out all the forms and sent them off to the DHSS but they disallowed it. They don't seem to think that a couple of missing toes are anything too serious.'

Her friend burst in indignantly 'Fine, but Dora is a war widow. Her husband Fred was awarded the Victoria Cross posthumously. Then she lost most of her family in the blitz. For years she wouldn't take the widows pension and now when she needs the money the government won't give it to her.'

'But why didn't you apply for the widow's pension? 'Petrie asked bewildered.

Dora smiled. 'I didn't feel I ought to ; after all. I was able to earn my own living.'

Petrie looked at Dora anew. He saw an elderly woman in a tweed coat and boots lined with some sort of artificial fur, a small nondescript hat perched on her head. She was breathing heavily from the exertion of walking and seemed in some discomfort but there was a twinkle in her eye. He made a mental note to take this one up directly with the Minister even though he rarely did that, preferring to go through channels by writing to the Department responsible. The Ministers were constantly having their ears bent by Members with requests about constituents but Petrie rarely looked for favours such as this.

'Well I will certainly look into it for you Mrs Heard and see what I can find out. If I could have your address and a telephone number that would help. '

Petrie took the necessary information including the PRSI number. He gathered up his papers and made ready to leave. He watched Dora shuffling slowly and painfully towards the door.

Petrie was pensive that evening as he ate dinner with Marjorie. He explained to her about Dora but she was not particularly sympathetic.

'Well if I understand what you're telling me Robert the woman was entitled to the widow's pension but chose not to take it. That's really her decision.'

'I suppose so but if you could have seen her Marjorie. It's just that the contrast in terms of living conditions between the people at the church village hall and the people that I met at the Flats was so stark. '

'That may be so Robert. But I think the responsibility of the state is to provide equality of opportunity. Forced redistribution of wealth is a socialist aspiration not a conservative one. '

'I understand the theories very well Marjorie but it seems to me the practical effect is that we are creating a Society of haves and have nots. It's nothing I can point to directly and say that's it. It's little things like when I walk down the Strand in the mornings there are homeless people sleeping in doorways. I don't remember that growing up as a child'. He sighed in exasperation.

Marjorie was uncompromising. 'We all look back with nostalgia on our childhood Robert. There was poverty when you were growing up. Maybe it wasn't so visible but it was there. Look you're a Tory member of parliament and you have a working-class constituency. You're conscientious. I've watched you; you do the best you can for your constituents. But what that does not mean Robert is that you sacrifice your principles or those of your party.'

Robert became defensive, 'All I'm doing is speculating Marjorie, reflecting on my day. I'm not some kind of Colonel Blimp type - my country right or wrong. I need to be able to integrate my experiences with my political philosophy. Hopefully to broaden and deepen it. It would be nice to have some support from my wife in this. '

Marjorie looked at him with a mixture of disgust and exasperation, 'you are hopeless Robert. I often wonder whether the wrong one of us entered politics.'

Robert was taken aback by the speed at which the conversation had degenerated. The solid comfortable fabric of his marriage suddenly seemed to him under threat. He tried to defuse the situation. 'We're both tired Marjorie it's been a long day for me, let's not talk about this now. '

Marjorie smiled wearily at him.' That's right Robert let's avoid conflict at all costs. You are a sweet man and I love you dearly at least I think I do most of the time. '

Chapter Seven

The first indication that the revised delinquent receivables policy of the Metropolitan Electricity Board was having unintended side effects became apparent with the Boat Show fiasco. Quite simply, the conference centre where the Show was being held forgot or omitted to pay its electricity bill for the month of November. And on the 10th of January supply was abruptly cut off. To be sure the system had sent a warning notice printed in red but large institutions had never taken these kinds of notices particularly seriously in the past. Fortunately, the loss of power occurred in daylight hours so the ten thousand or so people who happened to be in the centre at the time, while inconvenienced, were not really at any personal risk.

The newspapers had a field day, the tabloids indulging in lurid speculation as to what might have happened if the power supply had been cut off in hours of darkness while the Show was opened to the public. There were editorial comments on the draconian measures being introduced by the new managing director of the Metropolitan Electricity Board. The editorial in the Guardian deplored what it saw as the abrogation of social responsibility by the Electricity Board and proceeded to castigate the privatisation programme of the Tory government. The Telegraph took the opposite point of view. It noted that the management of the conference centre had been given ample warning over the fact that power supply would be disconnected if they did not pay. It applauded the more business-like attitude demonstrated by the Electricity Board and attributed this to the Tory government's privatisation programme which, of course , it fully supported. The Times editorial speculated on the role of the Boat Show in British society. Chaddick Spencer, was completely unfazed by all the publicity and went out of his way to compliment Brett Johnson on how effectively his instructions had been implemented.

'Great job Brett. We'll get payback from this system yet. I think all of the publicity is great. It will let people know that we're running a business around here and not some kind of charity. '

There was some political fallout. People who went to the Boat Show tended to have a lot of disposable income which generally meant that they voted Tory. The disruption of their winter ritual caused a number of them considerable irritation. When the newspapers began to divulge the background for the disruption, several of them phoned party head office to complain. The complaints ran along the lines of the' government's privatisation scheme is all very well, all for it myself. But I'm not too sure that we want some damn cowboy running the show, mucking up major social events.' This kind of input was smoothly masticated by the press office machinery and duly reported in a weekly briefing to the Prime Minister.

Martin Housegood, the Prime Minister, was a man in his late forties of medium build, orderly and precise in his habits. He was not a great orator neither was he seen as a visionary but what he had done was successfully managed a national campaign which brought the Conservatives back to power after ten years in the wilderness. Rodrick Walpole Became Prime Minister and rewarded Martin with the post of Chief Whip. From the Chief Whip's office, he engineered a series of stunning legislative successes for the party which rolled back the ten years of socialist reform. He had great tactical sense and shrewd anticipation. Many problem situations were headed off before they ever became apparent. He was cool and self-effacing and, for a Chief Whip, remarkably popular with the backbenchers. When Walpole developed a heart condition late in the first term it was unusual but not entirely surprising that in the subsequent election for Party leader Martin Housegood was an easy victor.

Housegood was briefed on the great Boat Show black-out as it was being called, two days after it happened, by his press secretary, and the chairman of the party, Lord Overton. It was not by any means the only item in the briefing; indeed, it was not even the major item but it drew Housegood's attention.

'This American that we have got running the Electricity Board is a bit too flamboyant for my tastes', Housegood said. Lord Overton interposed, 'It's a storm in a teacup Martin. It's the slow season for the news boys, they have just blown it up out of proportion.'

Housegood smiled and pressed his fingertips together. 'We have a by-election coming up in Stepney in about a month. The polls show that we are ahead by about seven points. We have been hammering away at a 'steady as she goes 'theme like the McMillan slogan in the sixties: "You've never had it so good". So far it's paying off. What you don't do gentlemen in that kind of scenario is gratuitously introduce a topic of controversy such as privatisation. We have a working majority of four, if we lose this seat, it becomes a working majority of two. No, no, we need to nip this thing in the bud. We need our cowboy to cool it at least until after the by- election.'

His companions looked at him with a new respect and nodded silently.

'Who do we know that's on the board of Directors, Freddy'

'Sir Peter Stephenage, the Merchant banker.'

'Ah yes, Stephenage of Guthroyds. It seems to me Freddy, that we are going to need some help from the banking community when we start the privatisation of the railroads. Why don't you have lunch with Stephenage and explain our little dilemma to him and you can talk also about our forthcoming needs relating to the railroads.'

Lord Overton inclined his head gracefully. 'Just as you say Martin'. They moved on to other matters.

Stephenage and Lord Overton had lunch a couple of days later at the Carlton Club. The discussion of the Government plans for railroad privatisation took place over soup. Dinner was taken up with a discussion of Sir Georg Solti's upcoming visit to the London Symphony Orchestra to conduct Verdi's requiem. It wasn't until coffee that Lord Overton brought up the subject of the difficulties with the Metropolitan Electricity Board.

'The PM is concerned that the American's style is too flamboyant, Peter. We have the by-election in Stepney coming up and one wouldn't want anything untoward to happen which would adversely affect our chances. Obviously, the whole idea behind the privatisation is that the Metropolitan Electricity Board is now a private company. Indeed, our Press Office put out a statement about the Boat Show affair which says that the Metropolitan Electricity Board was acting quite within its rights. This is in the sphere of the private sector. The government clearly can't attempt to regulate that; on the other hand, it's incumbent upon every citizen and every corporation to exercise social responsibility, words to that effect. The point is, we are concerned, but we can't directly do anything or be seen to be doing anything.

Stephenage smiled 'So you would like me ,as a Director, to have a word with our American friend?'

Lord Overton demurred. 'Well nothing official Peter, you understand.'

'Quite understand, Lord Overton. It just seems to me as a director of the Metropolitan Electricity Board that this kind of publicity might have unanticipated adverse effects from the company standpoint. And I think I really should have a word with Chaddick Spencer.'

'Quite so, Peter, quite so.'

Peter Stephenage made arrangements to see Chaddick Spencer the following week. He understood very well what was expected of him. If he could somehow defuse the abrasive management style of Spencer the party would be suitably appreciative and put some work his way. Of course, it had not been stated as baldly as that and the principals would be deeply shocked if anybody characterised it in that manner. But for all that, the transaction had taken place.

From the outset the meeting with Spencer did not go according to plan. Peter had suggested lunch at his club in the City. The American responded that he was too busy to do that but would be happy to meet Peter at the Metropolita Electricity Board itself. They arranged to meet for lunch and then a chat afterwards.

Lunch as it turned out was in the staff canteen, which was a whole new kind of experience for the Merchant banker. Chaddick Spencer obviously relished his hamburger and chips drenched in ketchup while Stephenage picked fastidiously at what had been labelled as an egg salad.

'They didn't do burgers when I first got here' Chaddick Spencer explained to his less than impressed guest, 'But when I told them that I planned to eat in the staff canteen everyday they soon put them on the menu. It's taken them a while to get the hang of it, but they are not half bad now.'

In the noisy atmosphere of the canteen, Stephenage found it difficult, if not impossible to broach the subject that was on his mind. When they returned to the American's office, the Merchant banker found himself on the other side of a very large desk. Spencer lit up a large, foul smelling cigar which further disconcerted Stephenage.

'So then Peter, shoot, what's on your mind?'

'Well the reason I stopped by to chat Chaddick is I'm a little concerned with all the publicity we have been getting with this Boat Show situation.'

'Nothing wrong with a little bit of publicity.' Spencer shrugged.

'Yes, well I am not too sure that this kind of publicity is helpful to the company's image.' Stephenage persisted.

Chaddick Spencer was unconcerned. 'It's done nothing to the stock price. In fact, when I looked this morning it was up a bit.'

Stephenage was growing irritated with the flippant dismissals.

'I do not want to appear critical but it seems to me that this particular type of management style could be interpreted as smacking of the ill-considered or cavalier.'

The cigar was firmly extinguished in the ashtray on the table.

'Listen here Stephenage, there's nothing at all cavalier or ill-considered about this policy. A commercial enterprise charges for the product it supplies, in our case, megawatt hours. If somebody doesn't pay for what they get then service is cut off. There is just no other way to run a profitable business. What you are watching is the transition of a not for profit utility company to a money-making venture. That's what I was hired to do. I would suggest that your job as a director is to represent the interests of the shareholders. What shareholders expect is a reasonable dividend and capital appreciation of the value of their stock. And you sit there and tell me that the actions I have authorised are not consistent with those objectives.'

'There are other considerations besides the profit motive.' Peter Stephenage retorted.

Chaddick Spencer was emphatic. 'Not in my rule book there ain't. It doesn't do anybody any good to get confused between running a business and running a charity. From my point of view, I took over a fat, sloppy, inefficient public sector operation and I'm trying to get it to straighten up and fly right. You want to make this an issue in the next Board of Directors meeting, you be my guest. But you know exactly how I feel about it and I assure you this is the polite version. Is there anything else on your mind?'

Stephenage considered the value of continuing the conversation and decided a graceful retreat was probably the only face-saving option available.

'Well, I see you feel strongly about this issue Chaddick and in fact, view it as a point of principle. I appreciate the vigour and forthrightness with which you represented your point of view. Of course, as our Managing Director you continue to enjoy my full confidence. But you should appreciate that I do have some reservations about this. With that being said I have no wish to blow this matter out of proportion. I have taken up enough of your time and in fact, I have another appointment back in the City so let's leave it at that and I will see you at the Board Meeting.'

The American was all smiles. He got out of his seat and came around the desk, pumping Stephenage 's hand vigorously as he walked him to the door. 'Well, great to see you Pete old chap. I'm glad you took the time out to let me know how you feel on this. It's important that there are clear lines of communication between me and my directors. That the way I like to have it.'

Stephenage was ushered swiftly out the door. As soon as it was shut, Chaddick Spencer's hearty smile completely evaporated. 'Pompous prick 'he murmured under his breath and returned to his desk.

When Stephenage returned to his office he phoned Lord Overton and recounted his conversation.

'Sorry Freddy but the man is a complete Neanderthal. He has no appreciation of the subtleties and obviously it was out of the question given my reception that I raise any of the political aspects.'

'Quite right, Peter, the fellow's a loose cannon. The next thing we would have him bleating about political interference which would compound our problems. I will brief the PM. We appreciate you made the effort Peter and we won't forget it.'

Chapter Eight

Cedric Hargreave lived in a house in Hampstead Heath which was surrounded by a high wall. It was a multi-million-pound piece of real estate as it was situated in a very desirable part of London. The five bedroom house was occupied by Hargreave, a cook and a manservant.

Hargreave Was Scrooge like. Indeed, if he had even bothered to read A Christmas Carol he would probably have viewed it as a tragedy in which the hero abandons his principles. Hargreave was a severe, gaunt man in late middle age who had never married. He had come by his money the old-fashioned way, inheriting it. The original Hargreave fortune had been made in Victorian times by an enterprising younger son who had gone to Burma and founded an import export firm with teak as its initial major commodity. The business had been expanded during Edwardian times; manufacturing capability was added in the United Kingdom where the focus was on furniture and paper products. Cedric Hargreave inheriting an enterprise with an annual turnover of 20 million pounds had, through market expansion in Europe, expanded the operation by a couple of orders of magnitude until it now had a turnover in excess of 400 million pounds annually. His own net worth was comfortably in excess of 50 million pounds.

Hargreave worked long hours and exerted total control over his empire. He had no fewer than 30 direct reports and complete disregard for any modern management theory. He wielded telephone and fax like weapons, querying and probing his operations mercilessly. Managers who stood up to the onslaught were well rewarded for their efforts but the burnout rate was extremely high.

On this night in mid-January, however, Hargreave was uncharacteristically nervous. He was contemplating giving up control of the one aspect of his core operations in the UK which was inherited from his father. Hargreaves made and distributed tourist novelties. In fact, because of the strength of their distribution channels they had virtually cornered the market in this unlikely commodity. A recent profitability study had shown Hargreave that the cost of manufacturing the novelties in the UK had been steadily rising over the previous five years whereas their sales price had barely kept pace with inflation. This led him to conclude that he should shut down his UK plant, buy the tourist novelties from a third party and make his money purely on the distribution. It made perfect business sense but it involved surrendering control of an aspect of the operation. Moreover, he had inherited it from his father and was almost sentimental about it. It was as close to getting emotional as he was capable.

His guests for dinner tonight were the Chen brothers from Hong Kong. They were proposing to supply Hargreave from their operations in the Philippines. He had meticulously researched the company and satisfied himself that for price and reliability they were far and away his best source of supply. Nonetheless, they were foreign, which made him nervous and he would be dependent upon them , which made him even more anxious.

He had given careful consideration to where the meeting should take place. Mark Finch his regional manager in Hong Kong had advised him that there were aspects of doing business in Asia which made it different from the western model. Particularly, Asian businessmen wanted to know the kind of person they were dealing with. Building a relationship was an essential prerequisite in establishing satisfactory business dealings. This, to Hargreave, meant some sort of encounter in a social setting. He agonised whether to host dinner at his club or at home. The public character of a restaurant was unimaginable to him. In the end, the feeling of security involved with being surrounded by his own things in his own environment outweighed the invasion of privacy which he felt the dinner would entail.

The grandfather clock in the hall chimed the hour. It was six in the evening. The Chens were due to arrive at seven, chauffered by limousine from the hotel in which they were staying. Dinner was to be served at eight. He had come home from the office early, around 3 o'clock, and spent the last few hours checking all the arrangements. He was driving the cook mad with questions about the menu and querying the selection of wines. He finished dressing. His manservant had laid out a dark blue pinstripe suit. He looked at himself in the mirror, carefully combing back his hair and rather wishing he had found time to go to the barbers. The evening stretched in front of him with all the appeal of a visit to the dentist. It wasn't so much having to meet the Chens, as it was the idea he would have to host a dinner whose primary purpose was to establish a social rapport. This meant holding a conversation on social topics other than the business issues of direct interest to him. Hargreave had little time for social graces. He compensated as best he could. His research staff had prepared a binder for him on the visit. He had extensive biographies of the Chens, knew all about their families, their hobbies, and their interests. He had watched travel videos on Hong Kong, for although he had visited the city many times over the past five years , all he ever did was travel from the airport to his hotel, conduct business in the city and return. Hargreave regarded foreign travel as a necessary evil to be got through and certainly not something to be enjoyed.

By way of background he had very little in common with the Chens. They were both married with large families; he was a Bachelor. The Chens were passionately involved in horse racing and he knew nothing of the subject.

This is going to be unbearable he thought. *Do I really need this business arrangement?* The business analyst in him responded emphatically 'Yes, you do. *I'll go down and review the briefing binder some more and that will take my mind off things. Maybe I'll have a Sherry to calm my nerves.* He almost never drank.

The furniture in Hargreave's house was polished mahogany. Dark and ornate, it occupied high ceilinged rooms with velvet curtaining and heavy flower-patterned wallpaper. Unusually some arrangements of fresh flowers had been placed in the Hall, the dining room, and the two reception rooms. But they did little to alleviate the impression that one was walking into a Victorian mansion.

Hargreave sat in the living room, in the armchair by the fire, with a small glass of Sherry beside him. On his knees was the briefing binder. His manservant was polishing the glasses which they would use for drinks. The house was completely silent except for the grandfather Clock ticking in the Hall. At precisely 7 o'clock the doorbell rang. Hargreave swiftly placed the binder in a drawer and stood up to receive his guests.

Andrew Chen, the elder of the two brothers, could have been anywhere between forty and fifty five years of age. He was, in fact, fifty two. He was dressed, like Hargreave, in a dark pinstripe suit with a white shirt. His younger brother Phillip, thirty four, wore a light grey suit and a striped, coloured shirt with a white collar. Andrew had been educated at Cambridge, his younger brother at the University of Pennsylvania.

'Good evening. Cedric Hargreave. It's good of you to come.' Hargreave extended his hand, stiffly towards the elder Chen.

'Indeed, a pleasure to meet you Mr Hargreave and extremely kind of you to invite us to your home for dinner.'

The evening proceeded smoothly, conversation over drinks ranged from the weather to the kind of trip the Chens had had from Hong Kong to impressions of London and the latest political events. Hargreave found himself warming to the elder Chen who exuded an air of sobriety. The younger brother Phillip was given to cracking jokes and making irreverent comments. He even tried to engage the manservant in conversation once or twice with very little success. It's the American education, Hargreave thought to himself.

At 8 o'clock they moved to the dining room. It was an impressive room with a long table that could seat twenty as the centerpiece of the room. Andrew Chen paused to look at the portrait which hung over the fireplace.

'Your father, Mr Hargreave?'

'Yes' Hargreave responded. 'It was painted just after the war. I was about seven at the time. I remember father being quite irritated at having to take time away from work to sit for it.'

The portrait showed his father seated with his legs crossed and a book open on his knee. The artist had captured the severe angular features very well.

'A very distinguished looking man.' Chen observed.

'Yes, he had a very commanding presence which I think the artist captured quite well.

I was always somewhat in awe of him.' Hargreave replied.

'You were an only child then Mr Hargreave .'

'Yes, my mother died shortly after I was born. My father never remarried.'

'Phillip and I come from a family of six. We have four sisters. I am the eldest in the family and Phillip the youngest. My father had wanted more sons but he had four girls before Phillip arrived. In Asia we favour large families. '

It was the first time the conversation had taken a remotely personal turn all evening. Images rose unbidden to Hargreave mind the subdued voices of the servants the day of his mother's funeral. His had been a solitary childhood spent with books and toy soldiers. Hargreave mentally admonished himself.

'Don't go getting maudlin and sentimental now of all times. You need your wits about you for this business deal.'

The dinner menu was simple. The Chens were health nuts. Consommé followed by fish, cheese , fruit, and sherbet. Not much alcohol was drunk; 1 bottle of wine was sufficient for the meal. The dinner conversation flowed smoothly and was wide ranging. Phillip Chen proved to be a witty and acutely observant raconteur. He regaled them with tales of college life in the United States. As they ate dessert, conversation began to turn toward business topics. The Chens were very optimistic about the prospects in South East Asia. Hargreave was careful to warmly endorse this point of view.

'Perhaps we should go into the drawing room for coffee gentlemen.' he suggested. As they sat in the drawing room drinking coffee and sipping port, the real business of the evening began.

'My business problem gentlemen' Hargreave began, 'Is not much different than a lot of manufacturers in this country. Competition is stiff yet manufacturing costs continue to climb. This puts pressure on my margins such that , in the case of these tourism products , I've scarcely been making a profit at all in the last two years. I have to get my manufacturing cost down so it makes sense to look for a source of supply over in Asia where labour is much cheaper. But do I really want to go to the trouble of establishing a manufacturing plant over there ? What I have is a pretty effective distribution channel built up over the years so I have concluded that the best course of action is to seek a third party source of supply for the base commodity in

Asia and concentrate on strengthening the distribution channel in my home markets. '

The Chens heard him out impassively.

Andrew was about to respond when his brother interjected.

'I'm sorry to interrupt the conversation but there is a phone call I really must make to Hong Kong. I wondered if I might use the phone. It really shouldn't take more than five minutes. 'His brother looked at him with annoyance.

'Certainly, Phillip. Roberts will show you upstairs to the library.'

Phillip was led away by the omnipresent Roberts.

'I quite understand your dilemma Cedric, May I call you Cedric ? 'Andrew began. 'By all means Andrew'. Hargreave was elated at the prospect of being on first name terms. It meant the evening was going well. The elder Chen continued. 'Most businesses in the developed world are being impacted in one way or another by the globalization of markets and the need to control manufacturing costs. If I may say so, what differentiates your situation is that you have correctly recognised the problem and identified an appropriate long-term solution. So many businessmen are fixated on symptoms rather than root causes and even if they correctly identify the problem they only have the resolve for palliative measures. '

Hargreave realised that he was being flattered but enjoyed the experience all the same.

'Let's get down to specifics of how we can be of assistance to you.' Andrew Chen continued. 'Perhaps we should wait for my brother Phillip. I must apologise for him. He has yet to perfect the art of delegation in business. '

Hargreave thought inwardly of his 30 something odd direct reports and winced. For the next few minutes, they talked about horse racing; or at least Andrew Chen did. Hargreave accompanied occasionally with a noncommittal grunt. The Chens planned to attend the Newbury races before they returned home. After a time, they heard movement upstairs and the sound of a door closing. Phillip Chen was bounding along the landing and taking the stairs at a fast clip. The lights went out suddenly. The room was plunged into darkness. They heard a muffled curse from the stairs and the sound of someone falling. Hargreave could hear Andrew Chen pushing back his chair and stumbled to where he believed the door was. Hargreave stood and crossed to the windows where he pulled back the heavy curtains to allow pale moonlight to stream through the room.

The manservant arrived with a Flashlight. They gathered at the foot of the stairs and found Phillip Chen lying motionless, his face covered in blood. Andrew Chen fell to his knees beside his brother his face awash with grief and concern.

'I'll phone for an ambulance.' Hargreave said. As he did so he thought, *my God this is a nightmare and to have it happen in my own house.*

Five minutes later the situation looked a lot less dramatic. Phillip Chen was very much alive with no bones broken. The blood had come from a wide gash on his forehead he had received from the banister of the stairway as he fell.

He would be taken to hospital anyway to be x rayed for possible head injuries. But he was not a stretcher case. Hargreave was being profusely apologetic. Andrew Chen, learning that his brother was not seriously injured, recovered most of his composure.

'You're sure you don't want me to go to the hospital with you Andrew ?'

'No, I don't believe that will be necessary Mr Hargreave .'

Hargreave noted the reversion to last names. The conversation was taking place in candlelight as power was still not restored. Hargreave was interrupted by his housekeeper who wore a bewildered expression.

'Sir, I have just got off the phone with the Metropolitan Electricity Board. It's not a power outage. They've cut us off because they say we haven't paid our bill.'

Andrew Chen shot Hargreave a look of disdain and contempt which was quickly replaced by a mask of impassivity.

'There's obviously been some mistake Mrs Curtis. I'll discuss it with you in a moment in the kitchen.'

'Yes Sir , but.........'

'In the kitchen Mrs Curtis.'

Andrew Chen began speaking as if nothing untoward had occurred. 'On reflection Mr Hargreave I think it would be best for my brother and I to return to Hong Kong as soon as possible. Tomorrow morning preferably. We would like to have him see the family physician back home and I'm sure his wife would never forgive me if I didn't bring him back as soon as possible.'

'But he doesn't seem that badly hurt.' Hargreave blurted out.

'You might not think so Mr Hargreave but you would forgive a brother's concern. Our business will have to wait for a later time. Now if you'll excuse us. Are you ready Phillip?'

Philip Chen stood up supported by two St Johns ambulance men, the left side of his head heavily bandaged. Hargreave could only watch helplessly as his meticulously researched business partners of choice walked out the door. He was experiencing an intensity of feeling and emotion almost unparalleled in his adult life. Frustration, shame, humiliation all welled up inside him. All he could think was, someone was going to pay for this. He strode back to the kitchen.

'Telling me in front of my guests that we didn't have a power outage because it's alleged we didn't pay our bills was an act of singular stupidity Mrs Curtis. You have been with me and the family over 20 years but I am sorely tempted to dispense with your services at this moment.'

Mrs Curtis looked ashen. 'I'm very sorry Sir , I never dreamt.'

'That will do Mrs Curtis.' He sighed resignedly. 'If I vent my spleen on you I'll only be shooting the messenger. Why don't you do something useful and make me a strong cup of coffee.'

'Yes Sir, immediately Sir.'

Hargreave went to the library, bringing the Candelabra, which was his only source of light and sat down at the Bureau where he kept all the household bills. 'It's no use.' He thought , 'I won't be able to see what I'm doing. I shall have to wait until morning.' It was inconceivable to him that the bills had not been paid. Cedric Hargreave was meticulous with the household accounts. He personally reviewed each, constantly questioned the housekeeper about what he saw were extravagances; joints of meat which he thought were too large, fruit bought out of season. The bills were always paid promptly and on time. However, he checked each one. Using a calculator, he re verified the total for itemised bills before paying.

Hargreave was convinced that anyone he did business with, whether an individual or an institution, would imagine that because of his great wealth, he would not pay attention to such detail and consequently overcharge him. So, he checked each bill and paid on time the amount which he believed was due, querying any discrepancies that arose. Even on the rare occasions where someone had undercharged him he still paid the right amount. When it came to the electricity bill therefore, he kept a careful record of the number of units used as shown by his meter readings and multiplied that by the rate per kwh. There were from time to time fractional differences between what he calculated and what the bill said but since the difference never amounted to more than a couple of pennies one way or the other he contented himself with paying what he felt to be the right amount resolving to question the billing if ever the difference got to be material.

He did not go to sleep are at all that night; rather he sat crouched in an armchair reviewing the events of the evening, alternatively feeling bewildered and humiliated. Principally he felt humiliated that this should have happened to him in his own house he who always prided himself on the correctness of his business relations. It was humiliating that the Chen's should think he had defaulted on an electricity bill of all things and that the outcome would be Phillip Chen injured while he was his guest. He was resigned to the loss of the business relationship. It was a question of face. After the events of the evening he could no more imagine doing business with the Chens than with the devil himself.

Soon after seven the next morning, the sun had risen sufficiently in a watery sky to provide the daylight he needed to review the bills in his Bureau drawer. His bookkeeping was immaculate. Each bill type was classified in a brown manila folder, each month carefully tagged. He reviewed the bills from the Metropolitan Electricity Board for the last six months. He looked at the check register he kept with the cancelled cheques associated with each monthly payment. There was no mistake. He never imagined there would be.

The bill had been promptly paid. The only discrepancy was a slight cumulative arrears of some six pence which had grown from three pence six months previously. This was a result of his own bill calculations not reconciling to the total shown and the Metropolitan electricity board billing statement. Surely, he thought this can be of no significance and certainly would not be material enough to cause the cut off of service.

Around 8:00 o'clock he left his house and drove himself to his office in the city, taking the electricity bills with him. Once in his office he summoned his chief accountant. Miss Ruth Houghton a woman in her 40s, arrived almost immediately. She was the exception in Hargreave's otherwise totally male-dominated management team. She had arrived at her current position by virtue of an almost religious devotion to her responsibilities. She was unmarried and appeared to have no other interests in life save the financial affairs of Hargreave limited.

Hargreave came directly to the point.

'My meeting with the Chen's last night at my home was disastrous. In the middle of dinner, the power supply was cut off and Phillip Chen stumbled in the darkness and sustained a head injury. The Metropolitan Electricity Board claims that service was disconnected for failure to pay their bills. '

The usually unflappable Miss Houghton gaped at him.

'Yes , I know it's inconceivable. I attend to the domestic accounts myself. Here are the bills for the last six months the record of payment and the cancelled checks. Please go over them and make sure there's nothing out of the ordinary so I know I'm not taking leave of my senses. Make note that there seems to be something wrong with the way they are extending the total bill.'

'Sir ?'She inquired .

'If you take the number of units of electricity that I've expended each month and multiply it by the rate you arrive at a slightly different total than the electricity board. '

Hargreave, content that he had put something in motion, turned his attention to the morning's business. The pile of faxes on his desk had come in overnight from Asia and the United States. The morning's business fell into a familiar pattern soothing his discomforture. At eleven fifteen, his secretary announced the arrival of Andrew Mayhew, his solicitor.

'Ahhhh, Andrew good of you to come at such short notice. There's something I want you to do for me.'

Andrew Mayhew was surprised. Cedric Hargreave rarely wasted time on politeness.

'Please sit down. Will you have some coffee?'

Mayhew accepted and took a seat in one of the upholstered leather armchairs that occupied a corner of Hargreave's office.

'I wish to bring suit against the Metropolitan Electricity Board's Managing Director and Board for breach of contract and associated damages in the amount of twenty million pounds. '

'I beg your pardon Cedric ?'

Hargreave smiled grimly. 'Yes, I thought that might get your attention Andrew. Perhaps I should explain.'

As Mayhew sipped his coffee, Cedric Hargreave explained the events of the night before. Initially his rendition was detached and factual. As he recounted the evening and its impact on the Chens however Hargreave became visibly emotional. 'My God' Mayhew thought with astonishment, 'the old bugger has a heart after all. '

'I have not slept at all Andrew thinking about this. I feel humiliated, violated even that it should happen in my own house. More than anything that I ever wanted in my life I want vindication and restitution. I want someone to be held accountable and yes, I want them to pay for the pain and the humiliation they've inflicted upon me. I am prepared to pay a great deal of money to accomplish my objectives. '

Mayhew placed his coffee cup carefully on the table in front of him. He took off his gold rimmed bifocals and looked at Hargreave.

'I understand what you're saying Cedric and I appreciate that you're very upset however the amount of damages you are asking for is astronomical.

Assume, for a moment, that the facts of the matter are as you have stated them to me ; there were systematic billing errors by the Metropolitan Electricity Board that created a small arrears and that as a result, they terminated your service without warning. You certainly have a case for breach of contract but we then get to the issue of damages. It's not as though one of your manufacturing plants was taken out of service and you had downtime. All that happened was you lost electricity at your place of residence and while that might be inconvenient it would be very difficult to sustain an argument that you will have been damaged to the extent of twenty million pounds. Direct damages would be in the order of a few thousand at most. The question would arise whether you could establish liability of the Metropolitan Electricity Board for consequential damages. That is the loss of a possible contract with the Chen brothers. Then it would have to be established that the loss of that contract would have cost you twenty million pounds. And I don't need to remind you Cedric, but I will for completeness sake, that if you file a suit and fail you become liable for the legal costs of the defendant , loser pays. '

Hargreave had sat perfectly still in the chair across from Mayhew. He listened intently; his brow furrowed in concentration. Without saying anything he walked over to his desk picked up the phone and called Ruth Houghton.

'Miss Houghton can you come over here for a moment please. Thank you.'

Thirty seconds later Houghton was in the room.

'The novelty products line. How much money did we lose during the past two years?'

Houghton didn't pause. Two and a half million pounds the year before last, three million last year. If we managed to control the costs we're hoping to keep the loss this year to 3.2 million.'

'And what were the financial projections if the deal with the Chen brothers went through ?'

'Well in the first year we were going to take a loss of six million. This would be attributable to the costs associated with redundancy and the closing down of the factory. But that was a one-time charge. There after we showed the operation domestically running a profit of three million a year and with the new distribution Channels from the Chen connection over in Asia an additional four million. So, seven million a year profit. That's just the novelty product line of course. Other aspects of the deal with Chen were that they were to give us new product lines for our distribution channels in Europe and the United States. We calculated that this would generate additional revenues of four to five million pounds a year. '

'How long have we been evaluating potential business partners in South East Asia along these lines ?' Hargreave asked.

Houghton smiled wryly it's' taken us two years '.

Hargreave looked at Mayhew 'would you say after hearing this Andrew that I've not been materially damaged?'

'it certainly adds substance to your claim, Mayhew said. But if I'm to play the devil's advocate as to what the Metropolitan Electricity Board will allege and I feel we need to do that, let's say they concede their liability for indirect damages which is far from being obvious. They would then contend that you have many business alternatives available to you so that your objectives could be realised by other business partners or by other means. In other words they will argue simply that even if it were true that they interfered with this business arrangement you were contemplating with the Chen's there are other fish in the sea. Your estimate of damages is precisely that and there is no way to know if in fact they would actually be realised to the extent you allege. They would seek to substantially mitigate your claim.

Cedric smiled. 'Yes Andrew, but where we've gone from is you at the outset claiming that the judge would throw the case out summarily to now giving me what amounts to mitigating arguments from opposing counsel. Is that not so?'

Mayhew reflected for a moment. 'I always thought you would have done well in the law Cedric. 'He stood up. 'If we are going to pursue this in earnest' Hargreave nodded vigorously 'Then Miss Houghton will need to prepare very careful financial statements that support what you've told me verbally. I will need to engage the services of another firm of solicitors to prepare the brief since this is not my area of speciality. I assume you would want Queens Counsel Cedric?'

'Yes .'

'Very well. I see no reason to take up more of your time right now' said Mayhew. 'I will put the matter in hand.'

Hargreave nodded.' I want regular status on this Andrew. Weekly if you please.'

'Certainly. Cedric. I'll show myself out.' Mayhew departed.

Chapter Nine

News of the impending lawsuit reached the office of the Managing Director of the Metropolitan Electricity Board about two weeks later. His reaction was predictable.

'The guy must be out of his tiny, fucking mind. 20 million pounds! It's crazy! Who is this character anyway?'

The solicitor for the Electricity Board was none too encouraging. 'The firm of Hargreave Limited has been in existence since the middle of the last century. It is a privately held firm but Cedric Hargreave is reputedly a very wealthy man and not noted for frivolous business undertakings. If he has decided to pursue the suit it is because he believes he has grounds and certainly from the legal talent he has assembled he's not sparing any expense on this.'

Chaddick Spencer grunted wearily. 'Okay fine. What exactly are the facts of this case?'

'Well, we're still trying to get to the bottom of it. But it would appear that we shut off service to Hargreave house a little over two weeks ago for non-payment of his electricity bill.'

Spencer was incredulous. 'For Christ's sake, how much was he in arrears by ?'

The company solicitor looked at the company accountant who was also at the meeting, willing him to answer.

'Well it would appear Mr. Spencer, that the amount was sixpence.'

'How much ?'

'Sixpence.'

'And for this we cut off this bum's electricity ? How could that happen?'

'Well , you understand that with the new system in place, one of our objectives was to streamline labour-intensive processes. Under the old system any account which was scheduled for disconnection would be reviewed individually before we took action. In the new system the process is much more automatic. It spits out disconnection notices and the engineers simply execute. There is no review. That saved us ten full time people a year. '

The American had been puffing on his cigar and was now completely enveloped in smoke. 'But surely whoever designed the system must have realised that there is an issue of materiality involved?'

Then he shrugged his shoulders. 'Screw it. Anyway, its only six pence. How's the guy going to be able to determine twenty million worth of damages from that situation?'

The solicitor eyed his mercurial client warily. 'It would appear from the brief that was filed that Hargreave was entertaining some potential business partners. The sudden loss of power at his residence created a most unfortunate situation in which one of the guests injured himself and moreover the guests were led to believe that the power outage had been caused by Mr Hargreave inability to pay his electricity bills. The consequence was that any opportunity for consummating the business deal was lost. Mr. Hargreave was gravely embarrassed.'

'Ok. Ok. So, the guy ends up with egg all over his face and it can be argued that we were a bit quick on the trigger in yanking his power supply. But screw it. The facts of the matter are that he didn't pay his bill in total even if it is only a few pence. So where does he get off trying to sue us for 20 million pounds?'

The solicitor looked even more pained.

'We have, of course, been reviewing in detail the billing history for Mr Hargreave and this has brought to light a discrepancy. It would appear that the error is on our side. ' The solicitor glanced meaningfully at the company accountant who was trying to make himself as inconspicuous as possible.

The American gazed at the unfortunate executive with fixed intensity. 'What you were telling me is that we fucked up .'

The accountant was apologetic. 'In a manner of speaking yes. But there's more to it than just the individual Hargreave account. As we dig into the billing histories it would appear that there is a systemic error in which customers are being billed fractionally more than their meter usage warrants. What's particularly distressing is that when we look at what is deposited to our bank accounts there is a difference between what was collected in the Billings and what was remitted to us. The amount per customer is only pennies but in aggregate it is quite a material sum. The shortfall is as yet unaccounted for.'

The American stood up in agitation.

' Are you telling me there's some sort of fraud going on. Is that what I'm hearing from you? '

The accountant avoided the American's gaze. 'I would hesitate to put such a construction on it or leap to unfortunate conclusions.'

Chaddick Spencer exploded. 'Oh, for God sake this British understatement makes me sick. There is a bunch of money gone missing and its unaccounted for. Where do you think it's ended up? In the widows and orphans fund? Some character's been helping himself to the small change in the till.' Spencer looked about him savagely. 'If this gets made public by being dragged through the courts it's going to knock the hell out of our share price. So, I guess we have no choice but to settle with these bastards. You Watson. 'He gestured with his head toward the solicitor , 'without letting the cat out of the bag find out what Hargreave might be willing to settle for. The internal audit guys have ten days to get to the bottom of this manure heap. If they can't I guess that we're going to have to call in the police. Jeez what a shitty day this has been.'

Chapter 10

Andrew Sweeney opened the door of his apartment and closed it quietly behind him. He called out his wife's name but there was no answer. He took off his trench coat hung it in the hall stand then went to the bathroom, locked the door, and vomited into the toilet bowl. His afternoon at work had been the foretaste of hell. At two o'clock he had been summoned to the office of internal audit where they had laid out before him what they were calling the Hargreave file. He was the analyst responsible for the billing algorithms in both the new and the old systems and so the interview had begun with an atmosphere of suspicion. How could it be that a pattern of systematic overbilling could have been replicated from the old system to the new? Andrew explained that he had lifted the code untouched from one to the other. He clarified that significant portions of the new system were in fact salvaged from its predecessor.

For the first hour, the questioning had been intense and antagonistic. How could this kind of error have been perpetuated without premeditation? How could it have gone undetected? He replayed in his head the responses he had made, somehow contriving to appear academic and detached.

'Well, it's not that surprising really. You see the billing algorithms are quite complex, involving a lot of rate conditions and exception processing. We thought it best when we were building this new system to take advantage of that portion of it's predecessor which had to do with the billing . To rewrite all that logic again from scratch, not to mention the effort in retesting it, would have been prohibitively expensive and also quite frankly risky. So, you see, given that it's the same code that's executing it's not at all remarkable that if there are errors in the old system related to the billing they would have been propagated into the new. Unfortunate of course but there it is.'

'But surely you retested the logic in the new system in some way ?' his interrogator asked.

'Of course, we did. There is a test bed of examples that we use every time we do maintenance on the billing. We executed the test bed running the new system against it and the results were as expected. We had no reason to believe that there was anything untoward in the billing algorithms. '

Calm, rational, unhurried answers had succeeded in reducing the levels of suspicion and hostility. The internal audit team now seemed prepared to accept that there was no collusion or premeditation in the perpetuation of the billing fraud from the old system to the new. Their efforts and attention would now be focused on who had access and opportunity in a time period which obviously dated back several years. The field of suspects would now be much broader and he hoped, for a time at least, the pressure on him would be reduced. He lay on the floor of the bathroom thinking: *this is some sort of bad dream, a nightmare. How could I have gotten myself into such a situation?* The awful prospect of detection, public humiliation, and imprisonment loomed in front of him. He had no idea what prison would be like never having been inside one. In fact, as he thought about it he didn't even know anyone who had ever been to prison. All he could conjure up was gleaned from documentaries and films on TV.

There was a pounding on the bathroom door.

'There's somebody in there mommy. I need to go really bad.'

He hauled himself to his feet. 'Ok Michael, I will be right out'.

Deirdre and his son had returned home. You look kind of grey Andrew', Deirdre remarked as he walked into the living room.

'Yes, they had Cornish Pasty for lunch down in the cafeteria. I think the mincemeat was a bit off.' He responded.

'Poor honey 'she said absently. 'You remember I have the drama society rehearsal this evening?. Must dash. There's cold meat in the fridge for you and Michael. Oh, and if you get a chance, help him with his homework would you? Some problem with set theory, he's been driving me batty all the way home. Can't think why they bother to teach the kids that stuff. I don't know any practical application it has.'

'I think it's to help them develop their reasoning powers Deirdre.'

She snorted.' I can think of much better examples of how to develop their reasoning powers than mucking around with sets. They're not likely to ever encounter a set in real life. But figuring out the tax the government is going to take out of their pay packet for instance, is a much more likely to be of use later on. Oh, never mind me, I'm just getting up on my soapbox. But you will take care of it won't you Andrew? The little beggar seems quite wound up about it.'

He went through the evening in a daze, his mind operating at two levels. On automatic pilot he prepared tea for himself and Michael and afterwards worked through the set theory problems.

All the while though he was thinking about what he couldn't help feeling was going to be impending disaster.

What am I going to do? He fretted. *Nothing,* an inner voice answered. *You considered the possibility that someone would stumble onto this when you put the scheme in hand. You covered your tracks. You dotted the I's and you crossed the t's . If anything, you're ahead of the game.*

It's taken them so many years to uncover the fraud the trail will have gotten very cold. Yes! he heard himself answering. *But at the time it seemed like an intellectual game a game of chess. Getting caught had no sense of reality. Now it's breathing down the back of my neck.*

If you lose your nerve you really will get caught. There's nothing to do but get on with your daily life exactly as before. Answer any questions they may ask accurately. Don't volunteer unnecessary information.

During the last two weeks of January working conditions at the Metropolitan Electricity Board had become anarchic. Brad Johnson in charge of the status meetings had always been thin but now he appeared emaciated. He was eating fast food and not sleeping well at night and had developed back problems. The field engineers were completely overwhelmed; first by the rash of notices to disconnect and then when the public hue and cry became deafening in short order, by the panicked demand from management that customers be reconnected. The engineering staff were working twelve to fourteen hours a day seven days a week. Retired employees were being brought back to the payroll on an emergency basis. Subcontractors were being used and still there was no let-up on the pressure. The manual processes pertaining to review of delinquent accounts, which had been eliminated under the new system, were now reinstituted. The upshot of all this was that the new system, far from saving on labour costs, had in fact doubled the payroll outlay not to mention the mayhem it had wreaked on customer service levels.

When he wasn't attending the status meetings Andrew spent his time working with the investigators from internal audit. As the days passed one week became two and with the investigations getting nowhere the auditors were becoming more frustrated and shorter tempered.

Parker Williams the head of audit, was having great difficulty with the chaotic nature of the source code involved in the old billing system. 'What I mean to say Andrew is that this stuff is a pile of junk held together with bits of wire and baling string.'

Andrew temporised 'Well it started out ok but you must remember it's been eight years in production and has a lot of heavy maintenance done to it. So, it's going to be showing wear and tear.'

'Yes, but there are over twenty major programs and literally hundreds of subroutines. We're still not sure we've accounted for all the code in production. Let alone analysed what's in it.' Williams sounded frustrated.

The auditor had embarked on an investigative strategy which hinged on analysing the source code in the system to identify how the fraud had been committed. Andrew knowing full well that taking this approach was tantamount to looking for a needle in a haystack had been more than happy to cooperate fully with this approach. He had accomplished the fraud by establishing variables in various programs and assigning them values deep in the subroutines whose purpose was primarily to support exits into the operating system. Since the variable names were just a jumble of letters and numbers which gave no clue as to their function, trying to figure out what was going on by just reading the source code of the system was like trying to break a cipher without the key. As each day passed without it being detected Andrew became just a little more hopeful that he would escape.

After two weeks with no progress in the investigation Chaddick Spencer was becoming more and more itate. He summoned his chief accountant. 'You guys have had this problem for the last two weeks and all you can tell me is that the old system is a crock of shit. I could have told you that. Basically, a bunch of amateurs is not going to crack this one. Whatever asshole pulled the stunt wasn't born yesterday. We need the equivalent of the FBI in here. What is that in this country?'

'I guess that would be Scotland Yard.'

'Fine then. Get their main guy on the phone for me. Let's see if we can't put a fire under this investigation.'

The accountant looked pained. 'Of course , if you feel this is the best course of action. But we would like to be as discreet about this as possible. We don't want to unduly damage the good reputation of the Electricity Board.'

Chaddick Spencer was contemptuous. 'Damage to our reputation did you say? Listen bonehead this shit hot new system is going to have our customers lynching us before too long. I should have thought our reputation was in the crapper already. If this fiasco is going to see me off I want it said *he may have been dumb but at least he wasn't '*There's been a major fraud perpetrated by someone in this organization that seems to go back six or seven years. I'm not going to cover it up or pretend it isn't there and we're going to get the bottom of it. Is that much at least clear in your head?'

'Oh perfectly. I can assure you sir.' The note of sarcasm from the accountant was totally lost upon Spencer.

'Then what the fuck are you waiting for ? Get on with it.'

Chapter Eleven

Dora Heard warmed a can of soup in a pot on the electric stove in her one-bedroom apartment. It had been a good day for her. This morning the young girl from downstairs had taken her to the post office so that she could get her pension and for the first time her medical disability payment. Speaking to the young politician the month before had produced unexpectedly swift results. She was glad her friend Hilda had persuaded her to do so. Last week a letter had come from the Department of Health and Social Services saying that they had reviewed her file and that due to additional facts brought to their attention of which they were previously unaware they were pleased to inform her that she had been found eligible for the disability benefit effective immediately. An extra £12.00 a week meant she had a little more latitude for the kinds of things she bought at the supermarket. That morning with her new found allowance she had treated herself to a fruit log which she was looking forward to after she had the soup and the steak and kidney pie she was warming in the oven. She would write a letter to the nice young politician who had obviously been the instrument of her good fortune. It would be a major undertaking with her arthritic fingers and all but she felt she owed it to him.

Dora listened with half an ear to the evening news being broadcast on the radio while she prepared her meal. The reporter was going on about an armed insurrection in some African country. All the news seems gloomy these days full of reports of violence and crime. Not nearly as bad as the war years in the early days when every news report told of Hitler's further successes and advances and it seemed that the very survival of the nation was at stake.

She ate her meal slowly. Everything seemed nowadays, to take much longer to do. Even the simple task of pouring the soup from a pot to a bowl took all her care and concentration; her arthritic hands refusing to respond to the messages her brain was sending, continuously reminding her of her ailment through a dull ache.

The fruit cake, an unfamiliar luxury, tasted wonderful. A bit dry perhaps but not bad for being store bought. Even three years ago it would have been no problem for her to make one but now the simple task would require physical dexterity of which she was unable. She sighed to herself as she cleared up. *It's a terrible thing to grow old. Don't be giving in to self-pity. You had a good life. You survived the blitz where many others didn't. With a little bit of extra money there's a lot you can think about doing. Going to the pictures maybe or on a day trip when the weather gets better.* When she was finished she went to the kitchen drawer, pulled out some note paper and a pen. At the kitchen table she began:

'Dear Mr. Petrie.' she wrote laboriously. She had posted his name on one of the presses in the kitchen so she wouldn't forget it. 'It was really good of you to help me a few weeks ago and take the time to help me with my benefits problem. Imagine my surprise when last week I got a letter from the DHSS saying that my disability allowance was approved. I really can't thank you enough. It will make such a difference for me the extra bit of money coming in each week.'

The handwriting was scrawled, the letters not well formed and she had difficulty keeping a straight line. *Oh well* she thought *I'm making the effort and that's the important thing.*

Suddenly without warning the lights went out. In fact, she noticed everything had gone out, including the tubular electric fire she used to keep herself warm. There was still light from the window from the streetlamps though. When her eyes became accustomed to the gloom she went to a cupboard and got out a couple of candles and some matches. *It's probably just a fuse in the building* she thought. *I'm sure the Superintendent will look after it. I'll wait a little bit and see if the electricity comes back on.* She put one candle on the table and the other on the kitchen dresser where she kept a photograph of her husband Fred in his uniform and one of her sister.

She noticed it was getting cooler in the flat. *What was it the weatherman had said? There was a sharp Frost expected that night?* She wasn't too surprised as it had been quite cold going to the post office that morning. She dozed as she sat in her chair. She woke up with a start. It must be a blackout. But why are the streetlights still on? Maybe the air raid siren had sounded and she just hadn't heard it. She really should have gone to the air raid shelter. Fred would be mad at her. She hoped he was alright wherever he was. His last letter had been a month ago. She looked around her not recognizing her surroundings. *Where is this place?* she wondered *I'm not at home.* She was so listless drowsy and confused. *God Fred I miss you so!* She drifted off.

It was two days before Hilda Blenkinsopp found her slumped in her chair with a half-finished letter on the table beside her. The weatherman said later on that the night of January 30th was the coldest in 30 years. A number of the homeless had frozen to death but there were a few old people like Dora Heard who had died of hypothermia. They were delinquent in their electricity bill payments and so had been cut off.

The press and the media gave the tragedy blanket coverage. There were photographs pf the deceased on the front of the newspapers juxtaposed with pictures of Managing Director Chaddick Spencer getting out of his jaguar in a cashmere coat saying 'No comment'.

The Electricity Board staff were besieged by reporters trying to get a new slant on the story. Bit by bit the sorry saga of the systems conversion leaked out. The Financial Times ran an in-depth article on the business risk inherent in such an ambitious venture as the Metropolitan Electricity Board had undertaken. The Times Leader talked about a complete absence of moral and civic responsibility, evidenced in the decisions of the Metropolitan Electricity Board's management. Tabloids focused heavily on the human-interest aspects, with biographies of the victims and coverage of their funerals.

Robert Petrie was pulling into his drive one evening about three days after the scandal broke. He was surprised to find a small mob of reporters and photographers waiting for him at the gate.

'Mr Petrie, how do you feel about Dora Heard's death?' one of the reporters shouted out.

'Who?'

Robert asked.

'Dora Heard. One of your constituents. She froze to death because the Metropolitan Electricity Board cut off her electricity supply for non-payment.'

'I'm very sorry to hear of the death of any constituent 'Robert replied.

'Yes, but you got her a disability pension. A half-finished letter to you was found with her when she died.'

Robert was half out of his car when the name registered and the face of Dora Heard flashed into his mind. 'I am very shocked. Mrs Heard was a very brave woman. She lost her husband and her immediate family in the second world war. Her husband was awarded the Victoria Cross you know.'

Cameras flashed; the reporters crowded in towards him. 'Mr Petrie, how do you feel about the actions of the Metropolitan Electricity Board?'

Robert responded. 'I would say they behaved in a very irresponsible manner.'

'Mr Petrie do you believe that events like this call into question the government's strategy of privatisation?'

'I'm not prepared to make a general statement of that kind based on one incident; however lamentable that may be.'

A woman reporter asked him: 'Mr Petrie, will you be attending Dora Heard's funeral?'

Robert began 'A member of Parliament has a very full.... 'He paused. Then he said decisively 'Yes I will. I will take no more questions now if you please. I need to get inside; my wife is expecting me.'

The reporters followed him all the way to the door to his house, bombarding him with questions, lights flashing, jostling to get close to him.

Marjorie was waiting for him just inside the door. She had been observing from the sitting room. 'What was that all about Robert?'

'Dora Heard is dead. You know the constituent that I got a disability pension for a couple of weeks ago?'

'What's so special about that?'

'She died of hypothermia when the electricity board cut off her power supply.'

'Oh God Robert, one of them.'

'Yes Marjorie, one of them.'

'What did you tell the reporters anyway?'

'I told them that she was a very brave woman. They asked me whether I thought this would have any impact on my view of the government's privatisation program.'

'And you said?' she asked sharply.

'I said that it was an unfortunate event but that I didn't necessarily think that it would affect my judgment on the policy. I have decided to go to the funeral tomorrow.'

Marjorie was startled. 'Whatever for?' She paused 'Well I suppose it can't do any harm. Concerned MP attends funeral of elderly constituent. I suppose the press will be there. Pretty good coverage, not much risk.'

He sighed. 'No Marjorie, its right up there with kissing babies' The sarcasm was lost on her.

'Well. Come into the kitchen. I got some lasagne from Marks and Spencer. We can have a bottle of Burgundy with it.' He hung up his overcoat and followed her in.

Marjorie busied herself serving up the food while he opened the wine.

'How was your day?' he asked her.

'Oh me? We are working on an acquisition at the moment. It's a friendly take-over and it's a stock swap with some cash involved. There is none of the tension associated with being in a bidding war for something but there are a lot of overseas holdings so there is a fair amount of technical detail. We are looking at the foreign exchange implications and also the tax liability'.

'Do you have to work any weekends?' Robert asked.

'Maybe a couple in March. We are going to try and wrap it up before the 1st of April. But nothing too horrific.'

'Maybe we can take a long weekend or something at the end of February and go to Paris?'

Marjorie was pleased. 'Oh Robert, how romantic. I think it's a wonderful idea. Let's check the calendar right now.'

They put their heads together over the daybook. 'Maybe the second weekend' Robert said. 'No, that won't do, there's a constituency association meeting. The third weekend.'

'The office has some kind of social function that weekend' Marjorie said. 'But I will just skip it'

Robert looked at her anxiously. 'Are you sure? I know how important these things are to your career advancement and all that.'

Marjorie smiled. 'It will be ok. Just remember to be extra nice the next time we go out to one of these things'. She looked at him archly 'Bed darling?'

He grinned 'I will just go and brush my teeth. Leave the dishes.'

It was the first time they had made love in over a month.

Chapter 12

'What do you mean the bastard won't settle? 'The Managing Director of the Metropolitan Electricity Board was not having a good day.

The company solicitor looked at him nervously. 'Well, as per your instructions we made quite a generous offer. The firm of Adolph and Swan, it would appear, have received very clear instructions from their principal. Mr Hargreave, it would appear, is not so much looking for financial reimbursement as public vindication.'

'So, what does he want? He wants me to publicly kiss his ass? Fine, I will kiss his ass.'

'It's no longer quite so simple as that. If Mr Hargreaves were an isolated incident we could, as you suggest, settle. But now there have been many similar instances and some with quite unfortunate outcomes. For us to publicly admit guilt or liability would expose the company to all kinds of potentially expensive litigation from many diverse quarters.'

'I see. So, what you are telling me is that he won't be bought off quietly. We are just going to have to tough it out?'

'It would seem the best course of action available to us.'

Chaddick Spencer sighed. 'Well, leave the offer on the table. But make it quite clear to the opposing guys we are all set to litigate this thing if needs be. We have to hope when our friend has had time to cool down he will figure a bird in the hand is worth two in the bush. Keep me posted as to the developments. Are there any other suits filed?'

It was the solicitors turn to sigh. 'Not as yet. But of course, its early.'

'That's a cheery thought.'

The intercom buzzed.

Spencer stabbed it as if he thought the device itself was responsible for his woes. 'Yes , what is it ?'

'Mr Johnson is here to see you. '

'Oh yeah, I'm just finishing up. Send him on in.'He started to light up a cigar. 'It seems', he remarked to no one in particular 'All I get these days are meetings full of gloom and doom.'

Brett Johnson walked into the room as the solicitor left. He looked haggard and his eyes were bloodshot.

'Christ Johnson. What happened to you?'

'These deaths Chaddick. I can't sleep at night because of them. Somehow I feel that I'm responsible.'

'Sure, you're responsible', Spencer replied. 'And I'm responsible for cutting off these peoples power supply. But then the welfare state is responsible too for not giving them enough money so that they can pay their bills. And their families are responsible for leaving them in that situation. But you know what Brett? We're screwed. We can take on the corporations and we can take on the politicos. But this latest fuck up. What we have is the windows and orphans lobby. And the press are going to hop on that bandwagon with a vengeance. So sooner or later they're going to be looking for heads and I'm going to be hung out to dry. You think I'm callous? Sonny boy if you lived through Nam and wanted to come back with a vestige of sanity from that hellhole you didn't think too much about the morality of what we were doing over there. The more sensitive guys that did, either got themselves shot or blown up. Or ended back Stateside with their heads totally screwed up. We had a good game plan here. The execution fouled up. That's all.'

Johnson was gazing dully out the window, not really hearing what was being said. Spencer strolled over to him until their noses were no more than a couple of inches apart. 'Now listen to me Brett. I'm not going to quit this job. They're going to have to push me. Part of the reason we are in this mess is because of this fucked up system. Now for that part you are responsible and I expect you to shoulder it. I don't need you to go into a self-indulgent guilt trip. I expect you to accept the consequences of your management decisions for better or worse and see this thing through with me.'

'You are always much tougher than me Chaddick.' Johnson said.

Spencer was having none of it. 'Tough is not how you feel Brett. Tough is what you do about it. Now are you going to take responsibility or am I going to have to cut you loose?'

Johnson shuddered and made a visible effort to get control. 'You warned me about the system Chaddick. I just didn't listen. Bad and all as I feel now if I bailed out and left you with my fuck up I couldn't live with myself. What do you think we should do?'

'I assume we have gone back to reviewing disconnection orders before we actually go and cut off the juice ?'

'Yes that has been in place for the last two weeks. Of course, it means another seven people on the headcount that we're not going to get rid of like we planned.'

Spencer shook his head wearily. 'Ah screw it. What does that matter now. The way I see it our credibility is shot. Our credibility with the public and our credibility with the Board. Any course of action we elect to pursue is going to need independent verification. Hire a bunch of consultants. I don't care who, as long as they are reputable. Have them do a proctoscopy on this system and tell them we want recommendations within a month as to what it's going to take to fix it. I will issue a press release saying that: 'Management is deeply concerned blah blah blah. We've taken measures suspending the automatic disconnection policy. Engaged consulting firm of Joe Blow and Sons to conduct an in-depth review of the system.' That may keep the wolves at bay for a little while but I doubt it.'

His boss was exhibiting the customary confident leadership that was his trademark. Johnson visibly brightened.

Spencer smiled.

'That's right Brett. Just because we're up to our ass in alligators doesn't mean we can't have a good time with it.'

'I will get right on a Chaddick.'

'Yeah keep me posted. Let me know who you select.' The intercom buzzed again.

'It's your wife Mr Spencer on line two. 'As Brett Johnson retreated out the door Spencer swore under his breath.

'Oh, Christ that's all I need.' He picked up the phone. 'Yes, honey what can I do for you ?'

The Long Island twang droned relentlessly in his ear. Spencer's face turned from one of weary boredom to growing annoyance. 'Shit Honey I don't have time to worry about what kind of china pattern we're going to get. Whatever you choose is fine with me.'

The tone on the other end of the telephone became distinctly sharper. Spencer exploded in exasperation. 'Honey we were talking about China patterns. How did we get from there to we have no home life? Yeah I know. I know I play too much golf. I don't give you enough attention.'

The voice was unassuaged. He had an inspired moment. 'Oh, sorry honey sorry to interrupt but Lord Malchum is on the line. Yes, that's right the one we met at the cocktail party. Yes, I'll be sure to tell him that you were asking for him. And I will remind him about the party we're having next month. Yes, and your regards to his lovely wife. Right. Yeah honey I'll be sure to tell you what he said as soon as I get home.'

Having got rid of his wife Spencer looked down accusingly at his groin. 'You have a lot to answer for ' he muttered. His secretary buzzed again.

'It's 11.30 Sir. Chief Inspector Maitland of the Yard is here to see you.'

Spencer was momentarily disoriented. 'The Yard. Oh yes Scotland Yard, the fraud thing. Okay send him right in.'

'It's not a him Sir it's a her. ' His secretary looked irked.

'You're shitting me. Okay yeah I know a sexist thing to say and all that. Send her in.'

The woman that was ushered into spencer's office was tall and had an excellent figure. Elizabeth Maitland appeared to be in her thirties. She returned his handshake with a firm grasp and made eye contact immediately. Used to sizing up people quickly he was impressed.

'Come on in and have a seat Inspector. That's what I call you right? You talked to my people. What did you find out? Has somebody got their fingers in the till or not?'

She moved unhurriedly to the seat he indicated and settled herself comfortably in it before answering his question. 'Well Mr Spencer it's Chief Inspector actually but we won't stand on formality. We have been working with your internal audit group for the last three days. It is quite clear that a fraud has been committed.'

Spencer was annoyed. 'God dammit I have been asking my people the same question for the last three weeks and can't get a straight answer out of them. How come you can give me a yes or no in two days. What are these guys good for anyway?'

Elizaberh Maitland was unfazed by his outburst. 'I assure you Mr Spencer your internal audit group is quite capable. In this case however more through inexperience than anything else they have spent their time trying to figure out how the fraud took place. This has led them to spend all of their energies examining the code of the system. It's the equivalent of looking for a needle in the proverbial haystack. We looked at it slightly differently. For all that it has a high-tech aura about it the basic principles of detection are the same. It's a question of means, motive, opportunity and above all in this case who benefited ? We know the billing algorithm that was being used on the commercial accounts was contrived so that it recovered slightly more than your receipts showed. And yet your books balanced.'

'If it were simply a programming error your accounting controls are such that the error would have been detected years ago. Someone made a compensating adjustment in your ledgers to conceal the over recovery from your consumers. That took premeditation and the amount embezzled, if we're right about how long this has been going on will represent several hundred thousand pounds. It went somewhere but certainly was not credited to the Metropolitan Electricity Board accounts. So, someone committed the fraud and the thrust of our investigative efforts will be to follow the money. If we can trace that we have our culprit.'

Spencer nodded appreciatively. 'I suppose I hoped you would tell me it was a horrible mistake. Of course, I know better than that. What next then?'

Maitland spoke decisively. 'I would like to assign you one of my detectives on an undercover basis. Say he's been brought in to help your internal audit division. Say he comes from an audit function from one of the banks. Our culprit is probably nervous that his little scheme has been detected after all of these years. It was a cleverly contrived fraud and he may be hoping to tough it out. If he becomes aware that the police are involved he may be tempted to run for it. Of course, we are relying on the discretion of your internal audit people. '

Spencer admired Maitland's clarity and responded in kind. 'Never you fear lady. I already gave those guys a going over. If you don't want to go public with this thing right now I certainly don't want to. I have enough bad press as it is without seeing the gory details of our fraud investigations splashed over the newspapers. Who are you assigning anyway?'

'His name is Stephen Goodchild. He has actually worked on a number of cases of bank fraud, so the cover will be plausible. Discovering where the money went will involve a lot of investigation of the electronic funds transfer.'

'Well let's hope you get your man. Fucking bastard.' Spencer scowled.

Maitland smiled coolly at him. 'Oh, we will find the person responsible. Never fear. Computer crime is unusual in that a significant amount of it goes undetected. In many cases even when a company discovers that fraud may have been committed they prefer to settle the matter quietly rather than treat it as the crime that it is. They fear that publicity would undermine confidence in their business. Once the matter is formally brought to our attention the detection rate is very high in excess of 90%.'

Spencer shrugged.' Yeah well I suppose there were a bunch of reasons why I might have swept it under the rug. Hey but it's not my style of doing business.'

He glanced at his watch. 'Shit, I have lunch in the city in 30 minutes. Sorry Inspector.'

Elizabeth Maitland stood up. 'It's perfectly alright Mr. Spencer. I don't believe there's anything further we need to discuss for the moment. Thank you for being so cooperative. We will of course keep you appraised of the progress of our investigations.'

Chapter Thirteen

The parish church was filled to overflowing for the funeral service. Dora Heard achieved a notoriety in death, never awarded to her in life. The regular parishioners were augmented by representatives of the veteran's groups. Large numbers of the press were in attendance and well-wishers from the general public had come to pay respects. The coffin was plain oak and unadorned. When Robert arrived, the vicar asked him to say a few words.

'I know it's a little unusual Mr Petrie but she had no close relatives remaining. Her neighbours would feel awkward and out of place talking in public. I will of course say something about how good a parishioner she was and how she always helped with volunteer work. But I thought it might be nice if someone other than me paid some sort of tribute. '

Robert at first declined but then thought: *she deserves more than just a few informal words from her local vicar.*

He sat in the front pew nervously biting his lips, trying to think of what to say. Surprisingly for a man in public life he was not a very good extemporaneous speaker. His rare interventions in Commons debate were meticulously researched and carefully scripted beforehand.

The service opened with the congregation singing "Abide With Me, "tentatively, at first but then with growing conviction. The atmosphere seemed suddenly charged with emotion. The vicar read a verse of scripture from Saint Paul and then indicated to Robert that he should say a few words.

He stood up and walked slowly to stand beside the coffin. The press reporters who had come expecting to file a human-interest piece sensed news. There was a jostling and a flashing of light bulbs as they repositioned themselves. He projected his voice without aid of a microphone to fill the small church.

'Dora Heard lived through the blitz. She lost both her parents and her sister to Hitler's bombs. She lost her husband fighting in Normandy- a brave man, who was awarded the Victoria Cross by a grateful nation for his efforts. I only met her once a few weeks ago. She had come to ask me to help her with the disability benefit. She struck me as a warm uncomplaining and cheerful woman. Now we are here today to mourn her passing.'

'There is always a sadness when someone dies even if as Christians, we believe they have gone to a better life. Although I didn't know her very well I am deeply grieved to be standing here today beside her coffin. Because Dora did not die of natural causes, she died of the cold. She died because the electricity was cut off in her flat and because she had not enough money to pay the bill. '

'Dora and her generation lived through the Second World war. She and people like her endured and watched loved ones die so that we might have our freedom and our Democratic way of life. And for those of us born after the war the events seem to have happened such a long time ago as to be something to be studied in the history books. For Dora and her generation however, the war years were the defining moments in their lives. How then as a nation have we expressed our gratitude for the sacrifices that Dora made? She died alone of the cold in an unheated flat.'

'I am grieved at her passing in this manner because I as a public representative bear more responsibility than the average citizen for what has happened. As a society we need to recognise that we are interdependent. If we embrace the philosophy which says that material prosperity belongs only to the strong and the weak must fend for themselves we will experience a spiritual death. We will create a society and a way of life which is the antithesis that for which Dora Heard and her generation sacrificed and died.'

He returned to his place. The congregation had grown silent during his eulogy. After a pause, the vicar began the 22nd psalm. Robert suddenly felt very tired. Dora was to be interred in the church graveyard, a rare occurrence as it was nominally closed to all but those who had existing family plots. Because of the circumstances of her death however and because she was the widow of a decorated war hero an exception had been made.

He resolved to slip away as soon as the service itself was over. The press and media would certainly turn the grave site into a circus. At the end of the service the vicar preceded the coffin carried by pallbearers down the aisle out through the porch into the grey sodden morning. Robert slipped out by the vestry door and made for his car. A couple of reporters, noticing his manoeuvre, raced after him.

'Mr Petrie have you any comments on the government's privatization scheme now ?'

'Mr Petrie in light of what you said just now can you comment on the government's social policy ?'

The shouted questions, the flashing cameras, the microphones thrust into his face, all became a meaningless babble. He kept moving purposely towards his car.

'I'm sorry I have nothing further to add to my previous comments.'

He broke the speed limit as he pulled the car onto the street and raced off. Only when he put several miles between the church and himself did he slow down. He found he was going in entirely the opposite direction of where he had intended. *What is happening to me?,* he wondered. His political convictions nurtured by social circumstances and honed in debate among his peers at University were becoming more uncertain. The waves of life's experience lapping slowly against the pillars of his political faith, were beginning to erode them.

A few weeks before Dora Heard would have been just a data point to him classified as a member of the constituency in a particular social class and within a particular demographic band, the over sixties. Now she was an old woman dead in her coffin. She had a face and a life history. He looked around at unfamiliar streets on the outskirts of the city. *Where am I?* He wondered. Probably halfway to Guildford. He found a place to turn and headed back as he was due at Westminster at one o'clock.

Chapter Fourteen

Stephen Goodchild rolled out of bed reluctantly with the alarm Clock set for 6:30. He stumbled to the bathroom and regarded himself sourly in the mirror. His mouth felt as if it were filled with cotton wool and his throat was dry. *Dehydrated.* He thought to himself. *Got pissed as a newt last night.* He was getting drunk too often. An emotional casualty of a failed marriage. He was well muscled with straight teeth blue eyes and blonde hair. He was thirty two. *A right pinup boy.* He thought miserably to himself.

The conversation started playing in his head.

'I'm sick of you never being home. '

'A police detective works long hours; you knew that when you married me.'

'It doesn't make it any easier to live with. Even when you are home your mind is still on the job. All I get are monosyllabic answers to any question that I ask you. It's like living with a robot.'

'Why is the house always a mess when I come home?'

'There's two of us living here darling'.

'Yeah, well I don't leave dirty breakfast things on the table.'

'With the hours you work more often than not you are not around for breakfast. How many cooked meals have I thrown in the garbage because you have had a quote-unquote last-minute emergency?'

Periods of solemn silence. In the early years of their marriage they had been carefree and bohemian. As the years wore on, however, each had found they needed and indeed wanted the conventional marriage. The lack of outward manifestation of those conventions had become more and more of a source of conflict to them. He wanted domesticity and order; she wanted a partner with regular work hours. As time passed, shared interests, mutual likes and dislikes, sexual compatibility, all withered with the unmet expectations each had of the marriage contract. At the end, whenever they saw each other they argued, so they went out of their way to avoid each other. He immersed himself in work and drink, she did extra shifts at the restaurant where she waitressed. Then two weeks ago she had come home and told him she found someone else. She was pregnant by her lover. The child couldn't have been his, they hadn't had sex in six months.

Here he was, in a bedsit in White Horse Lane. So, what was he left with? The job, the all-consuming job. He had wanted to be a detective ever since he was fourteen. With a computer science degree from Imperial College he applied to the Metropolitan Police Force and had been accepted. Two years on the beat and then he was transferred to the Criminal Investigation Division, fraud squad. Now he was a detective sergeant hoping to make detective inspector one of these days. His drive to do well in his chosen profession was all consuming in his twenties. The marriage was just fitted in around it as it were. Paradoxically as he hit thirty and began to reassess some of his priorities the years of neglecting his wife had already taken their toll and just as he started to want a more balanced life she had lost interest. Who was it that said that relationships were all a matter of timing? *Mine sucks,* he thought sourly.

As he went through the familiar morning routine of shaving and showering he willed himself to start thinking about his latest case. Reluctantly at first his thoughts turned away from his domestic problems and he began to focus on the fraud at the Metropolitan Electricity Board. It was a clever crime that had gone undetected for years and would have continued to do so had it not been for an unlikely combination of circumstances. The new system and ill-advised collections policy and a litigious miser had all conspired to create the circumstances leading to its detection. How long had it been going on? Five or six years at least. The crook had been cautious as not much money was siphoned off each billing period. But over the years it had mounted up. Best estimates put it in excess of half a million pounds. And the crook had been clever, not only programming the billing routines to divert the funds, but also faking out the General Ledger software package so that as far as the Electricity Board knew its books were balancing. Before Scotland Yard had been called in internal auditors had been poring over the code to try to see where the books had been cooked like wandering blindfolded in a maze. Now the approach was much more disciplined.

The Electrucity Board kept copies of the print files for the bills of the last year. The task force had calculated the total actually billed to the customers by the simple expedient of reprinting all the bills and adding them up. They then compared that to the amounts actually collected and remitted to the bank. Factoring out late receivables there was a discrepancy of anywhere between twenty and thirty thousand pounds each billing period which had been collected by the system but had not been remitted to the Electricity Board's bank. Where had it gone? They now had a comprehensive list of all the bank account numbers belonging to the Electricity Board. Someone had diverted the additional money to an unauthorised bank account.

Today and tomorrow they would run scanning software over the source code and do pattern matches to identify number patterns that corresponded to a bank account code and routing information for electronic funds transfer. Once they had the list of all occurrences by process of elimination they would with any luck find the wrong account number. That would give them the first link in the chain that would lead to the criminal. That was one line of investigation but only one. As his boss kept pointing out even with high tech crime the basic principles of criminal investigation applied. They were compiling a list of all Electricity Board personnel who had access to the system for the last six years.

Unfortunately, the security was lousy. They didn't even change passwords once a year. By going to the Personnel Department, they had compiled a list of names and were now running routine background checks. To this point nothing too sinister had shown up in terms of prior records. A few DUIs and one grievous bodily harm but so far nobody stood out as having a prior conviction for a crime of this kind.

They were beginning to check on people's financial situations to see if anybody showed up as maintaining a lifestyle unsupported by their salary or other income.

The Metropolitan Electricity Board controversy was all over the newspapers which had given the case a very high profile. Even though Stephen Goodchild was undercover there was considerable logistical support being given back at Scotland Yard.

He finished the mental review just before putting on his coat to head out the door. His mood had altered and he was almost enthusiastic. With any luck today they would identify the wrong account number and then the chase would begin in earnest.

He arrived at the offices of the Metropolitan Electricity Board to find a number of the internal audit staff having an impromptu tea break even though it was only nine o'clock in the morning.

'What's up Stephen ? Been a good boy have you? 'The speaker was an avuncular man with horn rimmed spectacles.

Fred Armstrong was assigned to the case from the Electricity Board side. Only the head of the Department knew Stephen's real identity. As far as everybody else was concerned he was on loan from Lloyds Bank to help with the fraud investigation.

'Alright thanks Fred. Maybe one pint too many but otherwise nothing to complain about. How are you doing with the scanning software?'

Fred paused with coffee cup in mid-air and looked at him blankly.

'Hello? Oh the software! Well systems is having a bit of a problem installing it right now. But they say they will have it operational by lunchtime. They won't be able to run it until tonight.'

Goodchild was visibly upset, 'Why in heaven's name not ?'

Fred was amused. 'well I realise that this fraud investigation is very important and all that but we do have a business to run. Production systems get priority during the day, particularly the online system, and then of course we have to run the billing at night. But there is a window of three or four hours when we could actually get priority on the machine. Remember son a little bit of patience goes a long way.'

Goodchild ground his teeth silently. Struggling to remain composed he asked 'Mind if I check in with systems to see how they're doing with the actual package installation?'

Fred Armstrong chuckled. 'Be my guest, that is if you can get them on the phone. You might actually have to walk down a couple flights of stairs to the computer Department to talk to one of them. A bunch of anti-social bastards if you ask me.'

Goodchild began to tune into the conversation going on around him.

'Well it's a charity do so I suppose we should go ?'

'it's one of the Yank's bright ideas.'

'What are they talking about ?' Goodchild asked Fred.

'Oh, there's a benefit dinner dance on Saturday. All the corporate staff are invited or rather expected to go. It's something the American introduced a couple of years ago when he first got the top job. His notion is that the Electricity Board should be a concerned corporate citizen or some such nonsense. Every Department has to do something to raise funds for local charities in their neighbourhood. The district offices do their thing and we at corporate hold a dinner dance. This year it's to benefit the inner cities. It's pricey enough mind you. Fifty pounds a seat. These charity dinners are all the rage in the States it would appear but they're not too common in our neck of the woods. You should go along; you get to see everybody in the Department. '

Goodchild was hesitant, 'I'm not too sure that would be appropriate.'

'Nonsense think of it as a little bit of fact gathering. I can point out all the …. 'Fred lowered his voice dramatically 'potential suspects. That way you could put names to faces.'

'When is it ? 'Goodchild asked.

'Next Saturday.'

'That's a bit short notice. I don't have a date.'

Fred eyed the wedding band on Goodchild's finger but didn't comment.

'Hey Vera! 'Fred shouted over to a girl sitting at a terminal, 'you going to this charity do Saturday night?'

'Hadn't planned on it Fred. There's a good movie on the box. I was going to put my hair up in curlers and watch it.'

'Stephen here needs a date, what do you say?'

'Our new boy 'Vera stopped chewing gum and looked at him appraisingly. 'Well it's a good flick. Roger Moore is James Bond, but I suppose he might be worth it.'

'There you are then 'Fred beamed happily. 'That's arranged. It's a formal do so you'll need a dinner jacket but I'm sure you can take care of that. Why don't I leave you to sort out the details. Some of us have work to do.' He meandered happily back to his cubicle.

Goodchild wandered over to Vera.' I hope you don't mind ?' he asked.

Vera was amused. 'If i had minded love I would have said so.'

Vera's dress style was a little unorthodox. She wore a short tight-fitting dress and a thick bulky wool cardigan. The upper half reminded you of your aunt the lower half would have done well in a bikini contest.

'I will need to get us a couple of tickets. They are on sale at administration.' She reached for her handbag.

'No that won't be necessary.' He said hastily. 'I will take care of the tickets.'

She looked at him sharply. 'Suit yourself but don't go getting any ideas.'

He grinned.' Don't worry I will be a perfect gentleman.'

'Well you don't look like an axe murderer but then you can never tell. Where's your missus anyway that you're not going with her?'

He fingered his wedding ring.' Oh we broke up a couple of weeks ago.'

She shrugged 'It happens. Talk to me when you've gotten the tickets. We will work out when to meet up and so on.' She turned to her terminal and turned up the radio which was permanently tuned to the Capital sration.

Well, Goodchild thought as he walked back to his desk, *it's a little unorthodox but Fred has got a point. I get to see these people in a social setting and form some impressions of them and I am supposed to be undercover.*

Chapter Fifteen

The newspapers were full of it. 'Tory MP blasts government social policy' said one. 'Dog eat dog society 'another. The tabloids picked a sensational headline and then supported the story by selectively quoting from Robert Petrie's eulogy. The Guardian and the Telegraph took a more balanced approach with the Guardian printing the eulogy in it's entirety. The furore caused consternation at Tory party headquarters. They first had to register who Robert Petrie exactly was. They quickly determined that he was the backbencher from the marginal constituency of Putney. The party press officer and party chairman held a meeting the morning after Dora Heard's funeral surrounded by the debris of the morning newspapers. Lord Overton was incredulous.

'You mean to tell me this fellow didn't bother to clear this with the party head office ?'

'I'm afraid not Lord Overton. It's just something he appears to have done himself.'

'For God sake we're one week away from a by election and this loose cannon hands the opposition a crowbar to hit us over the head with. The Prime Minister isn't going to be pleased by this. You know he doesn't like surprises. We're going to have to put some spin control on it. Work on a statement for the minister of Trade and Industry and also for the minister of Social Welfare.'

'What are we going to do about Petrie ? 'the press officer asked.

'Him? He's going to have to issue some kind of clarification or recantation or I don't know what. Write a speech for the bastard. Comments taken out of context, completely supportive of the government's position, whatever!'

'Have him here first thing tomorrow morning. Better make sure someone from the Chief Whip 's office is here also. God, some of these backbenchers, turnips for brains.'

Breakfast at the Petrie's house was acrimonious and heated.

'Look at the newspapers report. What possessed you to sound off like that? You said you were going to pay your respects to the poor old cow, but now you are off on some half-cocked crusade of your own.' Marjorie Petrie was livid.

'I said what I felt at the time Marjorie. I'm sorry I didn't distill it for every subtle political nuance.' Robert was unapologetic.

'My God the party managers will be furious. 'Marjorie mused to herself. 'You've ruined any chance you had for early advancement. I suppose you realise that Robert.'

'Sorry, Marjorie, I refuse to choreograph my life around party advancement.' Her husband replied.

'Oh, that's very fine for you Robert, very fine. But what you seem to forget is that we are in this together. With one of us pursuing a political career, the other one's got to keep a roof over our heads. Well I'm doing my bit every day of the bloody week. I have to work with some right turds in the City. Meanwhile, you indulge in quixotic crusades which will change precisely nothing. You can pretty much guarantee that your political career, if you have one after this, is going to be as an obscure backbencher. Its times like these that your feeble mindedness sickens me.'

'I'm sorry that you feel that way Marjorie. I guess that I don't have the same driving ambition as you do.'

'No, I suppose you can afford not to have Robert, with me paying the bills.'

'Come off it, Marjorie. You enjoy the high-powered job. And you are the one with the expensive tastes, fine wines, the winter holidays. So cut out the sob story, it doesn't wash with me.'

She looked at him resentfully and changed the subject. 'Just look out the window, it's a circus out there. 'The crowd outside their front gate was a motley crew of some twenty photographers and reporters. 'What are you going to say to those people?'

'For the moment nothing. I have said all I am going to say.'

Marjorie retorted.' Wonderful, just wonderful. Well I have to get to work and I'm certainly not going to deal with that shower on my own.'

'I'll take care of them Marjorie, while you drive away.'

'Why don't you bloody well do that Robert. It's the least you can manage.'

The phone rang. Marjorie exploded, 'Christ, another news hound. It's been ringing off the hook since 6.30 this morning'. She picked it up. 'Petrie residence, yes, who is this? Oh! Yes certainly. My husband is just here. Yes, I will get him for you'. She held her hand over the mouthpiece. ' Its Party head office.'

If Robert was nervous he didn't show it. He took the phone while she went to put on her coat. 'Petrie here. Not too bad thanks and yourself? Yes, the eulogy appears to have gained quite a bit of media attention. Quite unanticipated I assure you. Yes, that aspect of it is unfortunate. Indeed there are a number of reporters outside. No, I don't plan to comment further. Certainly, I can make time. Shall we say tomorrow then, at 9.00 am? Until then.' He slammed down the phone.

Marjorie confronted him 'I imagine they want your guts for garters?'

'It's nice to have a supportive wife dear. Yes, it was about the eulogy. They want to talk to me about it. '

She gave a snort.

Robert squared his shoulders. 'I have a meeting with the Chief Whip and the Party chairman tomorrow at nine. They don't want me to comment any further until they have seen me.'

'Bloody marvellous!' Marjorie exploded. 'You're right up there on their radar aren't you ? Well tonight we're going to go over exactly what you're going to say to these people and see if we can't salvage something from the wreckage of your career. '

'Your solicitude is touching Marjorie!'

'I'm not going to stand here trading debating points with you Robert. This is not some kind of verbal shuttlecock we're playing. Come on let's get a move on or I'll be late for my meeting in the City.'

He linked her arm as they walked out the door. 'Let's smile for the nice ladies and gentlemen of the press shall we Marjorie ?'

They emerged from their house smiling congenially.

'Mr Petrie any reaction to the press coverage of your tribute to Dora Heard?'

'Mr Petrie have you heard from Party headquarters ? 'There was a babble of voices.

'I have no further comment at this time.' Robert responded. He guided Marjorie to her car. 'Ladies and gentlemen if you could clear the way please my wife has a business appointment in the City.'

Finding that they were making no progress with Robert some of the reporters turned to Marjorie.

'Mrs Petrie have you any comment to make ?'

'My husband and I regret Mrs Heard's death. I am however fully supportive of this government's social policy. '

'Does that mean that you think your husband isn't ?'

'My husband is the sitting conservative member for this constituency. Of course, he supports the government's policy. Now if you'll excuse me.'

She rolled up her window and backed briskly out of the drive scattering reporters left and right as she did so.

Knowing it would rile her Robert blew her a kiss as she drove away.

It seemed there were reporters yelling at him wherever he went that morning. There were other obvious repercussions of the speech. When he attended the Trade and Industry committee meeting at the House later that morning members of his own party greeted him quietly, with attitudes ranging from confusion to suspicion to reserve. Not so the Labour Party members one of whom clapped him on the back saying 'Great speech Robert couldn't have done it better myself. Wouldn't have thought you had it in you.'

Where is this all leading me? He wondered? *A few spontaneous heartfelt words and it seems as if my life is a shambles.*

The proceedings of the committee held very little interest for him today. He knew there would be a major confrontation with Marjorie that night. He wondered what he would say. The blizzard of messages awaited him wherever he went...from the chairman of his constituency Association, from the news media, from well-wishers , from detractors. Overnight he had achieved notoriety and celebrity.

Robert left Westminster in the early afternoon and went to his health club. He swam a hundred laps and had a sauna afterwards. Uncharacteristically he went to a pub and had a small whiskey before getting in his car to drive home. *Well I best go and face the music* he thought to himself.

Marjorie was already there when he got home. She had laid out a plate of hors d'oeuvre and chilled some white wine. 'Hello Robert. I won't ask you what kind of day you had. Mine wasn't so good either. Why don't you get changed and come down and we'll have something to eat. We need to talk this through but let's try to be nice to each other while we do it.'

'I would like that.' He said simply.

After he changed they sat in silence for a few minutes. Then Robert began.

'I know you are very upset about this Marjorie.' He paused.

'I am Robert. I'm sorry that this old woman is dead but I really don't understand why you've decided to turn it into a cause celebre.'

'That's just it Marjorie, I didn't decide. It just happened. Now that it has, I have to admit the experience has had a profound effect on me. I have spent the last few days thinking very hard about my life and what I believe. '

She frowned but said nothing.

'It's as if, in a way, I've lived all my life to according to a script. Everything I've done has been premeditated, choreographed, very tidy and all in order. But this woman, she had a face and a name for me. And now she's dead.

'The problem Robert is that everything in your life to this point has come too easy for you. You've never really had to reflect too much on what you were doing because there were no really hard choices to make. Your social background dictated that you go to the right Public School and to the right University and after that you'd look for a career in one of the professions . This is the first time you've really encountered a slice of life.'

He sipped his wine and thought about her words. 'You may be very well right Marjorie but your background is not much different from mine.'

'No Robert my social background may not be different but my circumstances certainly are. You must understand that you were a man and I'm a woman. I went to Oxford on a scholarship. My family's view was, and still is, why waste time and money educating a girl. The proper role for a young lady is first to find herself a husband who will take care of her and then raise two or three children. So why waste resources with an expensive education. I was the only girl of four children, the second child. My three brothers had my parent's attention lavished on them. Getting to where I am, notwithstanding my social background, has been a bitter struggle for me Robert. My parents were opposed to my going to University and they most certainly do not approve of my working for a living. So, Robert, my life choices have been tough to make. Yours on the other hand have not been.'

Robert looked at her with amazement. 'How come you've never told me any of this before Marjorie? I knew your parents thought it a bit rum that you were working in the City but I had no idea that they had such an old world outmoded view of things.'

Marjorie sighed. 'Oh, I tried to tell you Robert from time to time, but you just weren't listening. You can be very self-absorbed you know.' She fiddled with the buttons on her dress. 'But all this is beside the point. What are you going to do?'

'Well what people obviously want me to do Marjorie is issue some kind of statement saying that it was all a big mistake. I'm expected to reaffirm my commitment to the party line. Then I'm supposed to keep my head down and wait for it all to blow over. '

She looked at him directly, 'But that's not what you want to do is it Robert ?'

'Marjorie, God knows I didn't go looking for this. But how I see the world now doesn't square with the political philosophy I've espoused for the last fifteen years. I can't just wallpaper over it and pretend it didn't happen. More than that I don't want to.'

His wife looked at him intensely. 'It will be the ruin of your political career you know that.'

Robert shrugged his shoulders. 'You might very well be right Marjorie but I will take my chances.'

She sighed and looked at the framed wedding photograph of them over the fireplace. 'You know Robert after the years of struggling with my father over my education I thought long and hard about the kind of man I wanted to marry. I wanted a man who knew where he was going, who had a clear idea of who he was and who was not afraid to let me live my own life. That's what I thought I was getting when I married you. You are re-evaluating your life and I wish you well in that, I really do. But I don't think I can stay married to a man who doesn't know who he is or what he stands for. Perhaps you'll get your composure back. I hope you do because I loved you when I married you and I think I probably still do.' Again, she looked at him directly, 'For now though Robert I think it's best if we separate. It may be cowardly of me but I don't want the pain and the uncertainty of living with someone in the throes of midlife self-discovery.' She was crying a little by the time she finished.

He looked at her helplessly, 'I'm sorry you feel like that Marjorie and I'm sorry that it's turned out this way.'

'I know you didn't Robert.' Marjorie said. 'We'll stop now if you don't mind. I'm feeling a little tired so I think I'll go to bed early. Perhaps it would be best if you slept in the guest bedroom. We can work out some details tomorrow.'

He knew better than to argue, 'I will just get my pyjamas and my shaving gear from our room. Is there anything I can get you Marjorie?'

'No Robert, thanks. I'm just very tired that's all.'

As he climbed the stairs slowly he thought to himself: *So that's how it happens. The thing you think can only happen to other people.* He got his things and lay down in the bed in the guest bedroom. His mind kept resurfacing memories. Recollections of the first time he had met Marjorie. Episodes from their carefree student days and their early married life. He wanted desperately to go to sleep but his mind wouldn't cooperate. Eventually though, after several hours, he drifted off.

Chapter 16

The company solicitor was in Chaddick Spencer's office to discuss the Hargreave suit.

'You made him an offer ? 'Spencer inquired.

'Indeed, we did Sir and, if I may say, an extremely generous offer. For prompt settlement with no fault admitted we offered Mr Hargreave one million pounds.

That might not seem excessive in the United States but in this country for a suit with such a tenuous basis as Mr. Hargreave it is an extraordinary offer.'

'And he wouldn't go for it ?'

'I met with Mr. Hargreave's family solicitor, who informed me that he discussed our offer with his principal, but that it was declined. Clearly it would have been inappropriate for Mr. Mayhew to have discussed with me what advice he gave to Mr. Hargreave but reading between the lines I sensed that he recommended Mr. Hargreave to accept and was quite taken aback when he did not.'

'What is with this guy then ?'

'Mr. Hargreave is a very wealthy gentleman but also very reclusive. So, it is very difficult to interpret his motivations.'

Spencer tapped his teeth reflectively with his pencil.' There's more to this than money. It's some kind of grudge thing.' He came to a decision. 'Tell Hargreave I'd like to meet him face to face. Have it out.'

The solicitor became agitated, 'Are you sure that's wise Mr Spencer? Even with legal counsel in the room.'

'No. No lawyers. You guys will only make sure it gets screwed up. Henry V. "The first thing we do let's kill all the lawyers." ' Spencer looked at him and chuckled. 'You probably think us Americans can't even spell, much less quote, Shakespeare.'

'Henry VI, actually. 'The solicitor murmured.

Spencer looked at him a bit unkindly. 'It's really simple. We've got a skeleton in our closet. It's called fraud. We need this thing put to bed before the investigation becomes public knowledge. We have tried money with him and he won't take it. So there has to be something else. We don't know enough about him nobody does, to guess what that might be. So, the only way to flush him out is to talk to him face to face, and that's what I'm proposing to do.'

The solicitor sighed, 'I'll see what I can arrange but, with your permission Mr. Spencer, I would like to brief you in advance on the legal aspects of this matter.'

Spencer nodded approvingly.' Sure! Work me up a briefing document, give me twenty-four hours to read it and then schedule a meeting with me so we can discuss it.'

The phone rang and Spencer picked it up. The solicitor gathered up his papers.

'Yeah who is it ?' Spencer barked. 'Berkhalter, The advertising agency? Put the son of a bitch through.'

'Hello yeah. I looked at your proposal for the image campaign. TV, radio, and print. Cuddly images of babies. Metropolitan Electricity Board - the caring company. There's such a thing as timing assholes. Right now, the caring company has had a bunch of its customers freeze to death. We cut off their power supply. We run this campaign anytime soon the media will crucify us. I'm not paying you guys six figures and agency fees to come up with a proposal that would turn us into the 'Bozo the Clown show' in short order. Right now, we have a black eye. I want some beef steak to apply to it. You figure out what that is. Maybe a year from now I can look at some of this stuff but just now it's horseshit. '

He paused to listen to the plaintive voice on the other end of the line. 'Listen Berkhalter, I don't care how many late nights or how many of your best people you put into this. I'm the customer and I'm saying this result sucks. You fix it or I'll get another agency. You have one week to come up with something better.' He put down the phone. 'Cocksucker', he muttered.

He turned to the solicitor.' Oh sorry about that pal. I didn't realise that you were still here.'

The solicitor closed the door quietly behind him.

Robert was a few minutes early for his meeting at Party headquarters that morning. There was the usual frenzied quality about the place. More so because of the by election due to be held in just two weeks 'time. They made him wait five minutes past the appointed hour just to show him who was boss. He had no doubt that they had been there some time previously, strategizing on how to conduct the meeting. When he went in he found Lord Overton, chairman of the party, and the Chief Whip, waiting for him. Seeing them sitting there a random impression ran across his mind. They looks like characters from Toad of Toad Hall. The chairman looked like a bulldog with dyspepsia, the Chief Whip looked like a ferret. He suppressed the urge to grin and thought himself *it's a nervous reaction.*

'Lord Overton, Mr. Graves.' Robert said in greeting as he sat in the chair they indicated,' You wanted to see me?'

Lord Overton came to the point without preamble.' Yes Robert. This Dora Heard business as you were well aware, has created quite a stir. Not good news two weeks from the by election. We want to hear your side of the story and then jointly decide what we're going to do about it.'

He felt like telling Lord Overton to get stuffed but instead what he said was 'I appreciate that Lord Overton. As you know Dora Heard was my constituent and died in tragic circumstances. I decided to attend her funeral and the vicar invited me at the last minute to say a few words, which I did. These were quite widely reported, and in some cases sensationalised by the tabloid press.

The Chief Whip intervened. ' If you were going to give a speech of that nature you should have cleared it with head office first. And at a funeral for God sake. This is not South Africa we don't make party political speeches at funerals. '

Robert looked at him coolly.' Perhaps you didn't hear me Mr Graves. As I explained the choice to have me speak came at the last moment. I said what I felt about the poor woman's passing and it wasn't meant to be a political statement.'

Graves wasn't having it.' You're either being disingenuous Petrie or you are incredibly naïve. How could that have not been a political statement with an army of media people in front of you.'

Lord Overton intervened.' Well there's no use crying over spilled milk. In a way I can sympathise my boy. After all, when you think of the way she died and she was a war veteran's widow, emotion of the moment and all that, I can see how one could get carried away. My thought Robert was that you needed to clear the air a bit; you caught the media's attention. Some of the trade rags have distorted your words and taken things out of context. What is needed is a clear statement from you reaffirming your commitment to the government social policy. Just for discussion purposes, I asked the PR boys here to prepare a draft of the kind of statement we had in mind.'

Lord Overton looked at the Chief Whip who passed around copies of the statement. Robert read the document slowly. There is no sound except for the noise of traffic outside. When he had finished he looked up slowly. 'I'm sorry Lord Overton but I don't believe I can make a statement like that.'

The gaze that met his nail was cold, unblinking, steady, without a trace of warmth. 'And why might that be Robert?'

'Well, it goes in for a certain amount of overstatement, don't you think ? ' Robert quoted:

"This government has an unparalleled record for development and improvement of social services."

'Basically, we mark time if we do that much.'

'Is there anything else that doesn't meet with your approval Robert ?' He ignored the chairman's sarcasm.

'Well now that you mention it Lord Overton.' "while deploring the specific circumstances of Dora Heard's death I fully support the government's privatisation policy."

'And what do you think is the matter with that particular statement ?'

'Simply that it treats the mess at the Metropolitan Electricity Board as an aberration. "Everything is fine in the best of all possible worlds." No adjustments need to be made to policy. The fact that there were ten people frozen to death as a consequence of that policy is neither here nor there.'

The Chief Whip exploded.' You two faced bastard.'

Lord Overton intervened once more.' We can discuss loyalty to party or absence thereof later. Let's just stick to the matter at hand shall we?'

'My sense of this discussion is that your views on these matters Robert have diverged so far from those of your party that a statement of support from you is unlikely to be forthcoming. '

'I think that states the position quite fairly Lord Overton.'

'This is of course a serious disappointment to those of us who at one time viewed you as having considerable potential.'

'I'm sorry that should be the case. 'Robert replied noncommittally.

'You will appreciate Robert that the government is balanced on a knife edge with this by election pending. And that publicity such as this is doing nothing for our ability to stay focused on the business of running the country and advancing our parliamentary agenda. '

'I respect the time you are taking with me Lord Overton but then again, I would say that there is a marked difference in how we see the situation. You see these issues as aberrations, unfortunate accidents as it were. I see them as symptoms of a fundamental malaise. There is a fundamental disconnect between the thrust of our political agenda and the human and social needs of the population. '

'We would appreciate Robert if you would make no further public comment on these matters. 'Lord Overton went on, before Robert could interrupt. 'Or if you feel you have to, you should at least give this office advance warning about what you intend to say. I remind you that you were elected as the conservative member for Putney and not as an independent. '

'Since Dora Heard,s funeral Lord Overton I have made no further comment to the press on these matters nor do I intend to. I am well aware of my dilemma. '

'In my own defence I would point out that since entering parliament I have never once voted against my party, nor abstained, nor ever missed a vote when for that matter. '

He looked sharply at the Chief Whip who turned to Lord Overton and said reluctantly, 'It's true what he says. He has a perfect voting record. '

Lord Overton's demeanour softened visibly. 'Well when it comes down to the crunch it's how you vote that carries the day. I'll brief the PM on this. He's not going to be too pleased. ' He got up and stretched.

'My advice to you, young Robert, is to keep your head down and say nothing and wait for all of this to blow over. Seems like a big deal now when everybody's got their knickers in a twist. Six months from now no one will care. I wouldn't want to see you permanently damage your career prospects. Now I have to go over to Downing St. The' meeting broke up.

When the Prime Minister was briefed in the context of overall prospects for the by election he paused before observing,

'Robert Petrie. "Yond Cassius has a lean and hungry look. He thinks too much and such men are dangerous."'

Chapter Seventeen

They had the bank account number. Dear God, what was he going to do? Andrew sat in the pub at his local High Street at one end of the counter, sipping a pint. One of the internal audit people had let it slip this afternoon.

'Whoever the bastard is Andrew, his goose is cooked now. This guy they brought in from Lloyds Bank is one smart bugger. He brought in some sophisticated scanning software. He figured out they had to be siphoning the money off through electronic fund transfers to some rogue bank account. Of course, we know which bank accounts are ours so it's just a case of scanning the codes to find the odd man out. Easy when you know how I suppose.'

On the one hand, he was amazed that the internal audit staff should be so naive as to talk about the progress of their internal investigation to anyone. On the other hand, at least, he knew the worst. He had to stop off on the way home and get a drink to steady his nerves. He couldn't go and face Deirdre in his current state. *The strain of living with his lie is going to kill me,* he thought. *That and not knowing whether they'll ever trace it to me.*

His mother's voice echoed in his head. 'They weren't supposed to find out there was a fraud in the first place. They were never supposed to find out there was a bank account. Serves you right Andrew Sweeney. You deserve everything you've got coming to you. Crime doesn't pay.'

'Shut up you sanctimonious old bitch. I could make a run for it.'

'And leave Michael and Deirdre behind with them not knowing ?'

No, Andrew thought to himself. *You don't run, you don't panic. They have a bank account number and that's all they have. They weren't supposed to get this far admittedly. But tracing that bank account to me is pretty near impossible the way I have set it up. And even if they do figure it out it's going to take them time.* He ordered another shot of whiskey. *What am I going to do? Go home to my wife and child. Enjoy my time with them. Hope to God the bloodhounds don't get any closer.*

When he got home, Deirdre was all excited about the prospects for the upcoming charity dinner dance on Saturday. 'I thought I'd wear the black velvet gown. Andrew did you remember to get fitted for your dinner jacket?'

'I'm sorry Deirdre I forgot.'

'You're hopeless. We hardly ever get a chance to go to social events like this.'

'London is a big town Deirdre. Renting a dinner jacket is not going to be a problem. I'll take care of it tomorrow I promise.'

Deirdre said sharply.' See that you do.'

Her good mood returned almost instantly however as she contemplated the prospect of an evening of wine and dance. 'God it's marvellous. It makes me feel like a student again. Great idea of your chairman or whatever he is to have this kind of event. What's the charity anyway?'

'Oh, it's for the inner cities. He's very much into the Electricity Board being socially conscious and a good corporate citizen and all that. Knowing him though he'll probably make it the subject of an ad campaign.'

'Don't be so cynical Andrew. I hope there are a few interesting people at our table anyway.' She looked at him slyly. 'Any handsome young men ?'

'There will be a couple of them younger than me certainly Deirdre. As too handsome, well I'll leave that to you. Have you organised a babysitter for Michael?' Andrew asked.

'Yes 'Dierdre answered. 'I got witchy poo from downstairs .'

Witchy poo was a Russian lady of indeterminate age who dyed her hair a garish reddish-brown colour. It stood up all over the place. She also applied rouge and mascara liberally so she looked perpetually like something from Halloween. Hence the nickname witchy poo. When Michael first had been introduced to her a couple of years ago he had been quite frightened and run screaming to his room. By now he was quite used to her.

'There's a shepherd's pie from Tesco's in the fridge for you Andrew.' Deirdre looked at him suspiciously , 'Are you coming down with something ? God I hope not. We're going to that dinner dance. I don't care if you're at death's door.'

'Just a little tired Deirdre that's all.' With the practiced skill from fifteen years of marriage he diverted her attention. 'Are you going to get your hair done Deirdre ? Don't you think you might like to have it restyled?'

She was immediately disconcerted. 'What's wrong with it Andrew ? I only had it done last week.' She went quickly to the mirror and gazed at herself nervously, fingering the ends of her hair.

He feigned indifference.' Oh well if you had it done as recently as that I suppose it must be alright then.'

'Andrew you're impossible. Marjorie did say something about it looking a bit skew wiff. I'll go to Vidal Sassoon downtown. God where am I going to find the time? I'll phone Marjorie now and see if she has any suggestions on what I can do with it. Andrew after you have had your dinner would you be a dear and help Michael with his homework?'

He sighed inwardly. He had hoped to be able to spend the evening unobserved, reading a novel, or at least pretending to, in order to mask his internal turmoil.

'It's that set theory stuff again.' Deirdre said distractedly. 'Michael seems to be having a very hard time understanding it and it's making him very anxious. You know how intense he is; he takes after you.'

'Okay Deirdre.' He replied wearily. 'I will get to it just as soon as I have my dinner. 'He thought about having some wine with his shepherd's pie but then he considered he had already had a shot of whiskey and a pint of Guinness and this was in the middle of the week. *If I keep this up I'm going to end up an alcoholic.* He thought. *The traditional weakness of my race. I'm going to have to lay off the booze. If I take refuge in alcohol my judgment is going to go and my tongue is going to be loosened and that's all she wrote.* He ended up having mineral water.

Michael was in his room at his study desk hunched over and biting a pencil. Andrew pulled up a chair. 'I hear you're still having some problems with set theory Michael. Is there anything I can do to help?'

'Oh dad , I will never get the hang of it.'

It turned out to be pretty basic stuff. Supersets, subsets, intersections of sets and union of sets. But Michael appeared to have a mental block. With as many examples that Andrew dreamed up for him he couldn't seem to get the underlying principle. Perhaps even more exasperatingly, he didn't really want to try. His attention wandered and he fiddled with the model airplane he was making.

Finally, Andrew exploded.' For God sake Michael, if you're not even going to make an effort I don't see why I'm wasting my time with you. Sometimes you have the attention span of a gnat. I give up with you!'

Michael looked at him pained and sullen. Andrew was instantly remorseful. *God now look what I have done.* He thought to himself. *Taking it out on my son.*

Deirdre had heard the outburst and came into the room. There was a glint in her eye and her lips were in a tight line. 'Take a break from the mathematics now Michael. Go in and have some milk and there is a piece of pie I left for you. When you've finished why don't you start on that English essay you've been set. You know the one about the River Thames. Andrew a word with you if you don't mind. '

He followed her into their bedroom. She closed the door and turned on him. 'Andrew I don't know what's going on with you at work but I can sure as hell tell you you're not taking it out on our son. Now in case you think I haven't noticed I can smell the whiskey on your breath. I'm getting somewhat sick of non-committal responses to any questions I ask or any attempt I make at conversation. But that's me. I'm a big girl and I know how to take care of myself. Michael is a sensitive child and he thinks the world of you. You obviously don't want to talk about what's going on at work and that's fine but if that's the way you want to handle it then I suggest you do just that. Handle it. Don't bring your baggage home and then start pissing all over our son.' She faced him hands on hips 'Got anything you want to say? '

'Only that you're right dear. I'm having a difficult time at work. This new system that's going in, or more realistically, not going in, has us all under an enormous amount of stress. You must have read something about it in the paper. People are screaming at each other all the time. Tempers are very short. It's a very difficult work atmosphere. But you're absolutely correct of course. There is no excuse for me taking out my frustration on Michael. I will go in and apologise to him and lay off the drink until this whole mess at work blows over. '

She looked at him appraisingly; 'You always were an honest man, I will give you that. Go tell Michael you're sorry. Read him a bedtime story. I will make us some hot chocolate.'

He walked back to Michael's bedroom where he found his son devouring the apple pie his mother had left for him. 'I'm sorry I got mad at you Michael and lost my patience. I'm having a hard time at work and it's making me very short tempered. '

Michael smiled up at him shyly.' It's okay dad. I know I don't concentrate very well on this stuff but it's just that I can't seem to get the hang of it at all.'

'Well Michael it's a bit abstract. It's not like adding up rows and rows of numbers. Why don't we give it a go again on the weekend when we're all rested? In the meantime, how would you like me to read another chapter of Beau Geste to you?'

'Thanks Dad. Thar would be smashing. '

He sat down on the bed with his arm around Michael's shoulder and was transported to CP Snow's world of sand and sudden death in the Sahara. It came as a welcome diversion to his troubles.

Chapter 18

Cedric Hargreave Looked at his solicitor intently. 'The Managing Director of the Metropolitan Electricity Board wishes to meet with me?'

'Yes Cedric.' Andrew Mayhew responded.

'And what does he imagine that will accomplish?'

'Who's to say. It certainly is a most unusual request. But then Chaddick Spencer is somewhat out of the ordinary.'

'What sort of man is he?' Hargreave asked.

'He's American; he's a veteran of the Vietnam conflict, twice decorated. He was previously the chief executive officer of a large utility company on the East Coast of the United States. There is of course no reason why you should meet with him Cedric. But the Electricity Board solicitor conveyed his request to me and of course I said I would take the matter up with you.'

Hargreave looked at the calendar on his desk. 'You will inform Mr. Spencer that I can meet with him in my offices at 9:00 o'clock this coming Friday for one hour. I regret that no other time is convenient for me. If he wishes to meet with me he should make himself available at that time. Is there anything else Andrew?'

'On this particular matter, no Cedric. There are however some affairs related to the family charitable trust of which you are the executor.'

Hargreave waved him to silence. 'No, I don't think I'll deal with that during office hours Andrew. Can you bring the papers to me at home this weekend? We can discuss it then.'

Informed of Hargreave's response to his request Chaddick Spencer vented his frustration. 'The snotty bastard. What it translates to is "show up when and where I say, or fuck you buddy." Tell that constipated Englishman I will be there.'

Two days later Chaddick Spencer arrived at Hargreave's office at five to nine. At precisely 9:00 o'clock he was admitted to see Hargreave. The furniture was dark heavy mahogany. The only artifact of 20th century technology was an antiquated telephone. Jesus he thought to himself. It's like something from Charles Dickens. He was ushered to a chair directly in front of Hargreave's desk.

Hargreave did not look up. *The bastard's Going to let me cool my heels for a bit.* Spencer thought. *The surroundings may be 19th century but the corporate power games are completely up to date. Put me in front of his great big desk to make me feel inferior. Oh well two can play at that game.*

So, Spencer settled himself comfortably in the chair and amused himself for a few minutes. He started by imagining Hargreave in the dress of a Vietnamese peasant. After a delay of about five minutes Hatgreave closed the heavy embossed leather folder in front of him. Instantaneously his office door opened his secretary came in and removed it soundlessly. Spencer thought: *He obviously has some way of summoning her. Probably a button on the other side of his desk.*

Hargreave looked at him coolly. 'You wished to see me Mr. Spencer. '

Spencer looked at him directly.' Yes Mr. Hargreave. It seems you have a bone to pick with me or my company and I'm here to find out exactly what it is.'

If Hargreave was surprised by the direct no nonsense approach of the American, his expression gave nothing away.

'Mr. Spencer, you are the Managing Director of the Metropolitan Electricity Board- an enterprise that is in business to supply electric power to individuals or companies upon payment of a specified tariff. I am one of your customers. Some two months ago you wilfully breached your contractual arrangement with me, your customer,and deprived me at my home of the electric power which it is your contractual obligation to supply. This your company did premeditatedly. As a consequence, I was caused a great deal of personal and professional embarrassment and have sought redress in the courts. If this constitutes in your parlance picking a bone with you then at least we are of one mind as to the issue in dispute.'

Hargreave finished speaking and gazed at him calmly.

Spencer retorted. 'So we fucked up, Hargreave. Okay. We have offered you a million pounds for your inconvenience as you put it. Now people tell me that I'm crazier than a junkyard dog to offer that amount of compensation just because the lights go out in your house one night. But there it is. I want this situation put to bed and I'm willing to pay a million sterling. And now I hear that you don't want to settle for that amount.'

'Perhaps you will find it difficult to understand Mr. Spencer but it is not merely a question of the money. '

"Good name in man and woman my dear Lord is the immediate jewel of their souls who steals my purse , steals trash ; tis something , nothing ; 'twas mine , 'tis his , and has been slave to thousands ; but he that filches from me my good name robs me of that which not enriches him and makes me poor indeed !"

'I would be impressed Hargreave if the advice weren't coming from Mr. Iago who was no Boy Scout if I recall my Shakespeare.' Did Spencer detect a gleam of amusement in Hargreaves eye? *Christ* he thought to himself , *I hope so.*

'Perhaps you don't understand the circumstances surrounding the power outage at my home Mr. Spencer.'

Spencer settled back into his chair.' Let me take a shot. You were planning to cook up a hot business deal with a couple of guys from Hong Kong called the Chen brothers. You wanted the deal because they could supply you with novelty products which you are currently manufacture here. Everything was going just peachy until we pulled the plug. One of the Chens hits his head and the next thing you know they're on the first plane back to Hong Kong. No prizes for guessing what happened to your business deal.'

Hargreave was nodding slowly, 'you seem remarkably well-informed Mr Spencer. '

Spencer grinned wolfishly , 'That's what they pay me for. Listen I'm sorry we managed to queer your deal but the Chens can't be the only game in town.'

'That is correct Mr. Spencer. However we researched potential partners quite extensively before selecting the firm of Chen brothers. From our perspective any other partner would be   second best. However, the loss of the partnership is not the only issue. There is the matter of loss of face.'

'Loss of face.' Spencer repeated the phrase slowly. Comprehension dawned.' Oh I get it. Out of this fracas the Chens think you're some kind of deadbeat. So, it's going to make cutting a deal in that part of the world much more difficult for you?'

'I compliment you Mr Spencer on your quick grasp of the business ramifications of this unfortunate affair. '

'There are other ramifications ? 'Spencer asked. 'You are very sensitive to the nuances of language Mr. Spencer. Hargreave responded.

Hargreave got up from his chair and came around the desk. 'Would you care for some coffee ? 'he asked.

'I'm going to have some. 'He gestured towards the corner of his office by the window where there were leather upholstered armchairs and a coffee table.

'Don't mind if I do' Spencer answered, thinking to himself,
he's coming out of his shell a bit at least.

Hargreave's secretary appeared soundlessly at the door. 'Coffee for two Miss Phelps if you please.'

They settled themselves comfortably in the armchairs. Hargreave gazed out the window at the abandoned docks for a while before speaking. 'We come from different worlds Mr. Spencer. I'm informed for instance that you fought in Vietnam and were decorated twice for bravery. I imagine serving in Vietnam was an experience where your life was fraught with uncertainty, not to mention danger. I on the other hand, have lived a life entirely of premeditation and order. It was known and understood from the day that I was born that I would inherit the family firm. I never contemplated any other future for myself. I have been successful in business, cautious with money, frugal, some might say.

He looked directly at Chaddick Spencer. 'The most traumatic and humiliating thing to happen to me in my adult life occurred two months ago when the Chens were my guests for dinner. It occurred due to the ineptitude or incompetence of your company Mr. Spencer. I am not one of those unfortunates that froze to death, I'm a man of some means and consequence and I intend to see to it that someone pays for my humiliation.'

Typically British. Spencer thought bitterly. *First offer you coffee and then kick you in the nuts.*

'There's just you and me in the room Hargreave so I'll admit it straight out. The new system is a fuck up. But since it's cards on the table time let me ask you a question. This manufacturing deal you were going to do with the Chens, you were going to get out of that part of the business yourself, right?'

Hargreave nodded.

'What were you going to do with the people on your payroll ? It just got downsized.'

Hargreave looked at him sharply, surprised by the sudden change of direction of the conversation. 'I don't know why it should concern you Mr. Spencer but the workers involved will obviously be paid redundancy money. I have kept the manufacturing plant open much longer than the business fundamentals would justify as it is.'

'I know Hargreave, you're a shrewd businessman and you take your responsibility as an employer seriously. I wasn't suggesting anything else. But facing up to the realities of the marketplace is going to mean a rough time for some of those people. It's unfortunate but we don't control the markets. I was brought into the Metropolitan Electricity Board to see to it that it ran like an efficient operation. So, what did I find? Rampant inefficiency, restrictive labour practices, you name it. The cost structures are twice what they should be and those costs are being passed on to you, the consumer. They in turn get factored into your cost of production. Result, lost competitiveness in international markets. The new computer system was a bottoms up, Big Bang, attempt to get some of this under control. And bluntly, I fucked up. I miscalculated the extent of inertia and resistance in the organization. I was naive about cultural differences between the UK and the US. We may speak the same language but that's the extent of it. And I overestimated the capabilities of the people I put in charge of the systems development effort. So, I guess I deserve having my head handed to me. Maybe I'm not the guy to fix this mess but you know, and I know Hargreave, that for this country to have any kind of standard of living the Electricity Board and other businesses like it are going to have to get fixed.'

Hargreave poured him some more coffee. 'Your candour is refreshing Mr. Spencer and I appreciate the points you are making but how does this help me with my problem?'

Spencer sipped his coffee and sighed. Well your problem turned out to be the icing on the cake. Oh, cutting you off because you were in arrears, that was a system fuck up sure enough. But the fact that the arrears were there in the first place is of concern. I suppose it doesn't make any difference to tell you; it would come out before this case came to trial anyway, but you remitted us the right amount. The difference, slight though it was, arose not because of sloppy programming. It was a case of fraud.'

Hargreave raised his eyebrows in surprise.

'Bills rounded up to the penny when they should have rounded down. These are fractional difference on each bill but multiply it by our millions of customers and it makes up over time to a tidy chunk of change. They tell me it's been going on for years. It wouldn't have been discovered yet except for two things coinciding. Your precise accounting and a new computer system which cut off power for even the smallest reported delinquency.'

Hargreave smiled bleakly, 'So that's why you've been so anxious to settle. I wondered why you were willing to come to terms so readily. But why tell me all this now?'

'Because as I say it's going to come out sooner or later. And from this get together I've concluded you're going to do what you want to do. I have no leverage over you. Believe me I've looked for some but you're privately held and you run a tight operation so I'm shit out of luck. '

'So, what are you doing about investigating the fraud ?'

'Oh, I let the internal audit guys chase it for a week then I lost patience and called in the police , Scotland Yard.'

'It seems Mr. Spencer that you have your hands full.'

'No shit Sherlock, as the man would say.'

Hargreave played idly with his coffee spoon. 'And what exactly are you prepared to offer me to settle this matter ?'

'Tell you what I will do. A full page of apology from the Metropolitan Electricity Board to Cedric Hargreave Esquire to run in all the major UK dailies and also the Hong Kong newspapers and a settlement of two million pounds.'

'Make it three million pounds Mr. Spencer. I sympathise with your dilemma but not that much.'

'Okay Hargreave, you win. Kick the dog when he's down. It will make a nice extraordinary item on your balance sheet. '

They shook hands.

Hargreave glanced at his erstwhile adversary. 'You know if it makes you feel any better I plan to use the money to help the workers at the manufacturing plant. If nothing else it will buy a little more time until I see what I can do.'

Spencer grunted. 'Yeah actually, that does make me feel a little better. '

Hargreave took his grandfather's pocket watch from his waistcoat pocket. 'Well I think this concludes our business. It's taken longer than I originally anticipated but then you are a very interesting man with whom to converse. Have you time for what do you call it, brunch?'

Spencer smiled. 'Sure, why not. Maybe you can give me some ideas about jobs unemployed Managing Directors of utility companies can find.' Both men were smiling as they left Hargreave's office.

Two days after the apology ran in the papers, Andrew Chen phoned Cedric Hargreave.

Chapter 19

Stephen Goodchild sat in the office of his boss Elizabeth Maitland. She laid back in her chair across the desk from him her breasts silhouetted against her blouse, a distraction. *He repressed his stray thoughts. Control yourself this is your boss you are looking at.*

'So where are we with the Metropolitan Electricity Board? 'Maitland asked.

'Well, we have traced the diverted funds to an account at the National Westminster bank in Temple Bar.' He responded.

Maitland smiled appreciatively and inclined her head, encouraging him to go on.

'The account was opened ten years ago. The assistant manager who handled the opening is retired and of course can remember nothing about the individual who opened it. It's just an account to him at this point.'

'Handwriting on the application papers ? 'Maitland asked.

'The information is typed. What we have though is the signature. The lab boys have it now.'

'And the account is in the name ?'

'Bradshaw.'

'I don't suppose there is anybody of that name at the Metropolitan Electricity Board?' Maitland smiled.

'No.' Goodchild answered.

'That would be too easy wouldn't it ? So, what's the activity in the account?'

'Well every quarter, to coincide with the Electricity Board cycle, anywhere between twenty four and twenty seven thousand pounds is deposited.'

Maitland stiffened. 'So, a hundred thousand a year. How many years has this been going on?'

'Ten years.' Goddchild replied.

'So, our friend, whoever he or she is has embezzled a cool million ?'

'That's about the size of it.'

'What else ?'

'Every quarter there's a rent check deposited for three hundred pounds. But I'll explain more about that in a minute. Since the account was set up there's been a monthly standing order for eight thousand pounds which is remitted to the account of Lazard brothers in Coutts. '

'And they are ?' Maitland inquired.

'Dealers in precious stones.'

'I see. And of course, you've interviewed the firm?'

'Yes. This is a settlement account in the name of Mr. Bradshaw established ten years ago. Every two or three months Lazard brothers get written instructions from Bradshaw to buy a specific consignment of gems, which varies from order to order. One time it can be diamonds next rubies. Their instructions are to deliver each package by bonded messenger to an address in Potters Bar.'

'And who lives there ? 'Maitland asked.

'A little old lady by the name of Mrs. Wilson.'

Maitland looked confused. 'Mrs Wilson has something to do with the Metropolitan Electricity Board ?'

It was Goodchild's turn to smile. 'None whatsoever. Mrs. Wilson has been at the address for the last five years. Before that, it was Mrs. Rutledge since deceased. According to Mrs. Wilson five years ago she answered an ad in the newspaper which advertised for someone to house sit an apartment for an absentee businessman. The ad specifically indicated that it might suit a spinster. Mrs. Wilson replied to the ad and got a response back requesting references from her. When she supplied these, she received a telephone call from the leasing agency who was handling the rental inviting her to come and inspect the apartment which by the way, is quite elegant. It's a one-bedroom. It comes with a great living room and a nice view from the 8th floor. I wouldn't mind having it myself.'

Maitland grew impatient.' Come on detective, you are not in real estate!'

'Okay. Well the deal was this she got this place for £300 a month with the stipulation that any mail that came there for Mr. Bradshaw should be forwarded to a P.O. Box at a post office near Heathrow airport. The way it was explained was that Mr. Bradshaw, while he didn't spend much time in the country itself, was constantly flying in and out and so could easily pick up his mail from there. '

Mirren sniffed. 'A likely story!'

'The price was right and Mrs. Wilson didn't have much money, so she took the deal. Every time a messenger from Lazard brothers arrived with his little box she took the little box, signed for it, trotted off to her local post office and forwarded it to the P.O. Box as instructed.'

'And the people at the post office near Heathrow? 'Maitland asked.

'Well that's as far as we've got so far. I've just had a phone call with them. No one has any specific recollection of the owner of the P.O. Box but I'm going out there to interview them all in detail this afternoon.'

Maitland sighed. 'We're dealing with a very clever thief. What he or she has done is convert their ill gotten gains into highly disposable assets, which are very difficult to trace. Our culprit has effectly laundered the money. How are the instructions to the Lazard brothers written?'

'It was done on some kind of home computer. Initially using a daisywheel printer and then about four years ago changing to laser printer.'

'Okay and the lab boys have all that correspondence ?'

'Yes.' Goodchild answered.

Maitland looked at him appraisingly. 'Well, you're right of course. Our best chance of getting a make on this character are the post office employees. He has been extremely careful to limit the times he's had to break cover over the years but he's had to resurface to retrieve those gems.'

She changed the subject. 'Background checks on Metropolitan Electricity Board employees past and present ?'

'Not too much to report. A couple of DUIs, one arrest GBH, one breaking and entering, but no one with an obvious MO like what we're looking for. The guy's a sleeper. '

'Financial background checks ?'

'We are working on it, but it's going to take a while. There are over 400 people on our list.'

'Need any more help ? 'Maitland asked.

'Thanks, but we've got people on it right now. I think if we added anymore, they would just start falling over each other. You know the syndrome. Nine women can't have a baby in one month.'

Maitland looked at him, annoyed.' I can do without the sexist metaphors. Let me know how you get on with the post office people. We **are** making progress. We know substantially more than we did three weeks ago. The problem is that the Metropolitan Electricity Board is in all the newspapers. They are living in a goldfish bowl. With all the media attention there's only so long we're going to be able to keep this under wraps. We're dealing with a clever criminal and if he's put on his guard it's going to become more difficult for us. So, we need to keep the heat turned up on this one. By the way how's your wife?'

'OK thanks.' Goodchild didn't feel like unburdening himself of his marital difficulties to Maitland, whose request was obviously perfunctory.

'Good, glad to hear it. Now I've got to run. I'm giving evidence down at the Old Bailey.'

Chapter 20

The evening of the dinner dance found Deirdre in a state of high excitement and anticipation. Her long black hair had been expertly cut that afternoon at Vidal Sassoon. She was wearing a black velvet evening gown cut low at the front with short ruffled sleeves. Her only adornments were mother of Pearl earrings and an antique brooch. She was also wearing three quarter length white gloves. The gown silhouetted her excellent figure. The overall effect was stunning.

Andrew fiddled nervously with his bow tie in the Hall mirror. Deirdre was talking to him quickly and animatedly as she always did when excited. He was only half listening. *Christ,* he thought to himself. *I have got to stop thinking about the situation at work or the stress is going to kill me.* His fears were worst late at night and early in the morning. He dreaded the thought of a knock at the apartment door, or someone tapping him on the shoulder at work. He knew it was irrational, as there was no way they could have traced it to him. The fear of discovery never really let go of him, however. He forced himself to listen to what Deirdre was saying.

'I wonder if they will serve white wine or champagne. I'd prefer the champers but only if it's a good bottle. None of this imitation sparkling wine stuff. Did you find out who we are sitting with?'

'I'm sorry Deirdre I forgot.'

'You're hopeless Andrew. You have a memory like a sieve. Be a dear and check Michael for me will you?'

Witchy Poo the babysitter was ensconced in front of the TV. Michael had retreated to his room as soon as she arrived. Andrew went in. 'Are you OK Michael ? 'his son was reading Ivanhoe. 'I'm ok, Dad.' His son replied.

'How's the book ?' Andrew asked him.

'It's not a bad story, but the language is a bit funny.'

'Well you will just have to make allowances Michael. It was written a couple of hundred years ago. '

'Knights and jousting stuff. It's hard to believe people did that kind of thing.'

'Well you remember I took you to see the suit of armour at the British Museum. ', his father reminded him.

'Yeah but it wasn't the same. They just kind of looked like, I don't know, Halloween costumes.'

'Well, the babysitter is here.'

'I know . 'Michael said gloomily.

'Your mother and I are going to be back late. You'll be OK?'

'Yeah, as long as that witch out there doesn't boil me and eat me.'

'Michael, Mrs. Rostov is a very nice woman. I'd like you to be polite to her.'

Michael grinned 'What's in it for me?'

Andrew smiled back.' Quite the little mercenary, aren't we? Tell you what, I will buy you a new CD tomorrow how is that ?'

'Oh, OK, I suppose I can be polite to the old bat.'

'Michael! lower your voice.'

'Don't worry dad, she's pretty deaf.'

'All the same.' Andrew leaned over and kissed him on the forehead. 'Goodnight son, sleep well.'

'Goodnight dad. Enjoy yourself.'

Deirdre called to him.' Come on Andrew the minicab is at the door.' Neither one of them wanted to drink and drive. The ride to the Hilton took forty-five minutes, with a build-up of traffic only as they approached Marble Arch. Andrew and Deirdre held hands in the back of the cab on the way. Deirdre chatted on merrily, not a care in the world. Slowly Andrew found himself getting caught up in the mood. It was cocktails at seven with a sit-down dinner at eight, which was to be followed by dancing. They got there about seven fifteen and joined the stream of people entering the hotel.

On the other side of London Stephen Goodchild, with a certain amount of apprehension, was picking up his date. The only time he had seen Vera was at the Metropolitan Electricity Board, and the employees tended to dress down, so he had no idea what sort of dress sense she had. Males, he reflected, had a much easier time of it. It was a regulation dinner jacket, white shirt, bow tie, and black shoes. So long as you owned or had rented one which was a tolerably decent fit, you couldn't go too far wrong. Women of course had much more latitude and that's what worried him. In the end he was pleasantly surprised. There she was, wearing a turquoise chiffon dress, a modest amount of makeup and a minimal amount of jewellery. The effect was to create the impression of a cool, self-possessed young woman.

He murmured awkwardly, 'You look very elegant this evening Vera.'q

She was much more direct.' Thank you muchly. You're looking pretty sharp yourself. Tell me, are those shoulders padded, or is it you?'

He smiled awkwardly. 'Not padded, no. What you see is what you get.'

'We must get a picture of you with me at the dinner dance and send it to my sisters. They will be madly jealous.' Vera giggled.

They drove down in his car. It had been agreed beforehand that he would drive to the affair and that she would drive back. She didn't drink, whereas he did. He spent the trip desperately trying to make small talk and thinking miserably: *I had forgotten what the singles scene was like. I'm just not cut out for this.* Vera however, just looked out the window and seemed unconcerned by the brakes in the conversation. Cocktail hour was in full swing by the time they arrived at the hotel. When they identified their table, they agreed to split up and mingle before coming back to sit down for dinner. Goodchild recognized a number of the faces although, sometimes he had to do a double-take. They looked so different in evening attire.

He had spent the last couple of days familiarizing himself with personnel records of eighty three Metropolitan Electricity Board employees. The profile he was looking at was someone male, clean shaven, and in his thirties. His visit to the post office at Heathrow had produced one clerk who remembered seeing the owner of post office box number 6478.

'I was just putting the letters in the pigeonholes you know. 6478 is at eye level so just as I was about to put the letters in a man opened it on the other side. I only really caught a glimpse of him and of course I only saw his face.'

Probing had narrowed the description to the profile he was now using. Although the post office clerk had been shown all the personnel photographs she resolutely refused to single any of them out.

'Have a heart detective. We're talking about my recollection of seeing this geezer six months ago. For what? Maybe fifteen seconds and only his face at that. I'm not going to be able to give you a more positive description than what you have already got out of me. And as far as putting that together with the faces you're showing me now you can just forget it.'

No amount of coaxing or cajoling would move his witness on the point, and he had consoled himself that she had at least halved the list of potential suspects even with the limited description she provided. There were eighty-three current employees and one hundred and seventeen former employees who were within the right age range and who were male. These individuals would have had access to the customer billing program modules. In a further development analysis of the signature on the Westminster Bank documents had led the handwriting experts to conclude the signer was making a deliberate attempt to disguise his handwriting.

Goodchild felt his villain was still employed at the Metropolitan Electricity Board. At this point there was no logical reason for him to conclude the perpetrator was a former employee. The fraud had carried over to the new system and even though all kinds of plausible arguments were advanced as to why it could have easily been grandfathered in without any additional intervention, somehow he just didn't buy it. Extensive background checks were now being run on all two hundred suspects. Profiles were being developed on personal habits, financial situations, and lifestyle. He was confident that this additional information would allow him to eliminate some more from the field. *If we could get it down to a manageable ten or twelve,* he thought to himself, *we can really start turning up the heat.*

His reverie was interrupted by the sound of a musical peal of laughter coming from a group halfway across the room. His eyes sought out the source. The woman he saw literally took his breath away. She was an older woman certainly, but her figure and posture were that of a young girl. She was dressed in a simple black evening gown with long white gloves. There was a mass of luxuriant black hair piled high on her head, tied with a bow and hung over her right shoulder. But it was her eyes that held his attention. They were dark brown and even from this distance they seemed to dance with life and a hidden fire. She was surrounded by four or five willing male admirers and seemed to be thoroughly enjoying holding court. As if feeling his gaze upon her she turned and looked at him steadily. He turned away hastily and began to examine a melting ice sculpture in order to hide his embarrassment. From the corner of his eye, he saw her gracefully detach herself from her male coterie and begin to walk, it seemed to him, straight in his direction. He examined the ice carving of a Swan even more closely, noting that the base of the neck had become perilously thin and concluding that the Swan would probably be headless before too much longer. A voice murmured in his ear.

'I often thought ice sculpting to be the quintessential ephemeral art form'

'Well they don't last very long if that's what you mean. '

Great he thought to himself. *Dazzling repartee*. He turned towards her. She was smiling at him in an amused sort of way.

'Hello, my name is Deirdre. Do you work for the Metropolitan Electricity Board ?'

'Actually, no, I'm on assignment there. An accounting job. Stephen is my name.'

'You look far too vigorous to be an accountant Stephen. You must have some rugged manly pursuits to produce a physique like that.'

Jesus, he thought, *she's flirting with me.*

'I'm parched for a drink. Let's say we go over to that waiter and see if I can snag one.' Confident in the effect she was having on him she took his arm and glided with practiced ease among the other guests.

He noticed heads turning as she passed. Women assessed her appraisingly. Men looked with admiration, some openly, some covertly, generally husbands with wives in tow. Her hands were gloved so there was no way for him to tell whether she was wearing a wedding ring. *Just enjoy the moment* he thought to himself. As they navigated their way towards the other side of the ballroom where the reception was taking place she made sly comments about some of the other guests.

'Interesting outfit she's wearing. It might do for a day at the races but hardly for a dinner dance, darling. He's put on a few pounds since he wore that dinner jacket last. He might want to be careful not to burst out of his flies. Flashing in high society.   That would never do.'

He was captivated, not by so much by what she was saying, but by the sound of her voice. It had a musical quality with a trace of an Irish accent. Her t's were given full weight not clipped, and the comments, barbed although they were, were made with affectionate amusement rather than malice. He found himself getting an erection. *Oh, shit* he thought to himself *you're not a glandular 16-year-old you're a 30-year-old man. A 30-year-old man who hasn't had any lately.* To impose self-control, he forced himself to listen more closely to what she was saying rather than to the intoxicating sound of the voice itself.

As they squeezed through an opening between two groups and conversation one of her breasts grazed as though by accident, against his arm. He felt his chest constrict. Finally, they reached a waiter standing impassively with a tray of assorted drinks. He seemed indifferent to whether there were guests present or not, and the notion of actually serving them seemed the furthest thing from his mind. She helped herself to a glass of white wine.

'You will keep me company won't you ? 'her eyes dropped quickly to his crotch and back. 'Something cold , I fancy.'

'Yes', he turned to the waiter to cover his embarrassment. 'A glass of iced water please.'

The waiter seemed slightly bewildered to have a guest actually talk to him, but after a moment's hesitation he produced the desired drink.'

'Yes it is rather warm', he said lamely. 'I suppose it's all these people in an enclosed place.'

'Yes', she replied, 'but at least it's not the tube at rush hour. That's one way to get to know your fellow man I can tell you. You get some right perverts among the city gentlemen when they're pressed up close to you. You being a man probably wouldn't notice it so much. Normally I don't pay too much heed. It's just part of the normal joys of commuting. I have kneed a couple of guys in the balls though, who were being really objectionable. '

She conducted this in an entirely normal conversational tone. She could have been telling him what she had for breakfast. He stood there, water glass in hand, mouth open. For him she was the only person in the room. An image of what she might look like naked flashed it into his mind. *For fuck's sake,* he thought, if *this keeps up much longer she's going to give me a heart attack.* He made a determined effort to put the conversation back on track.

'You're here with someone ?'

'With someone ? Oh yes, Andrew, but he's holed up in a corner somewhere chatting about his computer system. He hates these kind of social events. I on the other hand, social butterfly that I am, adore them. And you who are you here with? Silly girl whoever she is to leave you unattended.'

He reddened. 'Oh, just a girl from the office. This was a last-minute thing. I wasn't going to come but i had my arm twisted.'

'Well lucky for me it was. It's making for quite an entertaining evening having you around. '

The gong sounded for dinner.

'Ah time to put on the nosebag 'she said. 'I'm famished . It's been delightful talking to you.'

'Perhaps we can have a dance later? 'he blurted out desperately.

'Dance? 'she considered the question for a moment. 'Yes, that would be lovely. I adore dancing and Andrew doesn't care for it very much. How will I find you in the middle of all these people? Let's meet over by the ice sculpture at let's say 11.00 p.m. That gives me an hour before I turn into a pumpkin.'

She leaned over and gave him a peck on the cheek. 'Take care for now, don't eat too much. I wouldn't want you spoiling that manly torso.' She gave him an appreciative glance. 'Now what table am I at , fifty seven I think.' She turned and he soon lost sight of her in a throng of guests anxious to take their seats.

In the middle part of the ballroom Andrew stood clutching a large glass of whiskey and sweating profusely. The evening had started out well enough. He had spent the first half hour in Deirdre's company. She was as usual dazzling and vivacious, engaging acquaintances and strangers alike in a practiced small talk creating an illusion of warmth and intimacy in the conversation even though to his ears, the content was trite and superficial. He had no other role but to stand attentively beside her, which suited him fine because he was a very lazy conversationalist in this kind of setting. After a while though Deirdre disengaged herself from his circle and went off looking for new conquests. It was her way in these kinds of settings and he had long ago reconciled himself to it. He always felt hurt that she should seek other company than his own. It invariably brought back painful memories of the dinner dance at Trinity College.

After standing around aimlessly for a while, Fred Armstrong of internal audit at wandered up to him. Although he had resolved not think about it, the conversation had inevitably turned towards the fraud investigation, as he now knew it to be. Armstrong had let him in on the big secret that Scotland Yard had an undercover detective working with the internal audit function for the last three weeks.

Andrew had plied Armstrong with alcohol. Drunk, Fred had divulged every detail of the undercover investigation up to and including the discovery of the flat in Potters Bar and of the post office box at Heathrow. The revelations fell like hammer blows. The police were involved and had been indeed for the last several weeks; he was dealing not with a bunch of amateurs but a determined and sophisticated criminal investigation unit ; he had been partially identified by a Postal worker. It was more than enough to undermine his fragile self-composure. He suffered sharp stabbing pains in his stomach and his hands were trembling. Armstrong was too far gone to notice anything unusual in Andrew's manner. He wandered off, having spilled his guts, to relieve himself in the men's room.

Andrew took advantage of the opportunity to retreat to a corner. They had a specimen of his handwriting. They had a description, partial though it was, but who knew whether the Postal worker might remember additional details.

Sweet God let it be a nightmare he thought to himself. *Let me just wake up and find out it's a bad dream*. But even as he prayed he knew it wasn't true. The disgrace of being found out terrified him. What would Deirdre think, and his son Michael, not to mention his mother. The gleaming rails of the underground seemed very inviting.

How has my life brought me to this? he asked himself over and over again. *It's become a lie a subterfuge. Only now the lie is all consuming influencing my every waking hour driving my every thought and action.*

The gong for dinner sounded. With a great effort of will he brought himself to an awareness of where he was and drifted slowly to his table. He was one of the last to arrive; they had already started serving soup. Deirdre was waiting for him impatiently.

'Where have you been Andrew ? 'she muttered to him as he took the seat beside her. 'That bloody gong has been going for the last fifteen minutes. ' She sniffed suspiciously. 'You smell like a distillery. You've had a skinful already and it's not even nine o'clock. '

'Well whiskey is my companion for the evening with you doing your disappearing act. I need to find solace in something don't I dear?'

There were three other couples at their table. He only knew Peter Spencer and his girlfriend. Peter was regaling the males at the table with his account of the winning try in the England versus France match that afternoon. He had been at Twickenham with excellent seats just behind the French goal. Deirdre interrupted him in mid flow.

'Well it's all very well for you men to revel in the rugby union, but as a spectator sport there isn't much in it for us women. First of all, there are the scrums. All those men groping each other. Disgusting, if you ask me. Now, I prefer Australian Rules football. Nice clean-cut lads, tight shorts and sleeveless shirts. Much more interesting from a female point of view.'

Suddenly Deirdre was the focus of attention. *Which is exactly what she loves to be* Andrew thought, thoroughly disillusioned. She dominated the conversation all through dinner.

Stephen Goodchild waited for her at the half-melted ice sculpture with all of the anxiety and enthusiasm of an adolescent on his first date. *She's not really going to show up at all, she's just having me on.* He was still there twenty minutes after their appointed rendezvous time. Suddenly she was in front of him. She looked radiant.

'I hope I didn't keep you waiting. It took a while to finish up dinner. I was giving a woman's perspective on male contact sports.'

'Oh 'he asked, 'and what was that?'
'Oh. Basically, the more beefcake exposed the better.'
He was at a loss as to how to reply.
'So, are we going to dance? 'she asked.
'I have to warn you that I am not very good at it.'
She took him firmly by the arm. 'Never mind, I am.'

There were a number of options for dancing at the event. In the main ballroom the big band was belting out some fairly standard stuff that people could waltz to or whatever, but there were two other dance floors available. One had a disc jockey spinning discotheque records; the other had a variant of a heavy metal rock band. Deirdre selected the discotheque and they joined a pretty packed dance floor with couples gyrating to the sound of Depeche Mode. He started out self-consciously, just shuffling his feet from side to side. Deirdre had an uninhibited sensual style. She was completely un-self-conscious and obviously thoroughly enjoyed dancing. He found himself getting into it, eventually taking off his jacket and becoming completely immersed in the seductive rhythms of his partner.

'Deirdre, perhaps we should be going?'

Stephen Goodchild, being completely absorbed with his dancing partner, dd not notice the stooped, non-descript, middle-aged man who appeared at Deirdre's elbow. 'Oh Andrew, don't be so stuffy 'She said without interrupting her rhythm, 'it's early yet.'

'Actually, it's after two o'clock. The babysitter will be wondering what became of us.'

She came to a halt reluctantly. 'Always so responsible Andrew. Yes, I suppose you are right.'

For Goodchild, it was as if somebody had stabbed him unexpectedly in the stomach. He could not comprehend that she was partnered with this stooped, middle-aged, entirely non-descript man who was now standing beside her. She dispelled all doubt.

'Stephen, this is my husband Andrew. Andrew, Stephen. He has been good enough to be my dance partner for the last couple of hours.'

Andrew looked at him wearily 'I appreciate it, I have no talent for dancing, but my wife enjoys it very much.'

Goodchild stammered out some sort pf meaningless reply, his mind still reeling. *How could she be married to this cypher? Baby-sitter, they even have children*?

She turned to Goodchild and gave him a light peck on the cheek. 'Well it's been lovely meeting you; you are a great dancer. Maybe we will see each other again at this affair next year? 'she turned and without a backward glance, walked away arm in arm with her husband.

As she left, it seemed to him the life and animation walked away with her leaving him feeling angry and confused. Her parting words had an air of finality about them. No hope expressed that they meet again soon, no regretful parting look. It was obvious that for her the evening had been a chance encounter, an amusing dalliance, a flirtation. Maybe his pride and ego could have withstood it were it not for the husband. In God's name what did she see in him? Colourless and nondescript with a middle aged out of condition body, he didn't have position or status. He was only a systems analyst.

Money? He wasn't going to make much money working for the Metropolitan Electricity Board. The detective stopped. Unless of course he was helping himself to some. Andrew Sweeney had the means; he had the opportunity, and now it would appear there was motive. The motive being a beautiful wife. It gave her some reason to stay married to a nothing of a husband. Tomorrow Andrew Sweeney's life would be turned upside down and every aspect of it examined. His jealousy assuaged by this prospect, belatedly Goodchild remembered that he had come with a companion and he went off to see where she was.

Andrew sat in the taxi home with Deirdre sweating profusely. *I've had too much to drink*, he thought. He was still suffering from the shock of seeing his wife dance with the CID detective assigned to investigate the fraud. A drunken Fred Armstrong had pointed him out. 'Just between you and me old scout. Don't tell another soul'. It had taken all of Andrew's powers of dissemblement to mask his fear and anxiety at seeing them together. This latest dalliance of his wife was fraught with risk for him. *What stories had she regaled this detective with?* he had to know. 'You seemed rather taken with the young man you were dancing with Dierdre .'

She was looking out the window at the lights along the Edgeware Road. 'Oh, he was attractive enough in a beefy sort of way. Danced tolerably well. No conversation though.'

'Which left you to do all of the talking', Andrew observed. 'What did you have in common with him ? What did you talk about?'

Deirdre turned and looked at him sharply. 'It's most unlike you Andrew to take such a keen interest in my topics of conversation with a chance acquaintance. Surely you're not becoming possessive in your old age, you know how tiresome I would find that.'

He thought quickly. 'No Deirdre normally I really don't care. But it's just that Stephen Goodchild is interesting and that I discovered over dinner that he is not entirely what he seems.'

Now she was intrigued. 'Scandal, gossip, I love it. Tell me Andrew, what is it about this young man?'

He played coy. 'Ah now Deirdre. You tell me what you know about him and I will tell you his secret.'

'Andrew really this is being childish.' But she gave in. 'What did he tell me about himself ? That he was some sort of accountant. Now that I come to think of it he's a bit too virile to be an accountant. I said something of the sort to him.'

He forced himself to play along with her in their usual bantering style. To do otherwise would arouse her suspicions. 'Deirdre how very prejudiced of you. Accountants are human too, I think.'

'I don't normally associate accountants with burning ardour and unsuppressed lust. Our friend was pretty fixated on my knockers.

Of course, he was being a perfect gentleman about it.'

He flattered her. 'Well of course you're right as usual, Deirdre. He's not an accountant. What he is, is a Scotland Yard detective investigating a fraud.'

She was like an excited schoolgirl. 'Andrew, no, really. What kind of fraud?'

He was deliberately vague. 'Oh, something to do with customer billing irregularities I gather.'

'So, somebody's been giving themselves a little extra bonus at the company's expense ?' She was a quick study.

'That seems to be the way it is shaping up. But of course, everybody is very close-lipped about it. '

'So, he must have been at the dinner dance to scout out suspects ? She smiled and preened herself visibly. 'Well I obviously put him off his stroke. He danced with me for hours and never looked in anybody else's direction. Unless of course he thinks I'm a suspect.'

Andrew held his breath, but her chain of logic went no further. *Why would it?* He thought to himself sadly. *Deirdre is quite incapable of imagining that anyone would be interested in her simply as my wife.* He leaned towards her, hands on her knees, feigning animation.

'So, Deirdre , tell us, what did he go on about ?'

'When he wasn't drooling over my tits?', she reflected. 'Pretty adolescent really when I think about it. Spent most of his time complimenting me on my physical attributes. You know, what a good figure I had, what lovely hair and eyes. Basically as if I were a well-proportioned inflatable rubber doll. The fact that I had a mind seemed superfluous to him. An overgrown schoolboy in a man's body.'

She sighed.' But I suppose I shouldn't be too hard on him. Most males are like that anyway.'

'And you? What did you talk about?' he asked her

'Oh, everything and anything. Made some snide comments about some of the other guests and what they were wearing and how they looked. That seemed to amuse him.'

'So, he wasn't giving you the third degree?'

'God no, I should have figured out if there was any train of thought to his conversation. It would have come as a welcome surprise. No. Good body, nice buns, not too much between the ears. 'She flopped back in the seat. 'Christ, I'm tired. Aren't we home yet Andrew? What time is it anyway?'

'It's after three o'clock. Witchy Poo will be tearing her hair out. We said we would be home by one.'

Dierdre giggled 'She will have to take off her wig first. We had better give her a big tip Andrew.'

'I suppose 'Andrew too, sat back in his seat and reflected on what he had just been told. If he could believe Dierdre, and she was very astute when it came to men, there was nothing sinister in the detective's pursuit of her. He had simply been smitten by a very attractive, older woman. There had been no enquiries into their lifestyle or his own personal habits. *They are getting closer* he thought. *But I am still just one of a wide range of suspects and there is safety in numbers.* He closed his eyes and held his wife's hand.

Chapter 21

The following Monday, Stephen Goodchild was all over Andrew Sweeney. He went in early to Scotland Yard and gave very clear instructions to two detectives that had been assigned to work with him on the case. 'I want to know everything about this bloke. Where he was born, who his parents were, where he went to school, college, known associates, affiliations, financial background. Particularly financial background. Let's see if the Irish police have anything on him. 'He paused for a moment, 'Oh while you are about it you might as well check for any affiliations with the IRA. We've got seventy-two hours to pull together a detailed profile of this character.'

'What's up Sarge? 'one of them asked. 'Do you think you got something on him?'

'Let's just say that he has a very expensive wife to keep and I don't see how he is doing it on a systems analyst's salary. 'On a personal level, Goodchild's weekend had been miserable. He couldn't get Deirdre out of his head. He found himself fantasising about her. He found himself wanting her. It was like a physical hunger it was so bad. *Dear God*, he thought. *This is going to drive me crazy. I'm obsessed with an older, married woman. What's worse, the wife of a suspect in a criminal investigation.* He lectured himself, he rationalized with himself; it did hm no good at all. The weekend was spent indulging torrid daydreams of sexual intimacy with Deirdre Sweeney.

The next day the by election was held. It was a disaster for the Tories. Their margin of ten thousand votes in the general election was wiped out and replaced by a twelve thousand majority for Labour. Their working majority in the House was now reduced to two. The Labour opposition was jubilant. They chose to interpret the result as a blazing condemnation of the government's social policy. They served notice that they intended to table a motion of "No Confidence "in the government. The Torys retaliated that the by election had unique circumstances and the result, though disappointing, could not in any way be interpreted as an indication of how the country in general felt about the conduct of the government. This particular line of reasoning did not hold up very well in the face of a new Sunday Times public opinion poll which showed the government trailing Labour by twenty points.

The day following the election results the Prime Minister held what amounted to a crisis meeting with members of his inner cabinet, the Party Chairman, and the Chief Whip. The meeting was held at Ten Downing Street. Housegood was the last to arrive. The meeting was scheduled for eight p.m. He arrived at precisely one minute to eight.

He had deliberately chosen a casual setting for the gathering. The participants sat in armchairs round a fire and drinks were being served. 'Yes, I will have a glass of Chablis thanks. 'He indicated to the waiting attendant. 'Anybody else care to freshen their drinks before we get started?'

No one took him up on his offer.

'Fine, well let's not beat about the bush. 'He settled himself in his armchair. They all looked at him expectantly. 'Gentlemen, it's something of an understatement that we have a problem. We have just lost what was supposedly a safe seat and as a result, had our working majority reduced to two. Our popularity in the polls has gone, in four short weeks, from a situation where we were four percent ahead to twenty percent behind Labour. The catalyst of all this has been the unfortunate situation at the Metropolitan Electricity Board. We have had the spectre of several old age pensioners expire from hypothermia because their power was cut off. Bad enough as that was, our problems have been seriously compounded by the misguided efforts of one of our backbenchers, Robert Petrie, to become the conscience of the nation. Our entire social policy and our privatisation policy, which were major planks in our last general election manifesto, are now under siege. Indeed, they are threatened with total repudiation by the electorate.'

He paused and placed the tips of his fingers together.

'I think I may say, Gentlemen, that none of this was in the master plan. Ah, thank you. 'He accepted the glass of Chablis which appeared at his elbow and sipped it slowly before continuing.

The chancellor of the exchequer butted in. 'If it weren't for that bastard Petrie, we wouldn't be in this mess.'

Housegood thought about it for a moment and said 'Our difficulties might not be so pronounced but I don't think we can contribute the entire dilemma to our young backbenchers 'efforts however inconvenient they have proven to be. If we are forced to go to the polls with our current standing, we will return facing a Labour majority of a hundred against us. Does anybody dispute that assessment?'

No one did.

'Fine. We are certain that our friends in the opposition will table tomorrow a motion of "No Confidence "in the government. Difficult though the situation is, we are going to have to debate this motion and win. Moreover, we have to win decisively. Even if our margin of victory is small, we are going to have to ensure that the debate revolves around the core issues, our social policy, and our privatisation policy. We have to win this debate on its intellectual merits, both in the media and the minds of the public. This is the only way we are going to be able to remain in office and govern effectively.'

'So then gentlemen, this is what I propose we should do. The opposition will table a motion of 'No Confidence 'tomorrow I will promptly accept the invitation to debate the issue. I will, however, stipulate that the debate be a two-day affair. And because of the difficulty of scheduling it into already committed parliamentary business, it will be two weeks before we can actually hold it.'

He smiled, 'Howard Wilson observed once that a week is a long time in politics, two is an eternity. The opposition, of course will want to hold the debate immediately, since the momentum is all on their side. We, however, need time to frame the discussion and put context around it, both in the public mind and in the chamber debate which will ensue. We need to get past the emotional hysteria of the moment and get back to the fundamentals. Any questions so far? 'He looked around the circle. He had their rapt attention.

He weighed the impact of his words on them. He had arrived to a room of beaten and dejected men. In a few short minutes he had at least captured their interest. More than that they seemed reassured that their leader seemed not all that fazed by the precarious position in which they found themselves and indeed, was in the process of calmly articulating a plan of action.

'The country wants the party in power to stand for something and to have a plan of action. If we make the same mistake James Callaghan did in the 70s, appearing only to be concerned with staying in power, we will be dismissed in short order by the electorate. That is why I am convinced that we must win this debate on its merits and not just see it as a problem of parliamentary arithmetic. '

He stood up and faced them with his back to the fireplace.

'What is at stake in this debate gentlemen ? it is the future prosperity of our nation. People often forget that Britain is a trading nation. It's prosperity, and the empire it created derived from its trading prowess. People fret over Britain's decline as a world power in the post war years and all kinds of reasons have been given. But the heart of it is this; trading prowess made us great and gave us empire in the past. For our country and our children to have a prosperous future in today's global economy we must make the changes that are necessary to allow us to compete effectively. Either we adapt to the new economic order or our people face a future of declining living standards and mass unemployment while Britain will be confronted with continued loss of influence in the post-industrial world.

The conservative party must put in place the changes necessary to make the country competitive. They are painful to be sure and sometimes the execution can be tragically flawed in isolated incidences but for the nations good we must embrace change, not resist it. We must understand and adapt to the global economic forces which we cannot control. The choice is to embrace the challenge of the new age or to remain trapped clinging nostalgically to customs and practices from our glorious past. The country must decide between the party that has the vision and the courage to change the things we need to, or a party that is living with the pathetic and nostalgic delusion that somehow we can go on just as we always have.' He stopped and smiled at them.

'As you can see I am working on my speech for the debate but you get the general idea. So much for the big picture. We have two weeks to get this message out and to win this debate. There is a lot of work to do.'

'Freddy ', he turned to the party chairman ,

' I want head office to put together a PR campaign based on these broad themes.'

He looked at the cabinet members present. 'We are going to go on a media blitz. Each minister needs to explain how his Department is working to make this overall change happen. Sort of the perspective from the Exchequer, The Home Office , the Foreign Office , that kind of thing.'

He turned to the Chief Whip, 'Make it quite clear to the troops that this vote is a three-line whip and that if the government loses we will go to the country.' He smiled grimly. 'Given our standing in the polls , I can't imagine members would relish a general election right now.'

Lord Overton made to object. 'Don't we risk painting ourselves into a corner with this approach Martin?' House good shit him down.' We have no room for manoeuvre Freddie. Once we agree to debate the 'No Confidence ' motion the government has to win. We simply can't continue to govern if we lose the vote. So all we're doing is making it abundantly clear to even the most dim-witted backbencher what the consequences are going to be in advance.' He turned to the Chief Whip 'By this time tomorrow I want all the noses counted. I want to know exactly how the parliamentary arithmetic stands. Who we can count on absolutely, who the waverers are, and what the situation is with the minority parties. Oh and make sure our colleagues, the Northern Irland Unionists are onside.'

The Home Secreatary had been squirming in his seat for the last five minutes. Housegood now addressed him directly. 'Evan you have been looking unhappy. What's on your mind?'

'This is a Jolly good plan Prime Minister, don't get me wrong. But what are we going to do about the Metropolitan Electricity Board fiasco? And what are we going to do about Robert Petrie? Remember this is what got us into this mess in the first place.'

Housegood responded.' Well it's clear that the management of the Metropolitan Electricity Board is incompetent and so there will have to be a change made. Now whereas the Electricity Board has been privatised the government remains the substantial minority shareholder. We have what? thirty per cent of the shares outstanding? As a shareholder we are entitled to make our view known and I will do so. At the same time it would be helpful if the Board were to call for the resignation of their Managing Director. Given the current state of affairs I can't imagine they'll need much persuasion, just a little firm leadership. Freddie can you put that in hand?'

Overton nodded.

'Now, for Robert Petrie. 'He turned to the Chief Whip , 'I would like it made perfectly plain to Mr Petrie that the party expects him to vote with them on the 'No Confidence 'motion. Ideally it should be made plain to him that if he does not do so his constituency Association will not put him forward as the conservative candidate for the next general election, either in the next few weeks or the next couple of years depending on whether we ultimately win this vote or not. Mr Petrie has enjoyed the luxury of pursuing his private conscience. Now he must be reminded of his party responsibilities. Well then gentlemen we all have a lot to do. I won't delay you further.'

As they got up he went around and shook each one firmly by the hand. He departed the room briskly and the meeting broke up.

The following evening Housegood and his wife sat in a little sitting room they had made for themselves in one of the anterooms in Downing St. He was watching his performance on the television during the Prime Minister's Question Time in the House earlier that day. His wife sat opposite him in an armchair. She maintained an upright posture even when seated. She did not appear to be paying particular attention to the television. She was knitting a sweater for one of her nieces. He knew however that she was listening to every word that was being said, absorbing and dissecting it. Her glasses were on a chain around her neck, a relatively recent concession to an occasional forgetfulness. She didn't need them for near work; she suffered from farsightedness. If the hair was gray, the complexion was as soft and fresh as the day he married her thirty years ago. They had no children. They had never bothered to find out whose fault it was. Mary just accepted the situation and she devoted herself to his political career and the care of her parents in their later years.

On the television the Commons chamber looked like a bear pit, and indeed, in reality, it was. The chamber was crowded to overflowing. Members squashed like school boys on benches, tiered on either side of the table and ballot box. The leader of the opposition was on his feet haranguing the government benches, cheered on by his own jubilant party members behind him.

'Can I ask the Prime Minister if he will concede that the incompetent management of the Metropolitan Electricity Board installed by his government as part of their privatisation policy has brought about a frightful human tragedy. Cannot he accept the public verdict on his government's failed social policy expressed in his party's resounding defeat at the recent by election.' (This to multiple cheers from the Labour Party benches.) 'Is he deaf, dumb, and blind to the universal condemnation and outrage over the hypothermia deaths. Will he not recognise that he is leading a failed government with bankrupt policies? Will he not now take the only honourable option open to him which is to resign and dissolve parliament?'

Uproar ensued in the chamber with the Speaker screaming at the top of her voice for order.

Housegood watched himself on television making a reply. Standing completely dispassionately at the ballot box not a hair out of place and exhibiting no signs of stress.

There was an unmerciful din in the chamber. One northern accent could be heard to shout 'Wake up and smell the manure you dozy bastard. Quit now!'

Housegood proceeded firmly and unperturbed. 'The leader of the opposition has castigated this government using such blindingly original phrases as 'bankrupt 'and 'failed mandate.' His party has tabled a motion of 'No Confidence 'in the government, swept along as he and his colleagues are, by a current of banality and blinkered thinking. Let me be clear from the outset, this government is totally committed to its privatization and social policies. We welcome exuberantly the opportunity, which this recently tabled motion gives us, to explain the depth of our conviction.' Without seeming effort, he projected his voice to fill the whole chamber.

'Lest there be no doubt, we will debate this issue and we will win the argument decisively. We will win in the hearts and minds of our fellow countrymen, and ultimately, in this chamber.'

'What is at issue here is the future prosperity of our nation and its place in the modern world. The opposition rails against the government policy but has no alternative to offer of its own. (outrage from the opposition benches). They see no vision for the future, only tired old policies of the past, nostalgia not realism, pious aspirations, not clear-headed objectives. My right Honorable friend conceives the tabling of a motion of 'No Confidence 'as a masterstroke. This masterstroke will prove to be his undoing and that of his party. We will expose the opposition's policies for what they are; incoherent, ill-informed and intellectually barren. '

He sat down to roars of approval from his backbenchers.

The TV newscaster appeared on the screen. 'Scenes from Prime Minister's Question Time from earlier today , from the House of Commons where Martin Housgood, the embattled Prime Minister, gave a powerful and forceful performance. The 'No Confidence 'debate has been scheduled for 10 days 'time. What remains to be seen over the next 10 days is whether Martin Housegood and the Tory party with the most precarious of majorities in the House will be able to turn the tide of public opinion which has been running strongly against the government since the Metropolitan Electricity Board hypothermia deaths two weeks ago. '

He turned off the television.

'What do you think Mary? 'he asked simply. She continued knitting imperturbably.' You gave a good performance in the house Martin but then you always do. You rallied the troops. They need strong leadership at a time like this. How do you see your chances?'

He sighed wearily.' We're in a very tight spot. I'm not too sure we can pull it off. I don't know if I can get people to understand what's really at stake here. I'm sorry the Metropolitan Electricity Board messed up. I'm heartbroken those old people died as a consequence. But the country has to change. There's already one generation of chronically unemployed in Glasgow and Liverpool, unemployed parents with unemployed adult children. I want the next generation to have the opportunity for good jobs and a decent living. I want it to be something that everyone can aspire to, not just a privileged few.'

'We have got to change and we're not changing fast enough. The alternative is a permanent underclass of the chronically unemployed in our society, that we keep anaesthetised with social handouts. A world of have and have not. Whole sections of our population living out their lives with diminished expectations and few, if any, prospects. It breaks my heart to think of it Mary; to think that I might not be able to prevent it. I'm so frustrated. I can't even get some of our own people to sense the urgency.'

She stopped knitting and looked at him with a calm and steady gaze. 'Martin , I have been married to you for thirty years. You have been a good husband and you are a good Prime Minister. These next few days are going to be the most decisive of your political career, one way or the other. Knowing you, you have devised a strategy and you will execute it flawlessly. You'll count up the votes, you will marshal the arguments, you will rally the troops and you will twist some arms if needs be. Everything you do will be disciplined, controlled, and well thought out. If that is how things play out you will fight a good fight and you will fail.'

He looked at her with shock.

'Your problem Martin is that if you only tell people what you think about this issue you will fail to convince them. This time you are going to have to tell them how you feel. I suppose I'm the only person alive who knows that beneath that cool and controlled exterior that there is a warm passionate loving person. It's your best kept secret. Martin you want people in this country to undergo enormous wrenching changes and in the short term it will mean a lot of pain and for some a lot of suffering. But if people are going to put that much faith in a leader, it's not enough that they believe he knows what the right course of action is. To follow him they have to believe he cares about them too. And that, I'm afraid , means telling them how you feel.'

'That's not something I can do very easily Mary , you know that.' Her husband replied.

She came over and sat beside him on the arm of the chair. She took his hand. 'Englishmen are not expected to display or show emotion. It is interpreted as a sign of weakness and I have always thought it a cruel stereotype. You've asked me what I think Martin but really it's up to you.'

He sighed and squeezed her hand, 'I know Mary. I'd be much more comfortable reducing this to a problem in parliamentary arithmetic. Making lists; votes for , votes against , who could be persuaded , cajoled. People in the party have always seen me as a superb technician; calculate the odds and work to shorten them. That's how I've always seen myself. And now that I'm trying to be some sort of visionary, I'm not too sure if I'm cut out for it.'

He looked up at her. Her eyes gleamed with amusement. 'Well Martin, if you want to be a visionary I guess it helps to have a vision and you have that. Now all we're talking about is how you communicate.'

She got up and pulled him to his feet, walking with him over to the writing table. She pulled back the chair and sat him in it unresistingly. 'Write me a letter Martin.'

'I beg your pardon Mary ?'

'Write me a letter. Explain to me in terms you think I will understand, what you feel the issues are facing the country and also what you think we need to do about them. Remember you writing to me your wife of thirty years. Think of it as an early anniversary present.'

He looked at her in puzzlement for a moment, then comprehension dawned. He pulled the paper and pen toward him.

'I'm just going into the kitchen to get a sandwich. Do you want anything Martin?'

'Why don't you make me a pot of coffee Mary. I think it's going to be a long night.' He said with a smile.

Chapter 22

'So what have we got on this Andrew Sweeney fellow ?'
Stephen Goodchild looked expectantly at his constable.
'Andrew Sweeney, age forty, born in the Republic of Ireland, married to Deirdre Sweeney, nee Fitzpatrick, age thirty-eight, also Irish, one child, eight years old. Educated Trinity College Dublin with an honour's degree in theoretical physics. Joined the Metropolitan Electricity Board seventeen years years ago. No convictions or arrests, either in this country or in Ireland, we have checked with the Irish police.'
'Financial status?' Goodchild asked sharply.
'Now that gets a bit interesting. He earns forty thousand pounds a year as a senior systems analyst. She doesn't work, kid is going to a private school with annual fees of eight thousand pounds. The mortgage on his flat is two thousand pounds a month and she drives a BMW. So it's pretty clear he's not supporting that lifestyle on his salary alone.'
Goodchild felt a fierce internal exultation. *We have the bastard,* he thought to himself. He didn't let that show however to his constable.
'Well on the face of it, Mr. Sweeney has some explaining to do about his lifestyle. I think the next step is to brief inspector Maitland but I think we're probably going to want to talk to our friend.'
Goodchild had to hang around about half an hour before he got in to see Elizabeth Maitland. She listened attentively to what he had to say but seemed unconvinced.
'Why are you fixated on this one individual Stephen? What you're telling me is that this guy has worked in the I.T. department for a lot of years. He worked on the billing programs for the Electricity Board, so he certainly had means and opportunity. But then, as you have established, so did a couple of hundred other people that have worked in that department over the years. What makes him special now is that he has a lifestyle that can't be supported by his salary. That on the face of it doesn't make him a criminal. He may have perfectly legitimate sources of other income. I take it we are running similar checks on the other suspects?'

'Yes we are inspector but it all takes time. It's just that Sweeney is the first one to turn up something odd.' Goodchild wasn't going to tell Maitland at this stage the reasons he had focused on Sweeney. She could very well turn around and tell him he had allowed personal feelings to compromise his professional judgement.

Maitland went on. 'And from what you are telling me your suspect has a completely blameless record. Not so much as a traffic ticket.' She changed tack. 'This postal worker, try her again and take out a bunch of mug shots of some of these Electricity Board employees ; you should be able to get them from the personnel department. See if we can't get her to narrow the field a little bit more.'

She saw the look of dissatisfaction on his face. 'I know, I know , you think you have a live one. But most detective work is pretty routine monotonous stuff. Dot your I's cross your t's. We're going to have to turn up the heat on some of these people soon. I will grant you that. But not quite yet. I don't want to be stampeded; we have a little time. '

What Maitkand could not know was that time was going to be stolen away from her later that evening.

An inebriated Peter Spencer was being plied with alcohol at the Anglers Rest. He was spotted and picked up by an enterprising young female reporter from the Evening Star. She was looking for a new angle on the Metropolitan Electricity Board story and in Peter she found a willing and garrulous source. They were squeezed into a small booth in the raucous pub. For every pint of bitter that Peter Spencer downed Melanie Carruthers was careful to limit herself to a white wine spritzer. She was an attractive girl with a good figure and was quite shameless about using these advantages to cajole information out of her male information sources, for that is how she viewed Spencer.

She had spent the last hour softening him up by listening to him regale his rugby club exploits. She appeared to hang on his every word though, indeed, she cared nothing for the game and didn't have the vaguest idea what he was talking about.

'It must be pretty boring sometimes in the data processing department of an electricity board Peter, particularly given the exciting life you have outside.' Peter Spencer lapped up the flattery.

'Well it's not been boring since we started building the new system. After the conversion all hell broke loose. That's only the half of it now we have this fraud investigation going on.' She picked up on it immediately.

'Fraud investigation? That sounds very cloak and dagger Peter.'

'It's all very hush hush. They discovered that someone was siphoning money off the customer billing system and pocketing it for themselves. It's been going on for years. It's a big investigation.'

'Any ideas who might have done it Peter?'

'Could have been anyone really. Security system stinks.' For the next thirty minutes she pumped him for more information even though he was becoming more and more incoherent as the prodigious consumption of alcohol took its toll. In the end, he passed out, head down on the table in front of her.

'Drunken lout', she muttered to herself. She collected her handbag and raced back to the newspaper to file a copy for the morning edition.

It was a scoop for the Star the next day. "Fraud discovered at the Metropolitan Electricuty Board", read the banner headline. The Electricity Board story, which had been relegated to the inside pages for the last few days, was suddenly front-page news again. The reporters had its head office under siege.

Chaddick Spencer was on the phone to Maitland first thing. 'Well inspector our fraud is front page news. I'm going to have to issue a press release. I want to include the fact that Scotland Yard has been involved in the investigation for the last two weeks. It's going to come out now, sooner or later. And I have got to come up with something that makes us look less like total jerks. You okay on this?'

Maitland was resigned. 'Well Mr. Spencer, obviously we would have preferred to keep our investigation undercover longer, but that's not going to be possible. You have been very cooperative with us. So go ahead and issue the press release as you feel you must. I would appreciate an advanced copy of it over here. We will just batten down the hatches and wait for the inevitable inquiries.'

Spencer grunted. Appreciate it. 'Any progress on this case anyway?'

'Oh, we keep winnowing away at the field of suspects, but it's a slow and tedious process. We do have one or two candidates, however. You're probably already aware of this Mr. Spencer, but I should point out that now that your employees know a number of them are the target of a criminal investigation, you are going to have to handle some sensitive personnel issues.'

'Shit yeah. Personnel guys are all over that. Same time as I'm issuing a press release we're going to circulate an internal memorandum. I will shoot you over a copy of that too if you like?'

'I would appreciate that very much Mr. Spencer. '

'Well, let's just go and face the music then.' He rang off.

Maitland's phone didn't stop ringing all morning. Newspaper accounts became more sensational and distorted. "Deep seated fraud at the Metropolitan Electricity Board - linked to hypothermia deaths?" read one. In the House of Commons the government was accused of orchestrating a cover up. The Chief Superintendent summoned Maitland to his office.

'This fraud thing is getting completely out of hand. I understand your reasons for wanting to keep the investigation undercover Elizabeth but now all kinds of constructions are being put on it. The police force is being accused of colluding with the government. Our independence is being questioned and of course since the investigation is already several weeks old, we are getting the usual sniping at our competence. I had the Home Secretary on the phone, foaming at the mouth, demanding, would you believe, daily status reports. You would think we were trying to catch a serial rapist. We need some results and we need them fast!'

Maitland pursed her lips. 'I'm not sure that I would do anything different Chief. I had hoped for a bit more time for background checks on our suspects to narrow the field but I guess it's time for the more direct approach. We will just start in depth interviews.'

'Well any additional logistic support you need you just let me know. And you are going to have to keep me posted everyday Elizabeth since I'm going to have to brief the Home Secretary.'

Elizabeth Maitland walked back to her office shaking her head. When she got back she pressed the intercom. 'Get me Stephen Goodchild on the phone over at the Electricity Board. She drummed her fingers on her desk as she waited impatiently to be put through. 'Hello Stephen? I'm assigning seven more detectives to the case. We are going to need to interview all of our suspects. Yes! the gloves are off. They are to know they will be helping the police in a criminal investigation. No more cloak and dagger stuff. Did you see that post office worker?'

'Yes inspector', Stephen Goodchild responded.

'And?'

'Well we showed her the mug shots but she won't be any more specific than she originally was. The face of a middle aged and clean-shaven man.'

'All right Stephen. We can't expect miracles. I will come over there this afternoon myself. This fellow Sweeney that you're so interested in, let's interview him for a start. Set it up and I will sit in. Okay ?'

Chapter 23

Martin Housegood sat in his office at the House of Commons surrounded by the daily newspapers, which all contained the latest developments in the Metropolitan Electricity Board saga. The Chief Whip sat across the desk from him, studiously avoiding his gaze. They both had copies of the list of members of parliament. Housegood was being briefed on voting intentions on the upcoming 'No Confidence' motion.

'I'm afraid the arithmetic isn't looking so good at the moment Martin. Joe Pridget from Edinbourgh was in a car accident a couple of weeks ago. He is listed as critical in the Royal Free Hospital. With the devil's luck, Fred Brown of Manchester just had a stroke so he's not someone we can count on. I've counted eighteen of our own members who are threatening to abstain. The Unionist's are being very coy.'

'Have you explained to our backbenchers that this is a 3-line whip under a 'No Confidence' motion?' Housegood was pensive.

'Of course I have Martin! the problem is a number of these chaps are from rock ribbed Tory constituencies. The Dora Heard thing has upset a lot of people. The notion of the elderly widow of a Victoria Cross winner freezing to death because she couldn't afford to pay her electricity bills is not going over well in the Shire's I can tell you. Robert Petrie's funeral speech struck a chord.'

'So the reason for this revolt is these members are getting some support from their constituency associations ?' Housegood asked.

'That's it exactly Martin, otherwise we could take the ground out from under them.'

'Is the full meeting of the parliamentary party on for this afternoon like I asked?'

'Yes all laid on. Three o'clock.'

'Who is leading this revolt?'

'Jeffrey Price-Jones. You know he fought in World War Two with Montgomery at El Alamein and he's already announced he won't be standing for re-election.'

'So he really couldn't give a toss?'

Housegood thought for a moment. 'I'd like to meet with him privately. Jeffrey Price-Jones has done a lot for this country both in the war, under with twenty years of parliamentary service under his belt. I'm not sure whether a grateful nation shouldn't under the right circumstances offer him a peerage. Of course we'd have to discuss what these circumstances should be. What about the Unionists?'

The Chief Whip looked at him, 'Well they're going to want to know what's in it for them before they vote with the government. If they bring us down they're going to have to deal with Labour. The question they are going to have to ask themselves is whether their interests are likely to be better served under Labour rather than under the Tories. Would you do a deal with them Martin?'

'No Hugh, I won't do a deal with them. Even if it means the fall of the government. There is a fine line between the exercise of power and its abuse. My offering Price-Jones a peerage in exchange for his vote comes from having power and using it. If I start making concessions on the Irish question to the unionists simply to solve a domestic political difficulty, everything the Nationalists allege about British involvement in Northern Ireland would then be vindicated ; that in the last analysis we will subordinate that unfortunate province's best interest to our political expediency. No, the Unionist's must understand that if they vote against us they will bring down the government. They also need to consider the issues on their merits. There's twenty per cent unemployment in Northern Ireland. The issues of globalization affect them just as they do us. They have to decide what is best for their constituents. I will be happy to meet with them to explain this but they need to understand upfront there are going to be no deals.'

'You are not leaving me with a lot of room from manoeuvre Martin.' The Chief Whip was peevish.

'Well the question we have to ask ourselves, Hugh is, why do we want to stay in power? Is it simply because we like it for its own sake or do we actually have an agenda, some course of action we believe in, somewhere we want to take the country? if we don't have an agenda that's meaningful and that we can articulate maybe it is time for a change.' He smiled at the look of astonishment on the Chief Whip 's face.

'I know, subversive thoughts a for party leader to have, let alone the Prime Minister. We need to work on this block of eighteen. I want a personal profile on each one. The other side of it of course is that our PR campaign to get the message out needs to start having an effect. If we can get some grassroots support in their constituency associations they're going to be much easier to shake. So it's a long uphill climb but we have a week left.'

Chapter 24

Robert Petrie was having lunch with his father at the Reform Club. Ostensibly it was because Petrie senior had business in the City and just happened to have an available lunch date. Robert suspected however it was a direct result of his phone call a few days earlier, when he had broken the news of his split with Marjorie. Petrie senior was of the school which thought that once one's offspring had reached the age of majority, parents had no business meddling in their lives.

Luncheon fare at the club was unrepentantly British cuisine and consequently cholesterol laden. Both father and son wore pinstripe suits and white shirts and were indistinguishable from the rest of the lunchtime diners. The first half of the meal was spent discussing his father's business affairs, an upcoming trip his parents planned to make to the Canaries and problems his mother was having with her herbaceous border. They were well into their roast beef and Yorkshire pudding before his father approached anything like a sensitive topic.

'So, the government got itself into a bit of a pickle Robert? and you have been pretty vocal for a backbencher. Where do you stand on this 'No Confidence' motion?'

Robert smiled at his father. 'I'm rather out on a limb and the branches half sawn off.' There was a noncommittal grunt.

'The position I have taken is the main reason Marjorie left me but I'm not sure that there weren't other problems that would have surfaced sooner or later.'

'Not too sure it was a good idea for women to get the vote anyway Robert', was his father's comment.

Robert was amused in spite of himself. 'Well, that's a very Neanderthal thing to say father.'

Petrie senior was unapologetic. 'Religion and politics are not good subjects for marital discourse. Bound to cause trouble. This double harness business is tough enough without introducing inflammatory topics like that. I suppose I'm old fashioned. My model of marriage was the wife stayed home and minded the children, ran the household, husband went out and earned a living. Rules were pretty well defined. Now it's all equality of the sexes and marriage is a debating society. Awfully heavy sledding.'

'I don't know how it's going to turn out between me and Marjorie father. All I know is that it hurts like hell.' Robert said baldly.

If his father was embarrassed by the uncharacteristic admission, he didn't show it. 'So what are you going to do about this political brouhaha you've gotten yourself into Robert?'

'It's going to come down to whether I will vote for the government or not. The motion is worded that this house has 'No Confidence' in her majesty's government's social and privatisation policies. I thought a lot about it and the fact of the matter is I don't have any confidence in them. There's one part of me that says it's only a form of words, you should support your party, but that's what democracy is all about isn't it? words.'

'What does your constituency association say about it?' His father asked.

'Well, the chairman is sympathetic to my stand over Dora Heard with her being a constituent and all but they have made it abundantly plain that they want me to support the government in the 'No Confidence' motion or else I will not be adopted as conservative candidate in the next general election.'

'So if you go with your conscience you torpedo your political career.' His father accepted Brandy and a cigar from the elderly waiter who was bringing around the drinks.

Robert noticed it because it was a departure for his father, who rarely drank at lunchtime. It was an indirect acknowledgement that he was experiencing some of the stress that Robert was under, and sharing in it.

'What was it that Edmund Burke said Robert? "Your representative owes you, not his industry only, but his judgment: and he betrays instead of serving you, if he sacrifices it to your opinion." Not bad for an Irishman. '

'You know father I'm thirty years old but somehow I think I've only just grown up in the last couple of months. This business with Dora Heard brought home to me that parliamentary life is not just a debating society even though some of the time it would appear we're just a bunch of overgrown schoolboys. What we do, and what we say, impacts people in their everyday lives. I have never really understood that before.'

His father looked at him, solemnly puffing on his cigar.

'Now, now my boy, your mother and I have always been proud of you and what you have achieved at a very young age. You are grown now and I'm not going to tell you what to do. It wouldn't be appropriate. All that I will say is that whatever you do be sure you can live with yourself afterwards. There are a lot of things on the line, your marriage, your career, and your personal integrity. Whichever way it comes out remember you are our son and you always will be.'

His father took out a handkerchief coughed and blew his nose.

Roberts said simply, 'Thank you father. I really appreciate it.'

His father made a show of glancing at his watch. 'Is that the time Robert? Goodness I shall have to go. You should come down and visit us soon. Your mother worries about you, you know.'

'I will, I promise, the weekend after the vote. I can't really find time to travel before.'

They collected their coats from the cloakroom and walked out together on to the steps leading up to the club. It was a bright Spring day and overfed pigeons waddled everywhere. They shook hands and then walked in opposite directions. After a couple of hundred yards Robert looked behind him to watch the retreating figure of his father, a portly middle-aged gentleman, marching purposely along the Mall, swinging his umbrella.

Chapter 25

The interview with Andrew Sweeney was conducted in an interior office on the 8th floor of the Metropolitan Electricity Board building. The only lighting was fluorescent, the walls painted an institutional light blue, the furnishings utilitarian, plastic chairs and a Formica desk, with a telephone and a computer terminal. The interview was scheduled for three o'clock. At one minute to three Andrew Sweeney arrived and knocked on the door. Stephen Goodchild and Elizabeth Maitland were waiting. For Goodchild it was the first time he had seen Sweeney since the night of the dinner dance. Just the physical appearance of the man irritated him. An image of Sweeney's out of condition body in bed with his wife Deirdre flashed into Goodchild's mind. *How could she,* he thought, *It's physically revolting*. His rational mind intervened. *Get a grip on yourself. The man has a perfect right to go to bed with his wife.*

Stephen Goodchild's encounter with Deirdre Sweeney had turned into an obsession. He thought about her constantly. He fantasised about her. He played every detail of their conversation over and over again in his mind. *The woman has bewitched me,* he thought.

Maitland opened the interview. 'Good afternoon Mr. Sweeney. Thank you for agreeing to meet with us. You are aware that the fraud at the Metropolitan Electricity Board has become the subject of an official police investigation. My name is inspector Elizabeth Mirren of Scotland Yard and this is Detective Sergeant Stephen Goodchild. '

Andrew Sweeney sat impassively in the chair his legs crossed and said nothing.

'We have been running routine background checks on a number of the personnel both present and previous employees of the Electricity Board. The purpose of these interviews is to go back over some information given earlier to the internal audit staff and verify some details. Also, we have some questions arising from the background checks which we would like you to help us with.'

Andrew still said nothing and continued to gaze at her calmly.

'Well, if you have no questions at this point we will begin. You were the analyst who was responsible for the design and programming of the old billing system and also the conversion to the new system. That's correct?'

'Yes it is.' Andrew replied.

In the course of the next half hour they covered the same ground that the internal audit had. Sweeney's position was unaltered from his previous account. Yes he had been involved in programming the old system but was a junior programmer at the time. It was a long time ago, many people had access to code, almost anyone could have tampered with it. The billing algorithms had been taken over from the old system to the new without any alteration. The regression tests had worked he had no reason to suspect there was anything out of the ordinary.

Maitland suddenly changed tack.

'Mr. Sweeney you earn forty thousand pounds a year as a senior systems analyst with the Metropolitan Electricity Board.'

'That's correct.'

'And yet our investigation showed that you have a mortgage of some two thousand pounds a month, your son goes to private school, and your wife drives a BMW. Quite a high level of expenditure for that level of income.'

Andrew was rattled by that. 'What are you implying inspector?'

'At this point I don't imply anything Mr. Sweeney. It's simply an observation.'

Andrew Sweeney smiled back at her, 'If that's all it is, fine.'

Goodchild intervened, 'Don't be clever Sweeney. What we want to know is, where is the extra money coming from to help you support that lifestyle and your expensive wife?'

Andrew Sweeney was becoming visibly angry. He directed a look of disgust at Goodchild. 'Ah so that's how the wind blows is it? and with all the hundreds of people that have had their paws over these billing systems over the years why am I being singled out for such attention I wonder ?'

Maitland intervened, 'Please answer Sergeant Goodchild's question Mr Sweeney.'

'I will answer the question in one-minute miss whatever you are. Right now I can't help getting the feeling I'm being stitched up. You think I don't know what's going on. You people are having the shit kicked out of you because you can't find a suspect for this fraud business. And here's this mick Irishman who would do just nicely thank you very much. Not to mention lover boy here. Wants to have it off with my expensive wife as he calls her. Very convenient when I'm behind bars.'

Goodchild exploded. 'You fucking bastard, Sweeney.'

Maitland stood up and placed herself physically between the two men. 'Shut up both of you. Sergeant Goodchild you moderate your language. Mr. Sweeney these are senseless and baseless allegations. Nothing more than a smokescreen to cloud the fact that you have yet to answer how you maintain your current lifestyle on forty thousand pounds a year.'

'Baseless and groundless are they? Tell that to the three hundred people who were in the Hilton Hotel ballroom last Saturday night while your friend here practically undressed my wife in full view. Couldn't keep his paws off her. Slimy bastard.'

Goodchild screamed at him, 'I'll do for you Sweeney !'

Maitland was paralyzed by the turn of the conversation and the ferocity of the exchanges between the two men who were now both standing and squaring off with her in the middle. After a moment however she reasserted her authority. 'I've just about had enough of this. Mr. Sweeney sit down. Sergeant Goodchild outside. I want a word with you. '

She all but dragged him into the corridor. 'Is what this man is saying true ?' She whispered to him fiercely.

'Yes it is. I danced with this woman at the affair last Saturday. But I swear to God I didn't know she was his wife. That only became apparent when he showed up to ask her to leave for home.'

'Oh fine, wonderful. So you're messing about with the wife of a suspect in a major criminal investigation.'

'You were the one who decided that this was going to be some kind of cloak and dagger operation Detective Inspector.'

The truth of his remarks struck her. She made a visible effort to control herself. 'All right we're going to go in there and finish interviewing. Not a word out of you Sergeant. If there is I'm taking you off this case immediately. Is that clear?'

He nodded.

'And another thing. You don't go near that man's wife except on official police business and if you do, you do it in the company of a woman police officer. Got it?'

Again he nodded.

'Fine. Let's finish then. '

They returned to the office. Sweeney appeared to have calmed down in the interval.

Maitland took a deep breath and then began. 'Mr. Sweeney, Sergeant Goodchild assures me that he was unaware at the social gathering last Saturday that Deirdre Sweeney is your wife. He is a responsible police officer and will behave in that manner while this investigation is going on. Now as to your wild allegation that somehow you are being picked upon or victimised because you happen to be Irish, that is patently untrue. You happen to be one of quite a number of people who have had the opportunity to tamper with the system at the Metropolitan Electricity Board. You and many others are the subject of our investigation and scrutiny. You will be treated no better and no worse than anybody else. Let me now return to the original question. You would appear to maintain a style of life which cannot be supported from your salary as a senior system analyst alone. For the third time I am asking you if you would care to give us an explanation?'

Sweeney looked up at her and answered mildly 'Bridget Reilly was my aunt, of Arvagh in County Longford. I am the sole beneficiary of her estate which was quite substantial. If you bothered to check the tax returns that I filed for the last eight years you would see an item for unearned income in the amount of sixty thousand pounds a year roughly. I have never concealed the fact that I had sources of income other than my salary. I declared it on my taxes.'

Goodchild was scribbling furiously. Maitland straightened her crumpled dress. 'Thank you Mr. Sweeney. We will of course verify the information you have given us but on the face of it, you have answered all the major questions we have for the moment. You will appreciate that we may want to interview you again as matters unfold or as we have additional questions. I rather wish you had volunteered this information sooner in our interview. It would have made matters considerably less unpleasant. That would be all for the moment. Thank you.'

Andrew used the edge of the desk to lever himself out of his chair. 'Oh just one more thing.' She mentioned it almost as an afterthought. 'We are trying to match up some signatures on documents we have uncovered.' She placed two pieces of paper on the desk in front of him. 'I wonder if you could write the name that appears at the bottom of the page on the left. Try to copy the style of writing if you could.' It was a photocopy of an application to open a bank account in the name of Christopher Bradshaw. Andrew did as he was asked and then turned on his heel and left.

'What now?', Goodchild asked Maitland.

'Back to the Yard. Give the handwriting specimen to the lab. Then we have a phone call to put through to the Irish police.'

As they walked out the door of the Metropolitan Electricity building there was no longer any pretence about it being a police investigation. Several squad cars were parked outside on the street. A Detective Constable was waiting to chauffeur them back. They said nothing for the first ten minutes of the journey through the crowded London traffic.

Goodchild blurted out. 'I have really screwed it up haven't I?'

Maitland sighed and looked at him. 'Not your finest hour Stephen. But I think your instincts are right about Mr. Sweeney.'

Goodchild looked surprised. 'How do you come to that conclusion?'

'The man who perpetrated this fraud was resourceful and daring. We backed Sweeney into a corner and he puts us completely on the defensive. A mild-mannered, inoffensive systems analyst? I don't think so. Oh yes this is what he would have us believe but that is not the kind of man he is. So we are getting closer. He has this unexplained income; we question it and he gives us an answer. We have to prove him a liar. This is what we're going to do. You Stephen, are going to the emerald Isle to checkout this inheritance story as soon as I have cleared it with the Irish police.'

'When?'

'This evening, tonight. Flights leave on the hour, I believe, from London to Dublin.'

'But where is Longford? I don't even know where it is in the country.'

'You are a resourceful young man. You figure it out.'

Maitland made a phone call to the Irish police and saw Goodchild scheduled for an eight p.m. flight to Dublin. He would stay in the city overnight before continuing by train to Longford the next morning.

Upstairs in the executive suite, Chaddick Spencer was having a meeting with the chairman of his board of directors Sir Robert Winthrop. This was occasioned by a further fall of thirty pence per share in the value of the Metropolitan Electricuty Board stock.

The chairman was apologetic but firm. 'I'm sorry Chaddick but since the end of November last until today, scarcely three months, the share price has dropped in value over 30%. And there doesn't appear to be any end in sight. Clearly the board can't allow this to continue. I've spoken to several members of the board about this and we're in agreement. We have a quorum to call an emergency meeting next Friday. The board secretary has circulated the required notification.'

'Are you trying to fire me then Robert?'

'Someone has to be accountable for this management fiasco Chaddick. Your plan was sound enough I grant you. And the board bought into it. It's just that it's execution has been dismal. I want to be fair to you. If we set aside the computerization scheme for a moment, and God knows that's hard enough to do, other initiatives you have implemented have worked quite well. You contracted for new sources of power supply at improved rates. You negotiated some very significant labour contracts with the unions, and streamlined the electrical goods retailing operation.'

Spencer listened impassively to this litany of his virtues and accomplishments.

'What are you getting at Bobby?'

Robert Winthrop winced at the diminutive which he knew had been thrown in just to aggravate him. He persevered, however. 'The point, Chaddick, is that if one takes a detached view of your record as managing director what comes through is a quite competent and even, in some cases, an inspired performance. This more than merits our original confidence in you. One has to believe then that in the matter of executing the systems conversion, you were very poorly served by your management team.'

Spencer gave a wintry smile. Anyone knowing him well would have recognised the warning signals. 'Got any names Bobby?'

'Well that fellow you brought over with you. Ah what was his name? Bart Johnson was it?'

Spencer looked at him sourly, 'Brett actually.'

'I met him only the once you understand, but he struck me as being a bit anaemic, if you don't mind me saying so.'

'Let's cut to the chase here Bobby', Spencer gestured with his cigar impatiently. 'What you are telling me is that if I deep six Brett Johnson I will get to keep my job.'

Winthrop looked at him nervously. 'Well of course Chaddick, I can't prejudice in anyway the deliberations of the board in this matter, but I can say that I have talked to a number of the other directors. Their assessment of your performance is not out of line with my own. However they are equally insistent that in order to restore shareholder confidence in some measure management changes will have to be made. Were we to have your assurance that action will be taken to strengthen your management team I am reasonably certain that the board can be persuaded to persevere with you in the role of managing director.'

'Gee, swell Bobby. That's real British of you guys.'

Winthrop wasn't sure if this was meant as a compliment.

'Only one problem. As Jimmy Cagney said in strawberry blonde "that's not the kind of hairpin I am." Brett Johnson is a smart man and capable. His only fault is that he's not sufficiently ruthless. I told him time and again that the DP boys were given him the run around on the systems conversion that he should fire a bunch of them. You know what he said? He said I didn't understand the British way of doing things; he said I was being too harsh in my judgment. He also said that we needed to work with the people in place, to move the morale along, get a team spirit going, all sweetness and light and management theories. And a crock of shit. He should have tossed some of these guys out on their keisters the day he arrived. So where has he ended up? He's landed himself in it and me with him. But even if he was stubborn, he did what he thought was right. He was always honest with me the best he knew, about where we stood. So I'm not going to offer him up as some kind of sacrifice to cover my fat ass. Sorry pal, no deal.'

Winthrop was examining an imaginary speck of dust on his immaculate pin-striped trouser leg. 'I'm sorry you feel that way Chaddick, truly I am. You will appreciate however that the board has a responsibility to its shareholders and we will honour that responsibility. The meeting will be convened at three o'clock Friday in the boardroom. We would be grateful if you could join us at four.'

'Sure thing Bobby. I wouldn't miss it for the world. You might want to go over the terms of my employment contract in the meantime just to refresh your memory.'

Winthrop smiled bleakly, 'Yes Chaddick. I'm painfully aware that you negotiated a very generous severance package with us before accepting the position.'

'Two million in cash and I get to keep exercise of my stock options.'

'Yes, you will have done quite well out of this fiasco.' Winthrop spat the word out bitterly.

Chaddick was on his feet to propel him to the door. 'Hey Bobby, I was a hired gun. You knew that, a mercenary. Cheer up old fellow, it's only business. It's not as though England lost the Test Match. Just so you know though the board better be prepared to hear an earful from me. He adopted a gangsterish slouch. 'I ain't gonna take this lying down.'

'Well Good afternoon then Chaddick. Friday at four.'

Andrew Sweeney stood, back against the wall, in an alleyway several streets from the Electricity Board offices, his stomach heaving. After the interview with the detectives he had returned to his desk for a few minutes and then unable to maintain the facade of self-control any longer he got up and walked briskly out of the building. He passed the waiting squad cars, a few interested bystanders on the street, looking nervously behind him to see if he was being followed. The alleyway was littered with trash and broken bottles and stank of urine. A stray cat rummaging in the garbage looked at him indifferently.

The interview had terrified him. Even though he had a heavy overcoat on and it was not particularly cold, he was shivering. He knew without question now that they had discovered him. The illusion he had retained that somehow the crime would go undetected was gone.

Good God, he thought to himself, *I'm finished.* Stephen Goodchild he might have bamboozled, the woman, Elizabeth Maitland, he knew, would finish him. It was only a matter of time now.

He sank down to his haunches clapping his cupped hands together to get some sort of physical relief from the tension. He had gone for that asswipe Goodchild. In his anguish he felt a fierce sense of satisfaction that he had rattled the bastard.

He had turned the tables on the man at the cost of breaking cover. He was no longer a grey and anonymous man, one of many potential suspects, he was right up there on their radar and they weren't going to let go now. It had been a superhuman effort for him not to cry out in shock when that clever cow stuck the name Bradshaw under his nose. Getting him to mimic the signature. That at least wouldn't do them much good. He had signed the original application left-handed. His attempt at duplication had been done with his right hand.

He rubbed his knuckles reflectively. *'I can't Sister Josephine, I just can't.* 'A little boy with tears in his eyes trying to sign his name right-handed. The sting of the heavy ruler across his knuckles. 'You are just being wilful and stubborn Andrew Sweeney. Young gentleman write with their right hand. You're going to learn if I have to break this ruler across those fingers.'

How long would it be, he wondered, *before they put it all* together? Days, maybe a couple of weeks at most, there were a couple of more twists in the trail they hadn't uncovered but he knew all it would do was delay them, not stop them. He kept getting the image in his mind of the damned soul by Michelangelo on the roof of the Sistine Chapel.

That's what I am, he thought, *damned and disgraced. Jesus what have I done?* In the far distance he heard the sound of an ambulance or fire brigade. He thought of suicide, of flight. *It's no good I will have to tell her,* he thought. *Michael, Michael, what am I going to say to Michael ? they are the only two people in the world I care anything about. I will tell her somehow and then do whatever she wants.* When though? He resolved to tell her the following evening. He wanted just one more night with his wife and son as a family. He wiped his nose on the back of his sleeve and realised he had been crying a little. *I'd best get back,* he thought. *I will be missed and questions asked.*

Chapter 26

Stephen Goodchild stepped off the plane at Dublin airport. The location was completely unfamiliar to him. He had never before been to Ireland. He took a taxi downtown to the hotel where he was staying, The Royal Dublin. The Department budget did not run to any of the five-star hotels. The main thing that struck him was how green everything was. He commented on it to the taxi driver, a native Dubliner.

'Why wouldn't it be green? All it does is rain in this bloody country. You know what the saying in Dublin is? if you can see the mountains it's going to rain. If you can't see them it's raining already.'

He checked with the taxi driver on where he would be departing the next morning for the train trip to Longford.

'That will be Connolly station on Amiens St. They named all the train stations after the 1916 Patriots. Confused the life out of everybody for a while.' Although he had not wanted to make the trip, just getting away from London, his broken marriage, and his infatuation with Dierdre Sweeney was having a relaxing effect on him. So too was the pleasant banter of the taxi driver as they drove through the narrow, crowded Dublin streets to his hotel.

Checking into the hotel was a laidback affair nothing like the sense of frenzy of a similar operation in a big London hotel. It was ten p.m. by the time he checked into his room. He decided to go down to the bar for a couple of drinks before going to bed. He found it noisy and crowded. A few tourists, mainly locals, it being out of season. They were a cheerful talkative bunch. He fell into conversation with three men in their mid-twenties who were having a spirited post-mortem about a soccer match Arsenal had played against Everton in London the previous Saturday. He was struck by the ease with which they included him in their conversation and their willingness to buy him a drink, a ten minute acquaintance. It was a relaxing and cheerful environment. He wandered back to his room around eleven thirty and for the first time in weeks, had an untroubled night sleep.

The train for Longford pulled out of Connolly station on time at eight o'clock the next morning. It was not particularly crowded. He settled back to enjoy the four-hour journey through the Irish countryside. He was to be met by a member of the Irish police force at the other end who would helping him with the inquiry. The passing landscape of green grass, grazing sheep and cows was hypnotic. His mind began to wander. He found himself thinking about Dierdre Sweeney and what she would look like naked. Being in bed with her, caressing those long well-formed legs. He gave himself over guiltily to the fantasy and after a while dozed off.

He was met at the train station by a detective on the Irish police force. A bluff and hearty man with huge hands, one of which enveloped his, in a vigorous handshake. His opposite number had a red face that spoke of exposure to the elements and a fair amount of drink.

'You will be Stephen Goodchild, the Scotland Yard man. It's not often that we get a visit from the likes of you in these parts. You're very welcome all the same.'

His partner kept up a running commentary on the short drive to the police station. Stephen thought to himself, *The Irish are a very extroverted bunch*. Once they were settled in the police Sergeant's office it was time to get to the point.

'So what brings you to our town then Mr Goodchild? something to do with a fraud investigation in London I hear.'

'Yes, that's about the size of it. There's a case of fraud at the Metropolitan Electricity Board in London and an employee is helping us with our inquiry. The salary he is getting paid does not support the lifestyle he is currently sustaining in London. He has explained this to us by saying he is the sole beneficiary of the estate of a woman who lived in these parts, Bridget Reilly. And my purpose for being here is to verify the accuracy or otherwise of the information he has provided us.'

The Sergeant clasped his hands behind his head and rocked back in his chair. 'Bridget Reilly owned the farm in Arvagh. Four years dead, God rest her. She was a good woman, stayed home, minded the old people, inherited the farm after they passed on, never married. Left the farm to her nephew Sweeney I remember, although there were some that said it should have gone to her cousins the McBride's with all the help they gave her in the later years. So it would be him that you're talking about.' It was a statement and not a question.

'I suppose your best bet would be to chat with Matt Prendergast. Prendergast was the family solicitor. They are on the High Street.' The Sergeant chuckled. 'You can count yourself lucky it's Matt you're talking to. If it were his father now that's dead this 10 years, he used to conduct business on a commode would you believe, a blanket across his legs. Problems with his bowels. The farmers here didn't mind it so much. They were used to farmyard smells, but the city folk thought it a bit peculiar.'

Goodchild felt slightly disoriented by the conversation. 'Thank you Sergeant that's very helpful. And where would I find Mr Prendergast again?'

'On the High Street, just turn right when you get out of the station and follow your nose, you can't miss it.'

Goodchild found that he could and did miss it several times before finally figuring out that the offices were on the 2nd floor of a building above a butcher shop. When he finally did locate it he was confronted by a sign which said - out to lunch. There was no indication as to when lunch was, and when the office would reopen. There was nothing to be done but to go for lunch himself. Every second building on the Main Street seemed to be a pub. He stopped in to one at random and had a toasted ham sandwich and a pint of Guinness. He conducted a companionable conversation with the woman serving behind the counter. Wandering back about one thirty he found the solicitors office open. He explained who he was to a middle-aged woman who functioned as far as he could see as receptionist, secretary, and general factotum. He was given a grudging audience with Prendergast, the solicitor.

Prendergast turned out to be a slightly built man about the same age as Goodchild. The detective showed identification and explained the reason for his visit. The solicitor seemed unimpressed.

'Well no Mr. Goodchild, I'm not in the habit of discussing my client's business alive or dead
   with third parties. '

'I appreciate that Mr. Prendergast but you would be helping us in a criminal investigation.'

'So you say, so you say. And the local police know you're here then?'

'Yes. It was they who gave me your name.'

'Ah, it would have been Sergeant Hennessey that did that then.'

'Yes that was the man I spoke to' Goodchild replied.

'Well you won't mind if I just verify that now? I don't think I'm too happy divulging my client's confidences just because somebody I never laid eyes on comes into my office waving what he claims is a police badge under my nose. You will take no offence?'

Goodchild did take offence but wasn't about to say so. 'If you feel you need to take that precaution by all means Mr Prendergast do so.'

Prendergast called out to his secretary, 'Margaret would you get Sergeant Hennessey on the phone for me?' There was a delay of a few minutes during which the solicitor ignored Goodchild's presence in his office entirely.

'Mr. Prendergast, the Sergeant just stepped out for a few minutes on an errand. There expecting him back presently. '

'Oh if you just care to wait outside Mr. Goodchild until I have a chance to talk to Sergeant Hennessy. Margaret will get you a cup of tea.'

'I had hoped to catch the three o'clock train back to Dublin.' Goodchild said pointedly.

'Oh, never worry there will be another train about six thirty this evening and we should have finished our business long before then.' Prendergast replied airily.

Yes thought Goodchild to himself *and if I have to wait on the six thirty train that puts paid to any hopes I had of getting back to London tonight.*

The secretary seemed to take pity on him and vanished off to a pantry where she produced a pot of tea and some homemade cake.

'Made it myself', she muttered apologetically. 'Hope it's not too dry.'

He resigned himself to the wait and found himself taking interest in how business was conducted in the small country practice. Every few minutes the phone would ring and the secretary seemed to know who everyone was who called. She chatted with them about the weather, their mutual acquaintances, various ailments, and sometimes she put the call through to Prendergast. There appeared to be only one phone line so he assumed that callers got the busy signal the majority of the time. Coming from London it seemed hopelessly inefficient. But it had an easy familiarity which he thought quite beguiling. After an hour of Goodchild cooling his heels Sergeant Hennessey finally got through to Prendergast but not before a five-minute chat with Margaret on the subject of his wife's bunions. The solicitor seemed much more cordial when he was finally readmitted to the inner sanctum.

'Well Mr. Goodchild I had a chat with Sergeant Hennessey and he confirms you are who you say you are. You won't mind me taking the precaution? I'll be happy to answer any questions I can within reason of course.'

'You handled Bridget Reilly's estate when she died?'

'Yes, I did.'

'Could you verify for me please that Andrew Sweeney currently residing in London was the sole beneficiary? and how much did he inherit ?'

Prendergast paused and went to his files. He consulted some papers. 'After death duties and mortgages on the property were paid off the value of Bridget Reilly's estate was 74,326 Irish Pounds.'

'That's it, that's all?' Goodchild asked sharply.

'Yes, that's all there was. Her father suffered a stroke twelve years ago and soon after that they sold the livestock. They had some income from grazing rights and kept some chickens and pigs. But it wasn't really a going concern after the father had his stroke so in the end there wasn't that much left after the bills were paid.'

74,000 Irish pounds was not going to explain Andrew Sweeney's lifestyle in London for the last eight years, Goodchild reflected grimly. 'Would it be possible Mr. Prendergast to get a sworn affidavit from you? basically restating what you've told me.'

'I see no reason why not' Prendergast said. 'Bridget Reilly's estate went to probate so all of this information is in the probate office in Dublin with, of course, who the beneficiary was. Well, you have missed the three o'clock train so if you care to wait a half hour I'll make out the statement for you now and you can take it with you. '

Goodchild reflected that since there was very little else for him to do in Longford, he might as well wait. When an hour later he got back to the train station he attempted to use the public phone box to report his findings to inspector Maitland. He discovered that the phone box only took ten pence pieces and he needed to equip himself with two or three pounds worth of these in order to even have a three minute conversation. There was of course no change machine. *This place would drive me mental if I had to live here year-round* he thought. *That or I'd need to become more laidback than I am now*. After a few false starts he eventually got through to Elizabeth Maitland who sounded anything but calm.

'Where the hell have you been Goodchild? I've been trying all afternoon to get a hold of you?'

'Well I was at the police station', he replied. 'And then went on to the solicitor who handled Bridget Reilly's estate. Guess WHAT? she only left seventy odd thousand Irish pounds.'

Maitland gave a murmur of satisfaction. 'So our friend Mr. Sweeney has some explaining to do.'

'I'm going to head back to Dublin tonight.' Goodchild told her. 'It will be tomorrow before I can fly into London.'

'You won't be flying into London tomorrow', Maitland answered. 'That's why I have been trying to get a hold of you this afternoon. Sweeney is in Dublin.'

Goodchild was surprised. 'He's in Dublin.'

'Yes, his mother died apparently. He went over for the funeral. He didn't inform us he was going but then I suppose he didn't have to. I was so put off my stroke by our interview with him I forgot to warn him that we need to be kept informed of his where abouts. The mother's funeral is in Aughrim street, someplace in North Dublin and she's being buried in a Cemetery called Glasnevin. I want you to keep an eye on him, discreetly of course and make sure he plans on coming back to the UK. Remember Stephen, you are to watch him, nothing more. I don't want any unpleasantness with the Irish police. If it looks like he's trying to give us the slip, you will let me know immediately. We will issue the arrest warrant here and file for extradition with the Irish authorities. You clear on all of that?'

'Yes inspector. I will behave myself', Goodchild answered crisply.

'See that you do Stephen.' Maitland rang off.

Chapter 27

The call about his mother had come after midnight. It was his uncle Joe.
'I'm sorry, Andrew, but I have some very bad news. Your mother has passed away, God rest her. She had a heart attack earlier this evening. She managed to phone her neighbour, but by the time we got her to the Mater Hospital, she was in a very bad way. She died an hour ago. If it's any comfort to you, she had the last rites. I'm sure she's in heaven now.'

As his uncle talked, Andrew had a distinct mental image of his mother as he had last seen her: frail, white-haired, at her doorstep watching as his taxi pulled away. He had known he would get the phone call one day. Still, he had to cope with the feelings of shock and loss, surprised by their intensity. He hadn't realised he would care so much. He propped himself up on his pillows to carry on the conversation. Deirdre slept on beside him.

'I will catch the first flight I can in the morning, Joe.'

'I will meet you at the airport, Andrew,' Joe replied. 'Let me know what flight you're coming in on. What do you want done about the funeral arrangements?'

'It will take Matthew a couple of days to get back from Canada,' Andrew said. 'Have you told him yet?' Matthew was Andrew's brother.

'No, we thought we would phone you first.' His uncle sounded apologetic.

'That's all right, Joe. I'll phone him myself when we finish talking.'

Andrew got slowly out of bed. He would have to look up his brother's telephone number in Canada. He didn't phone him that often. The conversation with Matthew was brief, neither of them wasting time on expressions of grief which they did not particularly feel. Matthew would not travel until the afternoon of the following day. He claimed it was because he would not have time to go and get his passport, but Andrew suspected it was because he did not want to miss the important business meeting he kept muttering about with every second breath.

Andrew made himself a cup of coffee. How did he feel? Weary, mostly. He still had not been able to bring himself to tell Deirdre about his criminal activity. That was how he forced himself to think about what he had done now. It was a mantra for confronting reality. At times he thought fleetingly of ending it all or throwing himself on the gleaming tracks and being done with it. Now, however, he had an obligation to fulfil, to return to Dublin and bury his mother.

He finished his coffee and made a phone call to Aer Lingus. He booked himself on a flight from Heathrow to Dublin at eight the next morning. He went back to bed. What else was there to do? He slept fitfully. Childhood memories bubbled up into his consciousness. His Confirmation. The time when he split his lip against a lamp post while running away from some bigger boys, not watching where he was going. There were impressions of his mother, stern, severe, only occasionally happy, mainly around Christmas when he and his brother were opening their presents around the tree.

Initially, he fought the memories, painful recollections of an unhappy childhood. After a while, however, he allowed them to surface, acknowledging the painful feelings they evoked. In that manner, he drifted between sleep and consciousness until six o'clock, at which point he began to get ready for the trip. His moving around the room awakened Deirdre.

'You're up early, Andrew. Is anything the matter?' she asked him drowsily. He told her his mother had died. Deirdre was instantly awake. 'Oh, Andrew, I am sorry.'

'She was over seventy, Deirdre. She hadn't been in good health these past couple of years. I have to catch a plane in a couple of hours.'

'Do you want me to come with you, Andrew?'

'No. We would have to bring Michael, and it's a bit morbid for a boy of his age. Anyway, it isn't as though he was very close to Mother.'

Deirdre was up and putting on her dressing gown.

'Well, you finish packing. I'll go down and make something for you to eat. Have you ordered a taxi?'

'No, actually, I haven't.'

'Well, I could do that for you. Half an hour?'

'Fine. Oh dear, you'll need to phone work and let them know I won't be in for a couple of days,' Andrew said, then stopped in his tracks. He thought of the police. 'On second thought, I'll take care of it at the airport.'

'Are you sure, Andrew?'

'Yes, yes. It won't be any problem.'

He found most of the things he would need: a couple of white shirts and a dark suit. He didn't have a black tie. He would have to buy one in Dublin unless the funeral directors provided it.

Deirdre had cooked a breakfast of scrambled eggs, sausages, and toast. She was a good cook when she put her mind to it, but it didn't happen very often.

Traffic was heavy on the way out to Heathrow, and he just about missed his flight. The plane was full. Because he had booked so late, he found himself in a middle seat sandwiched between an overweight businessman and a nun. He resisted the temptation to have a drink, settling instead for tonic water. The sun was shining when he left Heathrow, but when they approached Dublin airport it was through a bank of heavy clouds. The plane landed under a dark threatening sky.

His uncle was waiting for him in the reception area. 'It's good to see you, Andrew. I'm only sorry it's on such a sad occasion.' It was a stylised ritual phrase, one of many he would hear over the next few days. I'm sorry for your trouble, Andrew. Her last illness was mercifully short. I'm sure she's in heaven now, Andrew. She's with her husband now.

He made a stock answer. 'It was good of you to come to the airport to meet me, Joe.'

'Sure, why wouldn't I? At a time like this, and I your flesh and blood,' his uncle replied.

When they got to the funeral directors, Augustus Wallace himself waited on them. Wallace was the third generation in the business. His main office was just outside the centre of the city. Even though he was situated on the main road, once you got inside, there was an air of sepulchral quiet.

He has put sound soak on the walls, Andrew thought.

In some ways Wallace looked like an undertaker. He had a very pale complexion, almost bloodless, but far from being cadaverous, he was positively plump. Wallace guided Andrew through all the various logistical arrangements, showing no surprise when Andrew informed him that he wanted his mother's remains taken first to her home. Wallace had stock phrases of encouragement, his favourite being, 'It's just what I would want for my own mother.' Andrew, in a moment of madness, wondered what would happen if he told Wallace that he wanted his mother cremated on a funeral pyre in her front garden.

Two days later, Andrew sat in the black limousine, which followed the hearse from the church to the graveyard. His brother and his uncle were the only others in attendance.

Each man was occupied with his own thoughts. They had left him alone with his mother for a few minutes, before closing the coffin. She had seemed so frail, old, and vulnerable, laid out like that, the life force gone. In her later years, he had thought of her as old and crotchety certainly, but in his mother there had never been any trace of the frail or the vulnerable. Sadness and pity for his mother welled up in him, feelings completely unfamiliar to him in his relationship with her when she was alive. Silently, he said a decade of the rosary for the repose of her soul, looking out the window of the mourning coach as he did so.

Did his mother have a happy marriage? Who knew? His father was a shadowy figure growing up, always working or in the pub, never around. Growing up, his whole concern had been his relationship with Ellen Sweeney as his mother. He never really considered or gave any thought to her as a person in her own right, with needs and hopes of her own. Selfish and juvenile, he thought sadly.

Perhaps the philosophy of life she had projected unto him, a philosophy of duties and obligations to be undertaken and met, was not part of her natural makeup at all. Maybe it had come about from her own experience of life. If she had taken another path, trapped in a lonely marriage, and gone and made another life for herself, what kind of childhood might it have been for him then? Certainly not the protected, cushioned one he had enjoyed.

What was it Oscar Wilde had said? "Children begin by loving their parents; as they grow older, they judge them; sometimes, they forgive them." With this new understanding and sympathy for his mother and her life came, inevitably, remorse. The phone calls he should have made and didn't. The times he should have spent with her, and somehow always managed to avoid. And what was he trying to avoid? The feeling of being stifled and repressed, which said as much about his own insecurities as his mother's possessiveness. His solution to the difficult relationship had been to run away to London after graduation. Avoidance, denial, proving to himself, but above all to his mother, that he was an adult. Marry a woman as unlike her as he could possibly find. Pursuing and marrying Deirdre had almost been like a compulsion. And when he found in the woman he married an absence of his mother's virtues of thrift and constancy, what was his response? To discuss his differences with Deirdre? No, to compensate by becoming a thief, and deluding himself that it was all done for love, when the truth of it was that the behaviour was driven out of his own emotional insecurities.

He murmured softly to himself, If you're in heaven now, Mother, looking down, have pity and forgive your unfortunate son. Even as he said it he knew what her answer would have been. You made your bed, Andrew, now you must lie in it. Indeed, I must, he thought. I'll be on a plane back to London in less than forty-eight hours. It's such a mess I have made with my life.

Stephen Denham watched from a discreet distance as Ellen Sweeney was laid to rest in Glasnevin Cemetery. The rain fell in sheets from leaden skies, and there was a bitter east wind off the Irish Sea, which chilled him to the bone. The last two days had been spent tracking Andrew Sweeney's movements and getting hopelessly lost in Dublin's one-way system while he tried to do it.

Following Sweeney around for the last two days and observing the overly elaborate rituals of an Irish funeral, it was hard not to feel sorry for the poor sod. He wasn't just a villain with a dishy wife, but somebody's bereaved son. Denham stood muffled in his parka in the shelter of an oak tree and watched as Andrew Sweeney and the other members of his family carried the coffin from the hearse to the graveside. Sweeney had no raincoat and was getting soaked as the mourners tried ineffectually to shield him with umbrellas.

It seemed to Denham that Sweeney had aged ten years in just a few days as he stood by the grave listening to the priest recite the prayers. Can't have been easy for you, you poor beggar, Denham thought, married to Deirdre Sweeney. I know the effect she has had on me, and if I were married to her, I would be crazy with jealousy.

Looking at him standing there, rain in rivulets running down his cheeks, Denham knew Maitland's concerns about Sweeney not returning to the UK were unfounded. Andrew Sweeney is not going to abandon his wife and child. And Christ, how much longer is this service going to go on? I'm going to get pneumonia out here.

That evening at seven o'clock, he watched Andrew Sweeney get on an Aer Lingus flight bound for Heathrow. He phoned in his confirmation to the surveillance team in London and boarded the next flight himself.

Chapter 28

They were waiting for him when he got off the plane. There was always a police checkpoint for flights from the Republic of Ireland. Unless there was an IRA flap on, it tended to be pretty perfunctory. Normally one bored-looking detective scanned the incoming passengers for signs of anyone or anything looking suspicious. Tonight there were three at the checkpoint, two of whom were obviously looking for him. They were clean-cut, and the two of them seemed awfully young. *I really am getting middle-aged,* he thought to himself.

'Mr. Andrew Sweeney?'

'Yes.'

'Would you mind coming with us, sir? There are a few questions we would like to ask you.'

The British, thought Andrew, *were invariably polite, even if they thought you were a crook.*

They led him through a winding maze of stairways to what was obviously an interrogation room. It was probably used by immigration. It was in the basement, and there was no natural light.

The detectives indicated a chair for him to sit on, but made no effort to question him. They were obviously waiting for someone. Andrew thought for ten minutes, and then decided he'd had enough.

'Well, gentlemen, what was it you wanted to ask me?'

'We are waiting on Detective Chief Inspector Maitland, sir. She will want to question you.'

'I have just come off a plane from burying my mother; I'm dead tired. Now, if you've got some questions, fine, but if not I'm going home to bed.'

The two detectives looked at each other uncertainly. 'I'm afraid we can't allow that, sir,' one of them said hesitantly.

'You're holding and arresting me, then. What am I charged with?'

It was clear they had received no instructions as to this eventuality. 'If you'll wait just one moment, sir.' One of them now had his back to the door. 'We will try to contact the Chief Inspector.'

Andrew met the man's gaze and held it. 'Why don't you do that.'

Maitland was already on her way to Heathrow and took the call on her car phone. She listened with irritation to the update from her sergeant and cursed under her breath at the London traffic, which was still moving at a snail's pace even though it was 8:30 p.m.

'Put me on the phone to him,' she said finally.

'Yes?'

'I hear, Mr. Sweeney, that you are not being very cooperative.'

'That's your point of view, Detective Chief Inspector,' Andrew replied. 'Your men met me off the plane and asked me to accompany them, as they have some questions. I have done that. Now they tell me they can't ask those questions. I'm supposed to sit around waiting for you, I gather. I'm tired. I've had a bad couple of days and I want to go home to bed.'

Maitland could hear the weariness in Sweeney's voice. But she was tired, too. And she'd had enough of tracking him across hell and back. 'Let me remind you, Mr. Sweeney, that you are a suspect in a major fraud investigation.'

Andrew stood his ground. 'Along with a couple of hundred other people, Inspector. If these questions are so urgent, please ask them. Otherwise, they can keep until tomorrow, unless, of course, you intend to charge me with something.'

'You are skating on very thin ice, Mr. Sweeney, and your attitude is not doing you any good at all.'

Andrew was not cowed. 'What questions do you have?'

'I make the rules, Mr. Sweeney, not you. When we conduct this interview, I intend it to be face to face, and Sergeant Denham will also be there.'

'Ah, the wife stealer,' Andrew answered. 'How could I have forgotten about him?'

I will strangle him with my bare hands, Maitland thought to herself. She had to brake suddenly to avoid rear-ending the car in front of her, which had stopped at a traffic light. *That is, if I don't kill myself first.*

'If you want to talk to me, Inspector, I'm happy to come to your offices anytime tomorrow morning after 8 a.m. Right now, though, unless your officers charge me with a crime, I'm leaving to go home. Oh, and just a minor point of correction, Chief Inspector. You don't make the rules. This is a parliamentary democracy. People's representatives make the rules, and you were sworn in to carry them out.'

'I'm well aware of my responsibilities, Mr. Sweeney, the main one being catching criminals and putting them behind bars. I expect you in my office at eight tomorrow morning. Let me further advise you that you are not to leave London without informing us and obtaining our approval. If you disregard this warning, it will, I assure you, result in the issuance of a warrant for your arrest. Am I making myself quite clear?'

'Perfectly, Detective Chief Inspector,' Andrew replied. 'I look forward to seeing you tomorrow morning. Now if you would just inform your colleagues that I am free to go?'

Chapter 29

At Ten Downing Street, Martin Housegood was having yet another of what seemed to be an interminable sequence of meetings with the wavering backbenchers of his own party. It was clear to him from these meetings that he had totally underestimated the impact Dora Heard's death was having on the Tory rank and file. The media coverage which had linked her death unequivocally with the government's policies was particularly damaging. There was still a group of six recalcitrant Tory MPs who were threatening to abstain. In vain it was pointed out to them that in a vote as close as this, an abstention was as good as a vote against their own party. Some did it out of fear of their constituency association and some out of conviction. They were two days away from the vote now, and still he hadn't managed to assemble a winning coalition.

The news was not all bad. The relentless public campaign by his cabinet ministers and himself, explaining the basis of the government's policy, was paying dividends in the public opinion polls. In two bruising weeks they had managed to cut the Labour lead from 20 percent to 7 percent, with a margin of error on either side of two percentage points. Public perception of his government now was not so much that they were out of touch with the plight of the common folk, but rather that what they were proposing was very bitter medicine. There was considerable uncertainty as to whether it was needed or indeed was the right course to pursue in the first place. The whole country, it seemed now, was engaged in the debate. Everyone had an opinion—economists, clergy, and of course, the media.

Housegood sighed to himself, *Well, win, lose or draw, at least I have them debating the right issues.*

There was a knock at the door of his office, and his private secretary entered. 'It's eight o'clock, Prime Minister. Major Price-Jones is here to see you.'

Housegood roused himself from reverie. 'Yes, of course, send him on in.'

In a calculated move, he set the tone for the meeting. He came around his desk and greeted Price-Jones at the doorway, pumping his hand vigorously. 'Ah, Jeffrey, very good of you to stop by. How is Margaret? I had a very interesting chat with her at the party conference last September.'

The response was gruff. 'Margaret is very well, thank you, Prime Minister.'

'Come in, sit down. Can I offer you some refreshment? Whisky perhaps? I have a very good Glenlivet.'

'Thank you all the same, Prime Minister, but if I could just have some mineral water.'

Martin Housegood experienced a sinking feeling. It was unheard of for Jeffrey Price-Jones to turn down vintage Scotch. He prepared the drinks himself, mineral water for the Major, a glass of Chablis for himself. *My alcohol consumption is certainly going off the charts,* he thought to himself. The two men sat facing each other in Queen Anne armchairs flanking the fireplace.

'Jeffrey, I might as well get right to it. Circumlocution will get me nowhere with a military man. I know you are having great reservations about this "No Confidence" motion, and I wanted the benefit of your perspective. I wanted the opportunity to explain in person the government's position.'

'You said there were a couple of things, Prime Minister?' Price-Jones sat well back in his armchair. Short and stout, his feet barely touched the floor.

'Yes, I'm aware you're coming up on thirty years of uninterrupted service as a Conservative member of Parliament, and of course I know you have indicated that you won't be seeking reelection. I thought it might be nice if there was some form of recognition of your lifetime of public service to the country both as a military man and as a member of the House of Commons.'

The Major was not to be drawn. 'Very flattering, I'm sure, Prime Minister.'

There was a silence; Housegood was forced to break it. 'Let's take the immediate issue first, Jeffrey. Where are you on the "No Confidence" motion?'

'Well, sir, as far as I'm concerned, there's no way I can vote with the government on this. The only issue in my mind is whether I will abstain or vote against. I have said as much to the Chief Whip, and I'm sure that's the reason for this meeting.'

'It's one reason, Jeffrey. It's a very serious matter for a member of Parliament to vote against his own government, his own party, on a "No Confidence" motion. I wanted to hear your reasons for contemplating such a course of action, face to face.'

Price-Jones was direct in his response. 'It's very simple, really. An old woman, the widow of a decorated war hero, died tragically. Her Majesty's Government policies are to blame for her death. This motion is bringing them to book for it.' The old man put down the glass of water he was playing with and looked Housegood squarely in the eye.

'I survived World War Two; I'm one of the lucky ones. I survived the Burma railroad and a Japanese prisoner-of-war camp, and countless thousands didn't. They gave their lives for this country. It doesn't sit well with me that the country's way of repaying them is to let their widows die of hypothermia.'

'That's grossly unfair, Jeffrey! Dora Heard's death was a tragic accident. It was no part of government policy to deprive her of the necessities of life. She died because there was poor management at the Metropolitan Electricity Board. It's as pure and simple as that.'

The Major was unyielding. 'I'm sorry, Prime Minister, but I see that poor woman's death as the unavoidable consequence of a pattern of neglect by this government, of the men and women in Her Majesty's armed forces and their dependents. You recollect that three times in the last six years I have sponsored a private members bill seeking to increase the benefits for services personnel, only to have no support from the front bench.'

Housegood had not been briefed about this. He decided to change tack. 'I'll grant you, Jeffrey, that we may have been remiss on that issue, but you will appreciate that we were elected on a platform of reducing government expenditures and rolling back punitive taxation levies caused by the Socialists.'

'I don't dispute that, Prime Minister, but you must appreciate that, as a survivor of the last war, I feel a responsibility for the dependents of those who did not come back. Call it survivors' guilt if you like. It's one of the reasons I entered Parliament thirty years ago. To make sure the country didn't forget the sacrifices those men and women made.'

'You realize, Jeffrey, that the government may fall, and your action would have contributed to that.'

The Major looked at him sadly. 'I realize that, Prime Minister. This is one of the most difficult decisions I have ever made in my life.'

'Would you at least abstain?'

'I'm a religious man, past my threescore and ten years. I'm expecting to meet my maker and comrades in arms quite soon now. I want to be able to look them in the eye. I will think about abstaining, Prime Minister. I understand the difficult position the government is in, believe me I do, but what this boils down to, in my mind, is a conflict between my responsibilities to the living and my loyalty to the dead.'

Housegood looked at him. What could he say? After half a minute, he reached over and grasped the Major by the hand. 'You do what your conscience tells you to do, Jeffrey. Let me handle the politics, and we'll manage somehow.'

The old man's eyes grew moist. 'Thank you, Prime Minister. I appreciate hearing that from you.'

'It's only politics, Jeffrey. If we didn't have rows like this from time to time, my job would get awfully boring.' Housegood decided to spare the Major any further emotional trauma. 'Well, Jeffrey, I'm sorry if I appear to be rushing you, but I have a meeting with the Foreign Secretary in about five minutes. Some problem in Belize.'

The Major collected himself. 'Yes, certainly, Prime Minister, I understand. Thank you for taking the time to see me.'

As soon as Major Price-Jones was gone, the Chief Whip stuck his head in the door. He had been waiting in an adjoining room. 'So how did it go with Colonel Blimp, Prime Minister?'

Housegood looked at him coolly. 'I don't think we will be able to count on Major Price-Jones's vote, Hugh. In fact, for planning purposes assume a vote against us.'

'Old fossil wouldn't budge, eh?'

'Major Price-Jones is a man of honour and principle, Hugh. Sometimes I forget that such people still do exist. A hazard of my job, I suppose. Whichever way this turns out, or however he votes, I plan to put him in for a life peerage.'

The Chief Whip looked at him, aghast.

'Oh, don't worry, Hugh, I'm not going soft in the head. Give me fifteen minutes with the Foreign Secretary, and then we can go over the latest vote tally.'

Chapter 30

Andrew Sweeney presented himself promptly at 8 a.m. at Detective Chief Inspector Elizabeth Maitland's office in Scotland Yard. She was there with Stephen Denham, who had been with her since six, briefing her about his trip to Ireland. As Denham briefed her, Maitland commented on what she perceived as his changed attitude towards Andrew. 'You seem to have come back with a much less jaundiced view of our friend, Mr. Sweeney, than the one you left England with, Stephen. Is it the benign influence of the Emerald Isle, I wonder, or something else?'

Denham was almost apologetic. 'I guess I'm not used to seeing villains in family situations. He could be just like you or me really, except for all this funny business he has cooked up.'

Maitland was understanding but unmoved. 'Most criminals aren't that much different from you or me, Stephen. They have similar feelings and impulses. What distinguishes them from us is that somewhere along the line they made a conscious decision to break the law. Andrew Sweeney isn't the Antichrist and he's not Albert Schweitzer either. He's an ordinary fellow who happens to have committed a crime. Our job as custodians of the law is to prove that he did it and to bring him to book. It doesn't do to get too emotional one way or the other about it.'

Denham shook his head ruefully. 'I guess I'm learning a lot from this case.'

'Most cases have a lot to teach. Whether that is wasted or not depends upon the individual's predisposition to learn from the experience.' As she spoke, she was methodically organizing Andrew Sweeney's file, preparing for the upcoming interview.

'Oh, I forgot to ask, what happened with the handwriting specimen?' Denham asked.

Maitland grimaced with disgust. 'A number of points of similarity but nothing conclusive. Any competent defense barrister would demolish it as evidence in two minutes flat.'

Once the interview with Andrew began, Maitland wasted no time on pleasantries. 'Mr. Sweeney, you remember my Detective Sergeant, Stephen Denham?'

'Good morning, Detective Chief Inspector.' Andrew ignored Denham.

'At our last interview, Mr. Sweeney, we discussed your financial circumstances and how you manage to maintain a quite expensive lifestyle on a systems analyst's salary. You said that your income was being supplemented from the estate of your aunt, Bridget Reilly. It may interest you to learn that my Sergeant has just returned from Ireland, having made enquiries to verify your statement. We were surprised to discover that the late Mrs. Reilly's estate amounted to no more than seventy thousand Irish pounds. The sum is clearly not sufficient to explain your current lifestyle. Moreover, it would appear, based on this information, that you have intentionally misled us in a criminal inquiry. I must ask you again, Mr. Sweeney, to provide a much more satisfactory explanation of your financial situation.'

Andrew Sweeney had regarded her impassively throughout this recital, his legs crossed, apparently quite relaxed.

'Your sergeant's information is quite accurate, Detective Chief Inspector, so far as it goes. My aunt's assets in Ireland, after death duties, amounted to seventy-four thousand Irish pounds, as you have indicated. But those were only her assets in Ireland.'

'Her assets,' Maitland repeated slowly, 'in Ireland.'

'Yes. My aunt was the beneficiary in her turn of, shall we say, a large gift from her brother Michael Reilly, a bar owner from Cleveland in the United States. Prior to his death, he transferred some five hundred thousand dollars to a Swiss bank account, making her the beneficiary. Interest on the principal from the gift was transferred to her building society account in Ireland on a predetermined schedule by the Swiss banking authorities. Some years ago, she made me a joint signatory on her account. She did this so that I could continue to receive the financial benefit after her death.'

'Why didn't you tell us all of this before?' Maitland asked sharply. 'Even if I believe it, which I do not.'

Andrew shrugged. 'With respect, Detective Chief Inspector, I cannot help what you choose to believe or not believe. The reason I was not forthcoming is that, from a tax point of view, it was a somewhat irregular arrangement. As I told you in our last interview, I may have declared all income from any source on my tax return and paid appropriate tax to the British authorities on it, but whether my uncle paid tax in the United States on the gift is something about which I would prefer not to speculate. If you check on his estate when he died, you will find that it amounted to no more than one hundred thousand dollars. Were you to do some further checking, however, you would discover that five years ago Michael Reilly settled a dispute with the Internal Revenue Service for back taxes and penalties of a quarter of a million dollars. Uncle

Michael was from the school of thought that accepted death as inevitable but taxes as not. There is also the possibility of a liability to the Irish authorities from the estate of my aunt. There you have it. If you want to report me to either tax jurisdiction, you are, of course, quite within your rights to do so.'

Maitland threw her pen down. 'I don't give a damn, Mr. Sweeney, about your taxes, and I don't believe one word of this cock and bull story you have just spun! As far as I'm concerned, you're my prime suspect for the fraud perpetrated at the Metropolitan Electricity Board. I know you did it, and I'm going to prove it!'

Andrew kept his face blank as he watched Maitland struggle to regain her composure. 'Allowing for one fanciful moment, Mr. Sweeney, that this latest stipulation is true, would you care to share with us the name of the Swiss bank and the account number where this munificent gift from your late uncle is lodged?'

'At this point, Detective Chief Inspector,' Andrew answered coolly, 'I feel I have answered more than enough questions. If you want to charge me, go ahead. Otherwise, I have a job that I'm late for. That is, of course, if I still have it after all the obvious attention I've been receiving from the police.'

Denham, who had been standing quietly in the back of the room during this exchange, looked at his superior. She gave an imperceptible shake of the head. 'For the moment, Mr. Sweeney, you are free to go. Do not, however, attempt to leave London.'

Andrew rose, nodded towards her and walked briskly out the door. As it closed behind him, Maitland put her head on her chest and closed her eyes. She remained immobile like that for some minutes after his departure. Eventually she looked up at Denham.

'He's one of the coolest customers I've ever come across. Of course he knows that getting proof against him from the gnomes of Zurich is a chicken-and-egg situation. They won't breach client confidentiality unless we can prove he has committed a crime. And we can't prove that unless they break client confidentiality. Well, we know his building society number in Ireland. From them we can get the name of the Swiss bank that's originating the wire transfers. I then have to put the wheels in motion to see if we can't get some sort of cooperation from the Swiss. That will be a slow and tedious business.'

Her eyes narrowed. She pressed her lips and thought. Then she said, 'I have become fixated on chasing the money trail to the exclusion of all else. We need to step back, Stephen. We need to go back over all the work that the internal audit at the Metropolitan Electricity Board has done. Before we were working with an enormous field of suspects. We focused on chasing the money angle as the only practical way of narrowing it down. Well now, we have it narrowed down to one suspect. Go over all the ground again, assuming that Andrew Sweeney is the one responsible. He has to have left some trace somewhere of how he did it.' She smiled at him wearily. 'It's frustrating, I know, but we need to remember the progress we have made. We have our man. Now we just have to tie him to the crime. I need to brief the Chief Superintendent.'

'Why didn't you charge him?' Denham asked curiously.

Maitland shook her head resignedly. 'Because at this point everything we have on him is circumstantial. Oh, there is a postal worker who would probably say that he might have been the man she saw, but then so might a million other people. He had the opportunity to commit the crime. He had the means and the know how to do so. There are some serious questions concerning how he finances his lifestyle. Set against all that is the fact that he is a model citizen. He has no priors. He doesn't even have a speeding ticket, for god's sake. He's provided us with an explanation of his financial situation. We may think it's a load of codswallop, but it's for us to refute. We have our suspicions and our conviction that he did it. If you're relying on circumstantial evidence to gain you a conviction, there has to be an irrefutable chain leaving only one possible conclusion, and we are nowhere near that. Oh, I could charge him, we have enough for that. An arrest would certainly get the Chief Superintendent off my back. We would be betting, however, that we could nail things down before the case came to trial. Nine out of every ten arrests I have made in my career have gone on to win a conviction. That's been so because I'd make my case before I'd make an arrest. This fraud may be high visibility and lots of pressure, but I'm not going to change my style just because of that.'

It was a much longer explanation than Denham had expected or indeed imagined he was entitled to. Maitland seemed, however, to have taken the opportunity to rationalize the position to herself as much as anything else.

The moment of reflection passed. 'Well, what are you waiting for, Sergeant? You've got your marching orders, so get on with it. Keep me posted.'

****

As Andrew Sweeney rode the tube back to the Metropolitan Electricity Board, his mood was one of resignation. This is the end game, he thought. They know it's me. It's only a matter of time before they prove it. I'm going to need to tell Deirdre soon, tonight or tomorrow. Still he procrastinated. He recoiled from the prospect of shattering forever the domestic harmony he had enjoyed for so long. Even so, a small part of him couldn't help playing the role of a detached observer to his predicament. You weren't so convinced that you had a life of domestic bliss before you're confronted with the imminent prospect of losing it. He bit his lip and tasted blood. Whatever happens, I swear to God, I will tell her by the weekend, he promised himself.

Chapter 31

Martin Housegood had gotten his wish: the debate waged in the public mind by the two political parties was squarely about the role Britain should play in the postindustrial age.

What was needed for the country to be competitive in the global economy? How was it to provide prosperity for all of its citizens? Neither party seriously questioned the need for improved competitiveness. What was at issue was how it could be achieved. The conservative government's model was a classic free-market approach. British industry, privatized and deregulated, would be forced to adapt and have to compete globally with little or no government support or intervention. The Conservatives argued passionately that any measures the government might take to shield British industry from the full effect of competition were merely postponing the day of reckoning. That to do so would be to further drain the nation's resources, rather than facing up to what was going to be needed long term to achieve wealth creation. The Labour Party argued for a social contract between government, labour, and business, which would seek to manage the process of change and cushion the social impact of the needed transition.

Housegood's strategy of fashioning the debate around the government's vision rather than allowing the opposition to castigate it for its tactics was successful in reducing the Conservative Party deficit in the opinion polls. On the eve of the debate, it had been slashed from twenty to four percentage points. As he had surmised, improved support at the grassroots level for the government resulted in significantly reducing the number of dissident backbenchers in his own party. That was the good news. On the other hand, the Ulster Unionists, confronted with a Tory Prime Minister who was adamantly opposed to doing a deal with them, had decided to vote to abstain, knowing it would bring the government down. They calculated that, in the ensuing general election, there was the strong chance of a hung parliament, which would give them the balance of power and a significantly improved negotiating position. Worst case, a Labour Prime Minister could be no more difficult to deal with than the current Tory incumbent. This left the outcome of the vote hanging on four or five members of Parliament who remained undecided going into the debate. Housegood found himself in the unfamiliar position for the first time since becoming Chief Whip and then Prime Minister of being unable to predict the outcome of a Commons vote.

As was usual with set piece spectacles of this kind, the debate had moments of high drama contrasted with periods of unremitting tedium. The passionately articulate competed with the self-important or the uninformed for their few minutes in the sun. Through it all, hour after hour, Martin Housegood stayed in his place. He seemed composed, unfazed, his usual Commons persona intact. Only occasionally did he offer any evidence of agitation. Once was when Robert Petrie rose to speak early on the second day. Petrie, looking pale and a little distraught, spoke extemporaneously to a hushed and silent house.

'Madam Speaker, I have served for the last three years as member for my constituency of Putney. My political views and my convictions have always had a rational basis. I have always recognized how our deliberations here affected people's lives. Until a few weeks ago, I must confess, I never fully understood what that meant. Then I met Dora Heard. On one level, she was just one more constituent with a problem. On another, she brought home to me in a way I had never experienced before the scale of my responsibilities as an elected representative. I cannot help but believe that Dora Heard is dead because of what we did or failed to do in this House.'

There was a rumble of dissent from the conservative benches, quelled by a sharp glance from the Speaker.

'Merely because a course of action appeals to reason as being the correct one to take, one cannot pursue it without giving sufficient consideration to the impact on the lives of the ordinary men and women of this country. No doubt this is obvious to many of the members in this chamber. For me, however, it has been a lesson lately learned. I understand the thrust and direction of my party's policies. I understand that Britain has to change. However, I have come to believe in the last few weeks that in its current policies, the price the government is asking of some of our citizens, such as the disadvantaged or the elderly, is too high. In a single-minded pursuit of material prosperity, we risk losing our soul. The unhappy fate of my constituent Dora Heard has made this painfully clear to me. Given that this is what now my conviction, I cannot in conscience vote with my party in this debate.'

Robert Petrie sat down to silence. Every member present knew that he had just committed political suicide. The debate would be wound up by Fred Graves, leader of the opposition, followed by Martin Housegood as the last speaker. The media focused much attention on the contrasting parliamentary styles of the two men. Graves was a powerful and eloquent orator. Housegood, on the other hand, was a cool, precise logician. His speeches invariably read much better after the fact than when he delivered them.

Graves delivered his concluding remarks with typical verve: 'This debate is about the soul of the nation. This government sees the issue merely as a matter of commerce. Truly for them, Britain is a nation of shopkeepers, and that is all we are. The only measure of our strength or of our worth as a nation is expressed in balance sheets and profit and loss statements. The Tories yearn for a new class hierarchy, a wealthy privileged few, an oligarchy of business moguls existing in a separate society from the rest of the population. This, Madam Speaker, is a recipe for divisiveness and despair.'

The rousing oration brought the opposition benches to their feet, roaring their antagonism at the Tory benches opposite. The Speaker, long since hoarse from trying to keep order in the debate, managed eventually to restore some semblance of decorum.

Seemingly unaffected by the hubbub around him, Martin Housegood rose to close the debate for the government. The opening was unremarkable: cool, balanced, factual, vintage Housegood. He recounted the long decline in British competitiveness since the Second World War. He contrasted the country's recent performance with that of other developed Western nations and also the burgeoning economies of Southeast Asia. The opposition benches were derisory, his own restive. As was his custom, he read from notes, reading glasses perched on the tip of his nose. Unlike Fred Graves, who looked as if he'd been serving pints behind the counter of a pub on a hot summer's day, Housegood was impeccably dressed. Just as people thought he was beginning to wind up his remarks, Housegood did something very unusual for him. He put away his notes, removed his glasses, and gripped the ballot box with both hands, staring directly in front of him at the opposition.

'My right honorable friend has accused us of framing this debate purely in financial terms, seeing it only in terms of balance sheets and profit and loss statements. This debate is not about that. It is about the hopes and dreams we have for the young people of this country, for our children and our grandchildren. Our world is changing. Daily it grows smaller and more competitive. We must come to terms with the new order, not because it is easy or we like it, but because we *must*. If we fail to do this, all that confronts the next generation is a future of declining living standards and reduced opportunity.

'Every parent hopes for a better life for their children. It is innate to work and sacrifice to make this a reality. Britain built an empire and for a time was the most powerful nation on earth because of our trading prowess. We need to recover and reignite that entrepreneurial zest. I am under no illusion as to what I'm asking the people of this country to do. I am asking them to change their ideas about education, work, pay, and benefits. That is difficult. Above all, I am asking them to change behavior and to become more in tune with the realities of living in a global village. I am asking them to do this for the sake of those who will come after us.' Housegood had the attention of his audience. Members stopped shuffling their order papers and there was a lull now in the heckling from the opposition benches.

Housegood's normally deep voice rose half an octave. Was he trembling? He continued. 'We can resist change, pine nostalgically for the good old days, mortgage the future by subsidizing the inefficient present. But change and the pace of change is relentless and insistent. We must embrace it or we will be swept away by it. Madam Speaker, this debate is about whether we fashion for ourselves and for our children a future of hope and opportunity, or one of melancholy and regret. It is a rallying cry to the nation to gird ourselves for competition and all that it entails. We will win the debate in this chamber. More importantly, we are winning it in the hearts and minds of the British people. Let us, then, have the vote, stiffen our resolve, and make a great beginning.'

An astute observer would have noted that on several occasions Martin Housegood appeared to be speaking directly to his wife, who was watching him from the visitors' gallery. When Housegood concluded his remarks, there was uproar again in the House. This time the Tories were jubilant.

At last the division was called. The MPs surged into the division lobbies. As Housegood walked through, he found Major Price-Jones at his side. 'I decided to cast my vote for the living, Martin,' Price-Jones said. It was a decisive ballot. The government won by 321 to 319. Once the result was officially tallied and announced, Housegood was surrounded by well-wishers.

His wife had somehow managed to get through to him in the crush. They embraced. As he kissed her cheek, he murmured, 'I'm exhausted. Help me away from here, Mary, or I fear I shall cry.' She gave him a fierce hug and whispered back, 'My husband is an old-fashioned romantic, but it will be our little secret.' Then firmly and courteously, her arm linked in his, she guided him through the crowded corridors out to his waiting car.

The next morning, Martin Housegood had a face-to-face meeting with Robert Petrie, their first since the Metropolitan Electricity Board affair had blown up. Housegood had regained his normal demeanour, cool and detached.

Robert Petrie was somewhat tentative. 'Good morning, Prime Minister. You asked to see me.'

'Yes, Mr. Petrie. I felt we needed a conversation about your future.'

'It would be inappropriate of me, I suppose, to congratulate you on your success, Prime Minister.' Petrie was sitting across the desk from Housegood, his body twisted sideways in the chair.

'Given the way you voted, Mr. Petrie, it would be, yes. Let us be clear with each other. You are a man of delicate conscience, given to introspection. In this recent affair, you came to grips with what it means to be a public representative. I have formed these impressions from your public statements and from your contributions in the debate. From where I sit, as your Prime Minister, this voyage of self-discovery and awareness on which you have embarked has been at the party's expense.'

Petrie, like a condemned man, listened as Housegood vented.

'You were adopted as the Conservative candidate for Putney. You ran on our manifesto. You were elected. You did not run as an independent. On matters of government policy, and particularly when there is a three-line whip, the party has the right to expect that you will support it. You are a man of conscience, Mr. Petrie, but these are challenging times when what is required is a national resolve. Given where the country stands right now, I have concluded that you are a luxury the party cannot afford. I have spoken to your constituency association chairman. You will not be adopted as Conservative candidate for Putney at the next election. Let me be clearer still. While I am leader of this party, you have no political future as a Conservative.'

Petrie listened attentively throughout. He sighed. And spoke. 'Thank you, Prime Minister, for your candor. I fully expected that this would be the inevitable outcome of the vote I cast. It comes as no surprise. I cannot agree with your assessment, however, that individual conscience has no part to play in the decisions an elected representative makes. "My party right or wrong" is not a maxim I wish to live by.'

Petrie smiled. He was exhausted, and yet strangely exhilarated, too. 'I have given considerable thought to what I wish to do with my life. I have determined to resign my seat in Parliament. I will be applying for the Chiltern Hundreds.'

If Housegood was surprised, he gave no indication of being so.

'I have decided that I should like to be a teacher,' Robert Petrie continued. 'You talked very eloquently last night, Prime Minister, about wishing to make a better life for those who come after us. Each one of us must consider how best to make his contribution to that better life. You will do it in your way and I hope to do it in mine.'

Housegood looked at him appraisingly. 'I think, Robert, you will make a very good teacher. Indeed, if Mary and I had been so fortunate as to have had children, we would have been lucky to entrust them to your care.'

He got up and walked around to shake Petrie's hand. 'I wish you every success with your future career.'

Petrie stood uncertainly for a moment, then turned and walked quickly out the door.

When Housegood's private secretary came in some minutes later to remind him of his next appointment, he found him still standing, staring at the door through which his visitor had departed.

Chapter 32

Across the river at the board meeting of the Metropolitan Electricity Board, Chaddick Spencer was getting reamed in front of the directors. The chairman, Sir Peter Winthrop, was leading the charge.

'I reiterate, Mr. Spencer, that to implement a policy of arbitrarily cutting people off from their power supply because of non-payment was a socially irresponsible act on your part,' Winthrop said.

Spencer sat at the other end of the long boardroom table from Winthrop, enveloped in cigar smoke. 'That's horseshit. You guys hired me to run a business. We have a commodity, electricity. We have customers who pay for that commodity. If you don't pay, you don't get the juice. Very simple.'

'Mr. Spencer. People died because of this policy.'

Spencer let a bit of ash fall onto the table. Winthrop couldn't tell if it was an accident or not.

'What they died of was cold, not the policy,' Spencer said. 'All of them got their notice for non-payment. We have practices in place whereby if people contact us and say they can't pay their bill, we work out some kind of planned payment schedule for them. These people didn't pay their bill and they didn't contact us, so they got cut off.'

'These are not automotive parts you're selling, Mr. Spencer,' another exasperated director chimed in. 'Electricity is a basic service. People are entitled to access to basic services.'

'That, fella, may be a good social policy, but it's a lousy way to run a business,' Spencer retorted with a snort of derision.

Peter Stephenage of Guthroyd's, which was a major shareholder, took a different tack. He was relishing taking his revenge for the cavalier treatment Spencer had meted out to him. 'Mr. Spencer, in four months the share price of Metropolitan Electricity Board stock has declined by over thirty percent. This happened while you were its managing director. Let the arguments of my fellow directors be what they may, I can assure you, sir, that from where I sit, a decline of that magnitude is no way to run a business.'

Spencer put down his cigar, stood up, and grabbed both sides of the table. 'Shortly after I took this job I came to you guys with a strategy for transforming this utility company from a government-run, public sector backwater into a profitable business. What I outlined for you was sound strategy then, and it's sound strategy now. We've had some problems with execution, but I'm not going to come in here and grovel, asking for forgiveness for my performance. This company needed overhauling. I figured out what had to be done. I set about doing it. It was change or die. The change turned out to be a lot more painful than any of us bargained for. In my book, that's just too damn bad.'

Stephenage was totally unimpressed; moreover, his temper was not improved by the forlorn efforts of the elderly director to his left to find a functioning hearing aid. He'd brought a handful to the meeting, and apparently none of them worked to his satisfaction.

The elderly gentleman kept banging the devices on the table, which caused them to emit a high-pitched whine. 'New-fangled gadgets,' the old man muttered. 'I don't know why I'm paying these medical men. I'd be better off with an ear trumpet.'

Stephenage tried to ignore the interruption. 'Mr. Spencer, saying that the strategy was fine apart from a few execution hiccups is like asking, "Apart from that, Mrs. Lincoln, how was the play?"'

Spencer rose to his feet. His chair fell backwards. His eyes were wild. 'I have had it with this crap,' he said. 'You guys say you wanted a commercially run business. You have your wishbone where your backbone should be. I've done the best I could. I'm not making any apologies. If you don't like it, you can kiss my ass.'

'We can do *what* with his ass?' the deaf director asked blankly.

At the other end of the table, the chairman had also reached the end of his patience. 'I think we have heard quite enough, gentlemen. I should like to propose we terminate the contract for employment of Mr. Chaddick Spencer as managing director of the Metropolitan Electricity Board. Do I have a second?'

'Seconded.' It was Peter Stephenage. 'All those in favor say aye.' Ayes filled the room.

'Passed unanimously,' the chairman said crisply. 'Secretary will record it for the minutes. Mr. Spencer, the board finds it no longer requires your services. Please be good enough to vacate the premises at your earliest convenience.'

Spencer was already gathering up his papers. 'And fuck you, too, buddy. I'm out of here, but you guys had better honour what's in my contract, or I will slap a lawsuit on you so fast your head will spin.'

Half an hour later in his office, chatting with Brett Johnson, Chaddick Spencer reveled in re-hashing the meeting. 'Went head to head with those guys and had a hell of a time. Managed to get a rise out of a couple of them.

But let's face it, they were a pretty constipated bunch. Forced them to fire me. They would have preferred, of course, that I take the British way out and resign. Hey, but nobody ever said I was gentleman. I'm sorry to have to tell you this, hot shot, but I guess you're next on the chopping block.'

Johnson smiled at him. 'I don't think I needed to go to college to figure that out, Chaddick. Anyway, thanks for not throwing me to the wolves.'

'You are being too kind to them, boy. At least wolves have teeth. All this crew would be able to do is gum you to death. Look me up when you get back to the States. I don't imagine you'll have much luck finding a job on this side of the pond.'

'What's next for you?' Johnson asked.

'I-guess I'll have to tell the little woman the good news.'

Chaddick Spencer's wife was arranging flowers in a Waterford crystal vase when he bounded through the door.

'Hi, honey, I'm home! Guess what? Got my ass fired today. You had best start packing the China. We are going back home. I'm going to need to sign on for unemployment. Oh, and about tea with Lord Melchum? I guess we can scratch that.' There was the sound of shattering glass.

Chapter 33

It was the same afternoon. Peter Spencer stopped by Andrew Sweeney's desk in a state of high excitement. 'I have figured it out, guy. I think I have nailed the bastard!'

Andrew, who had been staring vacantly at his terminal, tried to focus on what his assistant was saying. 'Figured out what, Peter? Nailed who?'

'The fraud thing, guv'nor. The internal audit boys were down in my cubicle again this morning back on their old kick. How was it done? I'm surprised they didn't talk to you about it. At first I was just pissed. We had been over this ground with them three weeks ago. But then I got to thinking. Whoever did it had to have changed the production link library when we cut over to the new system. He had to program the linkage editor to link in the subroutines with the dodgy code. The new version control software will have a record of all changes made to the link map and the user ID of whoever made them. They've secured the production library, so I don't have security access, but the internal audit boys do.'

It was as if he had been stabbed in the stomach. *Dear God, he's right*, Andrew thought despairingly. *I did have to change the link map to pull in the assembler subroutines. I'd forgotten all about it.*

Andrew struggled desperately to appear unconcerned. 'A good thought, Peter. You might very well have something there. So you're off to the internal audit boys on the third floor, then?'

'Yeah, see if my little bit of sleuthing pays off.' Spencer was excited at the prospect.

'Could I ask you to drop this report off to Brett Johnson? It's on your way and he's expecting it. It's an estimate of effort for a couple of emergency fixes they need made to the billing system.'

While Peter stood uncertainly, Andrew picked up the phone. 'Mr. Johnson? Andrew Sweeney here. Yes, I have the estimates you asked for. I'm sending down my assistant Peter Spencer with them right now. Yes. He will be able to explain the estimates to you.'

Peter gave him a startled look.

Andrew continued his conversation. 'Yes, Mr. Johnson, I've been running those tests on the last batch of changes. I will let you know how we're doing just as soon as the results are in.' He put down the phone.

'Don't worry, Peter; all it is, is some pretty basic estimate of effort stuff. Nothing earth shattering. Just read the memo on your way down and you'll be in fine shape when you see him. Then you should take your hunch on the fraud matter to the internal audit.' Spencer seemed a bit disoriented, but willing to do as he was asked. He took the memorandum he was being offered and wandered off, slowly perusing it.

As soon as Peter Spencer was out of sight, Andrew Sweeney grabbed his coat and hurried to the elevators. He descended two floors and went quickly to the computer operations area. He let himself in with his identity badge. Jack Forbes, the operator, was at his desk.

'Hi Andrew. What brings you here?'

'Oh, I need a tape from the tape library with some old testing conditions, Jack. The tea trolley was on the floor when I was coming in.'

Andrew held his breath.

'Bloody marvellous and I'm stuck in here,' Forbes answered.

'Well, if you want to get something, I can keep an eye on things, Jack.'

Forbes looked at him gratefully. 'Christ, thanks, mate. I could murder a Scotch egg right now. Won't be long.'

Forbes raced off in search of the tea trolley. He could not have been gone five minutes but it was more than enough time for Andrew to enter some commands at the console and then go and retrieve a tape at random from the tape library to justify the purpose of his visit.

'Got it, Jack,' he said, as Forbes returned. 'I wonder if you could mount it for me and start the program running. It's kind of a rush job.'

Forbes looked longingly at his Scotch egg and cup of coffee. 'Sure thing, Andrew. We will crank it up right now.' Andrew stuck around just long enough to see Forbes mount the tape and execute the command to run the program, the name of which he had provided.

It was a cool afternoon when he left the building, but he found himself covered in sweat, coupled with the feeling of nausea and breathlessness. He hurried to the tube station to make his way home. He wasn't out of the building five minutes before the whole Metropolitan Electricity Board computer system shut down. The program he had asked Jack Forbes to execute was written in assembler. It overwrote base registers and was designed to corrupt core memory, causing a fatal protection error which would shut the system down.

The operations of the company were instantly paralyzed. Engineers in the field, customers at the district office, the centralized billing and account maintenance function, all ground to a halt. One group affected was the internal audit. Stephen Denham, Parker Williams, head of internal audit, and Peter Spencer were crowded around the now disabled terminal. Peter had just finished outlining his theory to the two other men, and they had commenced a search of the version control system.

Denham was frustrated. 'Ah fuck it, now what's the problem?' The head of internal audit seemed mildly irritated at the profanity. They had to wait several minutes before anybody at computer operations would answer the phone. Williams listened to the agitated explanation being given at the other end of the line. He put down the phone and looked at the other two men. 'It appears we've had a total systems crash. We have to re-IPL the system. It shouldn't take more than about twenty minutes. Very unusual really, scarcely ever happens. Not like ten years ago. The system software is that much more robust. It's four o'clock now. Why don't we reconvene, say, in twenty minutes? I've got a few phone calls I need to make.' He looked expectantly at his visitors, willing them to leave.

He probably wants to phone his book maker, Denham thought with irritation. He took the opportunity to brief Elizabeth Maitland on the situation and the possibility they had of a breakthrough. She was excited.

'Christ, Stephen, I hope this lead plays out like you think. We could do with some luck on this case. I'll stay in my office by the phone. Let me know just as soon as they have the system back up and you've checked the audit trail.'

They reassembled expectantly at 4:20 p.m., and the system was still not up. Nor was it up a half hour later. Losing patience, they went down to the operations room, where the scene was chaos. There was a cluster of people around the master console. The chief operator was keying away furiously with spectators standing around him, arguing and gesticulating. Telephones rang off the hook. There was another cluster of people outside the operations room peering through the glass partition, shaking their heads, and talking urgently together.

'Detective Sergeant Stephen Denham, Scotland Yard,' Goodchild said, waving his badge at the people in front of the operators console. 'What is going on here?'

The operator looked up. 'We can't re-IPL the system. It won't accept the password.'

'What do you mean it won't accept the password? What is it?' Denham asked.

'For today it's PATERNOSTER. There are a few supervisory functions active. I've been able to access the data set which contains the password. It looks exactly the same as it did this morning. I key in PATERNOSTER and the system won't accept it. I'm buggered if I know what's going on.'

Chapter 34

Deirdre was at home when he got there. 'You're home early, Andrew. Is anything the matter?' She was seated in an armchair in the living room, reading a copy of *Cosmopolitan*.

He knelt down in front of her and took both of her hands in his. 'Deirdre, there's no easy way to tell you this, so I'm just going to say it. This fraud at the Metropolitan Electricity Board, I'm the one responsible. I have been embezzling money from them for years. Everything I told you about an inheritance from my aunt Bridget, that was all a lie. It's been Electricity Board money all along. The police have found out. They suspect it's me. Soon they will have the proof. They will be here looking for me in a couple of hours.' He slumped backwards, his head on his chest.

She looked at her husband uncomprehendingly. 'What are you trying to tell me, Andrew? You made some sort of mistake at work?'

He looked at her desperately. 'No Deirdre, not a mistake. I have committed fraud. I've committed a crime. God, there's so little time to make you understand.'

She looked at him incredulously.

'But why, Andrew? In god's name, why?'

He looked up at her. 'Because we couldn't seem to get by on what I was making, Deirdre, and I couldn't stand the thought of losing you.'

Deirdre was bewildered. 'But what possessed you to think you were going to lose me, Andrew? Yes, we had our financial problems. What young married couple doesn't?'

'I knew you weren't in love with me when you married me, Deirdre. You liked me certainly, but you weren't in love with me. I was a way for you to get out of Dublin and to get away from the monotony and claustrophobia of the place.'

She was looking at him, expressions of hurt, disbelief, and bafflement playing across her face. Tears glistened in her eyes. 'Andrew, you thought I married you because I saw you as a meal ticket out of Dublin? Have you never understood that I loved you then and I love you now, fifteen years later?'

It was his turn to look confused. 'But all the men you flirted with over the years; I don't care to think what else.'

She held his hands tightly. 'Oh Andrew, Andrew. I'm so sorry to have hurt you. I thought you understood. I flirt, yes. I like men to find me attractive, but that's my insecurity. I need constant reassurance that I'm still desirable. These men are not in love with me, Andrew. I know that. They're in lust with a post-adolescent fantasy. I'm not a real person to most of them. But I'm real to you, Andrew. I always have been. I know that. You love me no matter what I look like in the morning. You love me whether my hair is up in curlers or perfectly coiffed. Don't you understand how reassuring that is to a woman to know that she's loved for herself and not because she looks glamorous or can make amusing conversation?'

'I thought if I didn't give you a decent lifestyle, you would walk out on me,' he blurted.

She was crying openly. 'I can't comprehend it, the years we have known each other, lived with each other, and we've never understood each other at all,' she sobbed. Deirdre pulled a handkerchief from her sleeve and dried her eyes.

'This won't do, won't do at all,' she said, pulling herself together. 'You're in trouble with the police, and we must think of something.'

'Do you want me to give myself up?'

She looked at him astonished. 'Give yourself up? You must be crazy, Andrew Sweeney. If I had one complaint about our married life together, it was that I found you too stable and reliable. Secretly, I have longed for a little adventure. Now I find I've been married fifteen years to a twentieth-century pirate and never even knew it. Where are the ill-gotten gains?'

'In a numbered account in Switzerland,' he answered sheepishly.

'Unbelievable! This kind of thing only happens in the movies. We must get you away from here, out of the country.'

'It's no use, Deirdre. They'll be watching all the ports of exit.'

'Yes, yes, I know,' she answered impatiently. 'They will be watching for an Andrew Sweeney, but it's not an Andrew Sweeney that's going to leave.'

'I don't understand you, Deirdre.'

'Let me see.' She grabbed a copy of the *Irish Times* that was lying on the coffee table and flipped quickly to the 'What's On' column. 'Yes there it is. I thought I remembered it. There's a U2 concert in Dublin, and this, Andrew dearest, is Cheltenham week. It's going to be a zoo on the ferries. So much the better. Now we don't have much time. You need a Skinhead haircut and an outfit of black leather. You, Andrew, are going to become a middle aged U2 fan going across to Dublin for the concert. Even your poor dead mother wouldn't recognize you. How long did you say we've got before the police come?'

'An hour maybe. Two at the most.'

She seemed positively buoyant now. 'Okay, take a sheet off the bed, take it into the kitchen, lay it on the floor. Spread it out well. Put a chair in the middle and sit on it.'

'What are you going to do?'

'One of the few advantages of having to work in a hairdressing salon as a teenager in order to get enough money for the disco is that I know how to shave heads. Half an hour will have you bald as a billiard ball. Now I need to make a phone call.'

She picked up the phone and put it down again. 'No, the police will check the calls out of here. I'll use the public phone box. Get things organized, Andrew. I'll be back in ten minutes. I need to find an outfit for you.'

Leaving him still kneeling on the floor, she grabbed her purse and raced out the door.

She hurried to the phone booth. It was unoccupied. 'Hi, Margaret. Deirdre Sweeney here. Yes, it was a great night at the drama society. Listen dear, something of a rush. Andrew and I got invited to a fancy dress. We've decided to go all out. We're going as a couple of middle-aged band groupies.'

There was a roar of laughter from the other end of the phone.

'Yes, I know. Isn't it a hoot? Anyway, Andrew needs an outfit. Something in black leather. Could you manage something like that for us? Great, Margaret! You're a love. I'll send him on over. He should be there in about three quarters of an hour. Yes, it's tonight. I'll be sure and give you all the gossip tomorrow. Cheers, bye!' She wrote an address down on a slip of paper.

When she got back to the apartment Andrew was sitting in the middle of the kitchen floor just as he had been instructed. 'Okay. When we finish cutting your hair you need to go to this address. It's on the High Street. Ask to see Margaret French. She will provide the gear. They provide all the costumes for the drama society. Also, I checked on the sailing from Holyhead tonight. There are a few places left, not many. There's a travel agent two doors down from the costumers. Book yourself a ticket and pay cash.'

She was clipping his hair as she talked. 'The train leaves Euston Station at nine tonight. I will grab some mail from the downstairs apartment. It's for Fleming, but he's been gone for six months now. You won't need to show a passport at Holyhead, but the police might be checking ID, so the mail could come in handy. '

Andrew was dumbfounded. 'Deirdre, you think of everything.'

'Amateur dramatics. Keeps you on your toes.'

Within half an hour she had completely shaved his head. Together they quickly packed some toiletries, a change of clothes, and some underwear for him. Feeling self-conscious, he put on a cloth cap. Standing at the door, he looked at her sadly.

Deirdre was having none of it. 'We don't have time for the sentimental bit, Andrew. You need to get away. Where will you go?'

'I won't be able to stay in Ireland. It's too small a place. It would only be a matter of time before they found me. I need to go overseas; the States, I think.'

She was fussing over him, turning up the collar of his raincoat against the cold outside. 'Just make sure you don't get caught, Andrew Sweeney. When you've managed to work something out, send for me and Michael.'

He looked at her, startled. 'But Deirdre, I will be a fugitive. What kind of a life will you have?'

'I will have no kind of life if I can't be with you,' she answered simply. 'If you love me, Andrew, and I know you do, make it work. Goodbye now. Go quickly.' She hustled him out the door.

He collected the outfit from the costumers without difficulty. Margaret French thought the notion of him masquerading as a middle-aged rocker hilarious. To buy the ticket for the crossing to Ireland, he used the name that appeared on the mail Deirdre had purloined, Harry Fleming. The sailing would be full. There were only a few places left. He took a taxi down to Euston Station and changed clothes in the men's room. Looking at himself in the mirror, bald, clad in black leather, he was unrecognizable. *Whoever said clothes make the man had the right of it*, he thought.

The train to Holyhead was crowded; the only seats to be had were in a smoking carriage. He found one and spent the journey dozing fitfully.

Chapter 35

At the Metropolitan Electricity Board, the chief operator let out a jubilant yell. 'Finally, the clever bastard, whoever he was.'

It was seven o'clock in the evening. The unruly mob in the operations room had been replaced by a select few: the chief of internal audit, Peter Spencer, Stephen Denham, and Elizabeth Maitland.

Maitland, losing patience waiting in her office, had come over hours ago to see for herself what was going on. 'You're in finally?' Maitland asked him sharply.

'The problem was with the password,' the operator answered. 'Someone changed it from uppercase to lowercase. The editing software doesn't make a distinction. It shows everything as uppercase. When I would query what the password should be, it looked like—' He grabbed a pencil wrote PATERNOSTER. 'That's what I remembered it to be. In fact, what the system was expecting was "paternoster" in lowercase. The hexadecimal representations are different. Because it looked like the system wasn't taking a valid password, I've been assuming some really hairy operations problem and running all kinds of diagnostics for the last two and a half hours. It was only when I eliminated every other possibility that I realized *this has to be the password,* and voila! So it is.'

'Fine, we're in. Now the question is who modified the production link libraries?' Maitland was so absorbed in the conversation she absentmindedly swallowed a mouthful of scalding black coffee from the cup Denham had just handed her. 'Damn and blast. This case will be the death of me.'

Peter Spencer tapped the chief operator on the shoulder. 'Here, let me at the terminal, mate. I know what it is we're looking for.'

They changed places. Peter began to key rapidly. After less than a minute, he had the answer. 'Oh, Jeez, not Andrew!'

Maitland was already putting on her coat. 'That's it, then. We have him. Come on, Stephen, let's go pick him up.'

It was after eight when they got to the Sweeney's apartment in Turnham Green. Deirdre Sweeney answered the door, her eyes puffy and her hair a mess.

'Good evening, Mrs. Sweeney.' Maitland flashed her badge. 'Detective Chief Inspector Elizabeth Maitland. This is Sergeant Denham, whom I believe you have met. We're here to see your husband.'

'He's not here,' Deirdre answered. 'You had better come in.'

'Who is it, Mummy?' Michael's voice, nervous and apprehensive, reached them from his bedroom.

'It's only a couple of business friends of your father, Michael. Finish up your homework, and I will be in shortly to read your story, there's a good boy.'

She showed them into the living room, closing the door behind her.

'Where is he, Mrs. Sweeney?' Maitland asked.

'He's not here. He's gone.' She looked at them, distraught. 'Oh God, I'm sorry, I'm going to have to sit down.'

'Where, Mrs. Sweeney?' Maitland asked through clenched teeth. 'When did he leave?'

'It must have been three hours ago,' Deirdre answered. 'He came home early from work. I was surprised. Andrew never comes home early. He told me he'd been involved in a fraud, some sort of billing fraud involving the Electricity Board, and you were on the point of finding out. I still can't believe it. You're married to someone fifteen years. You think you know everything there is to know about them and then one day your husband comes home and tells you this. It's as if I've been living with a stranger.'

'You knew nothing of this before?' Maitland asked.

Deirdre looked at her, stunned. 'Of course I knew nothing of this. What do you take me for? He's caught up in some way with that dreadful billing business where those poor people died? I have been married to a monster!'

'Did he say where he was going?'

'He talked about needing to flee the country. I don't know what he was on about half the time. He kept saying he loved me and how he didn't want to lose me and how he had done it all just for me. As if I'm somehow responsible for what he's done!' Deirdre was wringing her hands and rocking backwards and forwards in her chair. She seemed so distraught Stephen Denham had an almost irresistible impulse to go and throw his arms around her to comfort her. All he could do was to stand protectively by her side.

Maitland called Scotland Yard. 'Yes, this is Detective Chief Inspector Maitland. I have a fugitive, Andrew Sweeney, wanted in connection with billing fraud at the Metropolitan Electricity Board. We have reason to believe he is attempting to flee the country. I want a watch placed on all ports of exit. What?' She paused. 'No, I don't believe Andrew Sweeney is either armed or dangerous. He is, however, very resourceful.'

While Maitland was on the phone, Deirdre tugged at Stephen Denham's elbow. 'Stephen—I'm sorry, Sergeant, could you get me a glass of white wine, please? I feel quite weak. The bottle is over on the drinks counter.'

Denham immediately did her bidding. He was beset by conflicting emotions: pity for Deirdre Sweeney's distressed state, relief that she had not known about the fraud, and an irrational resentment with Elizabeth Maitland for being so brisk with her, even though he knew Maitland was only doing her job. As he gave the glass of wine to Deirdre Sweeney, Denham's resentment of Maitland grew even more intense with her next question.

'Mrs. Sweeney, if your husband confessed to you that he had committed a crime and indicated that he intended to flee the country and this was some hours ago, why did you not bother to inform the police?'

Deirdre stared at Maitland. 'What kind of woman are you? He's my husband. I feel betrayed and abandoned, and I have a ten-year-old boy in the bedroom next door who was wondering why his daddy isn't home. I told him Andrew had gone away on a business trip. How am I going to explain to him what his father has done? How will we live with the shame and disgrace of it? And in the middle of all this, I'm supposed to calmly figure out that I should be informing the police?' She looked at Maitland defiantly. 'I'll tell you this, Chief Inspector, or whatever your title is, I hope you never find him. I hope he vanishes off the face of the earth. That way, my son won't have to endure the shame and humiliation of a trial and seeing his father put behind bars. I will divorce him, take my maiden name, and move away from here.'

The wine glass fell from her hand. She had scarcely touched it. Once again, she began the rocking motion back and forth. Denham was on his knees beside her to pick up the fallen glass and, by this point, looking with open hostility at his superior.

Maitland pressed her lips together. Inwardly, she rolled her eyes. 'I'm very sorry, Mrs. Sweeney. It's clearly been a great shock for you, and you are obviously distressed. However, we are going to need a statement from you just as soon as you are able. Can you remember anything your husband may have said, which would help us to determine his whereabouts?'

'I'm sorry, Chief Inspector. As I told you, he talked about needing to get away, to leave the country. He kept saying that he had done it all for me, wanting me to reassure him. I told him anything I thought he wanted to hear so that he would leave and get out of my apartment. Oh, what a spineless, worthless man he was. A liar and a thief!'

Denham felt a surge of excitement on hearing Deirdre talk about her husband in the past tense.

Maitland stared at her, trying to suss out whether Deirdre Sweeney was telling the truth. It was hard to tell. 'I must go back to the Yard and see about coordinating the hunt for him,' Maitland said. 'One or two last questions, Mrs. Sweeney, before I go. I'm sorry. Did your husband take anything with him when he left?'

'Yes. He packed an overnight bag with some clothes and a few toiletries, but that's all.'

'When exactly did he leave here?'

'I'm not sure as to the precise time.' Deirdre Sweeney looked exhausted. 'I think it was between four and five o'clock this afternoon.'

'Very well. I will leave Sergeant Denham here and also arrange to have a female police officer over within the hour. It would help us greatly if you would agree to let us look around. Your husband may have left some indication of where he might be headed.'

Deirdre agreed wearily. 'Yes, of course. Just as long as you don't upset Michael.'

'We appreciate it, Mrs. Sweeney. He may try to contact you again, so we will need to set up a surveillance, and as I said, we'll need your statement just as soon as you are able. Will you require medical assistance?'

Deirdre shook her head. 'No, what can a doctor do for me? I will be all right.'

'Very well, then, I will be going. Maitland looked at Denham significantly. 'Sergeant, I'm sure you'll take good care of Mrs. Sweeney. There will be another police officer to join you within the hour.'

She placed emphasis on the last sentence.

'I understand, Detective Chief Inspector,' Denham said.

Chapter 36

As the train approached Holyhead, Andrew's anxiety level rose in anticipation of boarding the ferry. As Deidre had predicted, it was a chaotic sailing. Cheltenham had been a good race meeting for the Irish. An Irish horse had won the Gold Cup. The returning punters were in high spirits. There were more police in evidence than usual, and they were checking more people's papers. A plainclothes detective scrutinised carefully the faces of the passengers as they cleared the inspection point. Andrew Sweeney's throat was dry and his palms sweaty as he waited his turn in line. The detective looked him over with professional thoroughness, but seemed mildly amused when, on asking the purpose of Andrew's trip, he was told it was to go and see a U2 concert.

It was a rough crossing. There was a heavy chop in the Irish Sea and a force six wind. Andrew was not a good sailor. He lay on the floor in one of the lounges below deck, feeling wretched for the four-hour journey. It was seven o'clock in the morning when they got to Dun Laoghaire. Andrew felt exhausted. He was tempted to check into a hotel but realized that delay could prove his undoing.

Once in the city centre he hurried to Busarus, the national bus terminal, and boarded a bus for Shannon Airport. It took over five hours, and he barely made the afternoon flight to Toronto. He used a Gaelic version of his Irish passport. He had two. One was in English and the other Gaelic. He had acquired the second simply by reporting the first one lost. He still had a valid Canadian visa from the trip he and Deirdre had taken to visit his brother Matthew three years previously.

When he got to Toronto he was tired from two nights of not having slept in a bed. In his wrinkled clothes, he felt grubby and vulnerable. He experienced the by-now familiar feeling of dread and nervousness going through customs and immigration. He knew the British police would have an alert out for him and that they would eventually trace his route of escape. It was just a question of how soon. Logically, he told himself, there was no way for them to have traced him in such a short time to the Air Canada flight from Shannon. Still, he went through the inspection with his heart in his mouth.

He booked himself into a nondescript hotel on the outskirts of Toronto. After a shower he collapsed into bed and slept unbrokenly for fourteen hours. The following morning, he went to a sporting goods store and bought himself hiking boots and a backpack. He boarded a bus for Montreal. Once he arrived, he took a ferry across the St. Lawrence and set out cross country for the US border. Andrew was not much of an outdoors man. Even though he had bought a map and a compass, he wandered in the forest for over twenty hours before finally intersecting with route 87 on the US side. He managed to hitch a ride from a trucker to Albany. Once there he boarded an Amtrak for New York. Only when the train pulled into Grand Central Station did he feel really safe and confident that he could lose himself, along with the hundreds of thousands of other illegals, in the Great American melting pot.

****

Andrew was sitting in McSorley's pub down in Greenwich Village two months later. Seamus McNamara, his cousin, had given him a letter from Deirdre. Eagerly he tore it open. It was written in her familiar sweeping scrawl.

Dearest Andrew,

I got your message to write you care of your cousin. I'm sure by now you've made it to New York. The first few days after you left I was terrified they might catch you. You were in all of the newspapers. The police really pulled out all the stops and they traced you as far as Toronto, but then you vanished. I have been the centre of attention. The house has been under surveillance. It was an awful strain in the beginning when I didn't know that you were safe, but I have been reveling in my role of betrayed and embittered wife.

Fortunately, the primary liaison on the police side has been Stephen Denham. You remember him, the blond Adonis. He is seriously in lust and quite obviously panting to go to bed with me. I do just enough to keep him on the boil. You know, the usual sort of stuff: flutter the eyelids helplessly and brush against his manly chest. Anytime he's around me, he's thinking with his cock. I'm just grateful it's not that suspicious old bat Elizabeth Maitland I have to contend with. She's far too clinical.

Things have finally died down a bit. I've started making noises about needing to pay a visit back home to Ireland to repair my poor shattered nerves. Denham is so besotted he'll buy any story I want to spin him. Of course once I'm over there I'll have much more room for maneuver. I don't think surveillance will be anything like it is in London.

I have a few ideas about how to make my getaway. One of them involves masquerading as a nun, but then how would I explain Michael. Never fear, though. In a few weeks I will have figured out something. America! Andrew, I'm so excited I wet myself just thinking about it. Oh, don't worry too much about Michael. I've told him you're a sort of Robin Hood. When I married you I knew I was getting someone who was deeply, desperately, in love with me. To be honest, I never expected a life of romance and adventure, but you're supplying that, too, you darling man. Keep the bed warm and take care of yourself. I will be seeing you soon.

Deirdre.

Andrew was smiling broadly as he folded the letter carefully and placed it in his breast pocket. His cousin looked at him. 'Looks like good news, Andrew. Fancy another pint of ale?' Andrew grinned at him happily. 'Ah sure, why not, Shamus, it's great news entirely. I might as well celebrate it.'

Printed in Poland
by Amazon Fulfillment
Poland Sp. z o.o., Wrocław